WIZ

...Tells the story of Izward a young computer genius who travels back in time to stop the evil Vulgor from taking over the universe.

...Izward lives inside an ancient fort known as the Institute in the middle of a river estuary. Its buildings have been converted to laboratories and their scientists are the best in computer technology. It has its own defences and is completely isolated from the outside world...

...Izward is owned and educated by the Mentors, the Institutes Guardians, who hope to use his genius to enhance their wealth and reputation. Izward leads a lonely life devoid of personal relationships. He spends his spare time playing and designing virtual reality games and experiencing the outside world through computerised images...

...Beyond the Institute's island fortress is the mainland known as The Abandon Zone. It is an unpopulated area of destruction, which is recovering from the effects of a Nuclear War...

...Izward leaves the Institute on an educational field trip and travels across the Abandon Zone with his tutor Wally Zeeman to an isolated lighthouse on the coast...

...and is transported back through time to a terrifying world of monsters and nightmares.

ALIEN W HALL

THE
WIZARD MASTER
Time Warrior of Tellurian

TRAFFORD

© Copyright 2004 Alien Hall. All rights reserved.

No part of this publication may be reproduced, stored in a retrieval system, or transmitted, in any form or by any means, electronic, mechanical, photocopying, recording, or otherwise, without the written prior permission of the author.

Printed in Victoria, Canada

Note for Librarians: a cataloguing record for this book that includes Dewey Classification and US Library of Congress numbers is available from the National Library of Canada. The complete cataloguing record can be obtained from the National Library's online database at:
www.nlc-bnc.ca/amicus/index-e.html
ISBN 1-4120-2389-0

TRAFFORD

This book was published on-demand in cooperation with Trafford Publishing.
On-demand publishing is a unique process and service of making a book available for retail sale to the public taking advantage of on-demand manufacturing and Internet marketing. On-demand publishing includes promotions, retail sales, manufacturing, order fulfilment, accounting and collecting royalties on behalf of the author.

Suite 6E, 2333 Government St., Victoria, B.C. V8T 4P4, CANADA
Phone 250-383-6864   Toll-free 1-888-232-4444 (Canada & US)
Fax 250-383-6804   E-mail sales@trafford.com   Web site www.trafford.com
TRAFFORD PUBLISHING IS A DIVISION OF TRAFFORD HOLDINGS LTD.
Trafford Catalogue #04-0217   www.trafford.com/robots/04-0217.html

10   9   8   7   6   5

To Wally and Jean.

– Together they would have ruled the Universe.

Contents

Location   The Planet Earth
Time Zone   The Present...................13

Location   The Void
Time Zone   Unknown...................25

Location   The Planet Earth
Time Zone   The Past...................33

Location   The Planet Earth
Time Zone   The Present
– Three Hours Later...................69

Location   The Planet Earth
Time Zone   The Present
–Two Years Later...................71

Location   The Planet Earth
Time Zone   The Past...................75

Location   The Planet Earth
Time Zone   The Present
—Three Years Later...................135

Location   The Planet Earth
Time Zone   A Long Time Ago...................153

Location   The Planet Earth
Time Zone   The Present...................339

Location   The Planet Earth
Time Zone   The Past
Extracts From:
The Mysteries Of The Universe Part II 345

Location   The Planet Earth
Time Zone   **Ancient Times**
Extracts From:
The Mysteries Of The Universe Part II 347

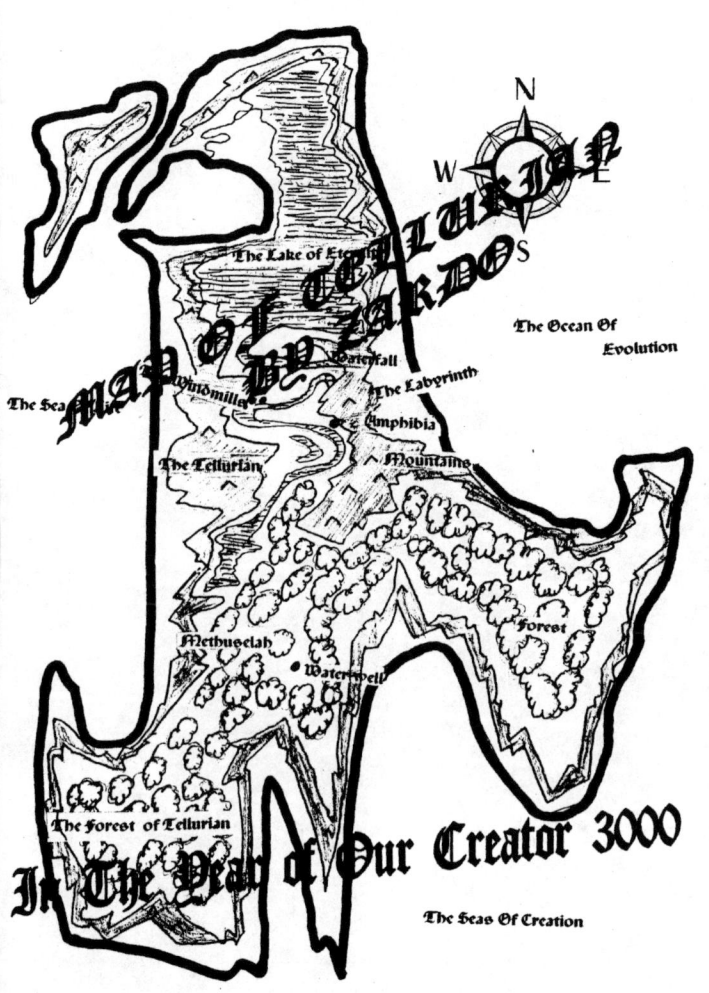

Location *The Planet Earth*

Time Zone *The Present*

Izward was bitterly cold and extremely wet. He was beginning to wish he hadn't come. The Estuary looked bleak and desolate and the sky above him had turned a stormy black. Rain clouds raced across the sky and he could hear thunder rumbling in the distant. A gale force wind had been raging across the peninsula ever since they had arrived and he wished to return to the safety of *The Institute* and its artificial climate control.

He tugged at his clothing trying to adjust to its feel. The materials felt alien and uncomfortable and he longed for the lightweight touch of his cyber-suit. He wondered how the Ancients had coped with such inferior garments. His *duffel coat*, for that's what it was called, was soaking wet. The rain had soaked clean through the material making his skin feel damp and clammy. He shivered and his skin prickled. Water dripped off the coat and into *wellingtons*, rubbery footwear that were supposed to keep the feet dry. They smelt of burning plastic and they certainly didn't work. Water pooled under his feet and made squelching sounds when he walked about. He couldn't think why his ancestors had worn them. They were smelly, heavy and extremely uncomfortable.

On his hands he wore *gloves*. A label informed him they were made from a substance called *wool*.

"Wool?" said Izward.

PETE his SERIES XI microcomputer burst into life.

"Wool comes from sheep, a creature now feared extinct," said a male mechanical voice from a holographic image just above his wrist.

The new Personalised Enquiry TErminals were compulsory hardware to all students in the Institution. They were microcomputers strapped to the wrist and programmed to the individual's need. Life in the Institute was lonely and students lived in isolation of their families. The Mentors, the Institute's founders hoped these tiny terminals would provide their maturing nine-year-old geniuses with substitute family figures. These artificial families were individually programmed to provide the student with the love and understanding of a real family member. Each holographic image stored the SERIES X1 memory chip and therefore the sum total of the world's knowledge. It was hoped these miniaturised mothers and fathers, brothers and sisters, aunts and uncles would satisfy all their student's biological and intellectual enquiries.

"Thanks," said Izward looking into the tiny male face now smiling up at him from his wrist.

"You're welcome Son," said the holographic image of a father he had never known, *"have a great day!"*

The hologram faded and PETE turned itself off.

To wear such an artefact was a privilege and Izward proudly held up his hands and stared at the sodden finger protectors. They hung damp and heavy on his hands and water dribbled off them onto his wrists. Again he cursed the absurdity of his ancestors wondering how they could have worn such ridiculous objects.

Drops of salty rain ran uncomfortably down his nose and into his mouth. He hated the taste of salt it made him feel sick.

"Ugh!" he grumbled and spat angrily onto the ground. He ran his tongue across his lips hoping the offending taste had gone but the salty taste was still there.

"Zeeman! Where are you?" he shouted above the roar of the waves. But his voice went unheard, swept away by the wind into the storm that was brewing over the river.

Behind him towered *The Lighthouse*. It stood tall and majestic against the darkening sky. He turned around to face it. The wind blew directly into his face. He shivered as the damp salty spray attacked his face once again. He half closed his eyes and squinted up at the building. The ancient monument excited him. He had never seen one before, except on his terminal. Being this close to ancient civilisation was really *cool*. He liked that word; it was the *in* word to use. All his mates at the Institute said it and the *NET* used it all the time.

"Cool! Real cool!" he muttered to himself as he stared up at the dome shaped top of the lighthouse. As he watched a beacon of light flashed across the sky.

"Wow! Real cool!" he said. "It's so cool!"

The lighthouse had been the main reason for the visit, a rare opportunity to experience *a real environment*. Zeeman, the boy's personal tutor had arranged the visit. He had wanted to postpone the trip until the weather had improved but Izward had insisted they kept to *The Schedule*. The Institute's directors had carefully planned his future and postponements of any kind would seriously affect his future status. The Schedule was Izward's gateway to prosperity and nothing was going to interfere with that.

Izward's world of computers and state of the art affluence was a million millenniums away from the ancient building in front of him. He gazed up at its carefully preserved features and wondered what life must have been like all those centuries ago. Today modern society relied on computers. They were installed in every home and Virtual Reality Networks became compulsive viewing. Home based Internet schools educated the family and T.V. shopping channels catered for consumer needs. In a world recovering from a nuclear holocaust most families stayed home and experienced life through their television sets.

Field trips into the *Abandoned Zones* were only for the privileged. Izward knew he was one of the lucky ones. Only the best young minds were recruited into the Institute. The future of mankind could one day rest on his shoulders and if his *Schedule* demanded a visit to the Abandoned Zone then that's where he was going. The Schedule was Izward's future and nothing was going to interfere with that.

The wind continued to blow and Izward waited patiently for his grey haired tutor to return. While he waited he recalled the events leading up to his present situation.

The Institute was built on the foundations of two ancient Military Forts situated in the middle of a river estuary. They had boarded a hovercraft and had crossed over to the mainland. Once outside the protective dome of the Institute he had suddenly heard thunder and experienced real rain and for the first time in his life he experienced a genuine storm.

They had boarded an automobile called *The Jetster* and had travelled along decaying tarmac and concrete roads. The car was the latest in vehicle technology and was a slim cone shaped hover vehicle that flashed and blinked with all the latest gadgets. They had quickly travelled through abandoned landscapes and decaying cities, silently sliding over ancient roads and motorways on a cushion of invisible air. He had enjoyed the ride. The sights of the ancient one's achievements had fascinated him. It had been much better than the Virtual Reality images he had been used to seeing.

They had come to a river and had crossed over it via an old metal suspension bridge. He had looked up enchanted by its ancient rusting towers. Once over the bridge they had turned right towards a ruined city. He had wanted to know the city's name but Zeeman had forgotten it. He had asked his family and *PETE*'s holographic circuitry had come to life. The face of his surrogate mother had floated on his wrist and she had informed him the city was called *Kingston* and it had been destroyed in a Nuclear War.

They had travelled on gliding noiselessly alongside a river whose waters had long since been polluted. It had looked red and dirty and he recalled smelling dead fish and rotting cabbages. They had entered the city and drove into a world of decaying silence. He had seen the architectural dreams of the ancients in ruins, left to decay where it had fallen. A thousand piles of rubble lay on top of a thousand more. The Jetster had sped on, its solar powered engine pushing it soundlessly through the deserted streets. It had taken several minutes to drive through the city and he had felt a strange sadness as the crumbling streets flashed by his window. He visualised the city's end and imagined the ghosts of its people haunting the streets at night. Finally on the outskirts of the city the vehicle had come to a standstill. It had floated quietly down to ground level and Zeeman had turned off the engine. The weather had deteriorated and a strong northerly wind blew rain clouds across the whole area. He had stepped out of the vehicle and an icy cold wind blew into his face. He had staggered to keep on his feet and had held onto the frame of the car for support. The wind carried a dampness that had prickled his neck and he had felt a cold shiver run down the whole of his body.

"Wow!" he had shouted still holding onto the car's door, "it's fantastic!"

Worried by the worsening weather Zeeman had issued yet another warning.

"You must stay close to me," he had insisted, "and don't wander off!"

"Whatever!" he had muttered more concerned with exploring.

Quickly he had scrambled back into the car and had changed into the ancient's clothing. Fascinated by the weirdness of such apparel and amused by the thought of having to wear such absurdities he had consulted Zeeman on how to use them and had then spent an amusing fifteen minutes getting ready. By the time he'd finished Zeeman had already changed. His ageing tutor had worn a long oversized coat, called a *macintosh*, and something called a *baseball cap*. Zeeman had put the cap on his head and he had seen obsolete writing on it.

N.Y.C. he had read slowly to himself trying to decode the old forgotten script. He had again consulted PETE and via the holographic image of his sister had been told it was the name of a city that once stood in a country called *America*.

They had set off and Zeeman had once again reminded him about the dangers of real environments. They had left the car and walked several hundred metres towards a broken down old gate. Bits of wood hung off it and it had long since lost the ability to open. He had climbed over it while his tutor had suffered the indignity of having to clamber through it. After a little more walking and several more fences they had reached the peninsula.

He had never seen anything like it. He had found himself standing on a narrow piece of uneven land about a kilometre in length. To his left had roared the angry sea and to his right the calmer waters of the river. Clumps of overgrown grass grew everywhere their reed like stems blown almost horizontal by the battering winds. Dotted about the land and covered with green moss and mould, were large rocky boulders half submerged in pools of water.

The landscape reminded him of *Terror-Saurus* a computer generated adventure game he had just started to play. Adventure games were *cool* and he spent most of his spare time battling ogres and monsters in imaginary role-play situations on his computer. However *logging-on* and contacting fellow gamesters throughout the world was his favourite pastime. To the InterNET community he was known as *The Time Warrior*. Most evenings, after he had finished *institute duties*, he contacted fellow conspirators and together they would fight to save hundreds of imaginary worlds from a thousand different evils. In his latest game he was *Neandoman*, a humanoid figure trying to survive in a world of flesh eating dinosaurs. His present surroundings had reminded him of that game and he had spent several minutes trying to match the rocky shapes with the names of some of the dinosaurs in his game.

"Look Zeeman!" he had shouted pointing his gloved finger towards a rock that towered high above all the others.

"Tyrannosaurus!"

Zeeman had laughed and had joined in the game.

"Triceratops!" he had announced indicating a clump of bushes with spiky edges.

"What about those?" said Zeeman pointing to several round lumps of rock sticking out of the ground. He had hesitated at first then with a large grin across his wet salty face he had shouted," dinosaur dropping!"

They had both started to giggle.

Above them storm clouds had been forming and a sudden gust of wind had blown Zeeman's cap high into the sky and the dinosaur game had come to an end. He had laughed as he had watched his tutor's comic attempts to recapture the cap. Several times he fell and had to scramble to his feet to resume the chase. With each new fall the more dishevelled his tutor looked. Finally Zeeman had followed the artefact over a sand dune and disappeared from view.

Warnings tend to be ignored especially when you're having fun. Ahead of him had been the lighthouse. It had stood tall and erect and towered high into the stormy clouds. He'd been tempted to explore it on his own. He'd looked around for Zeeman but his tutor had vanished. So he had decided to inspect the building on his own. A decision he now regretted. He had pulled his *duffle coat* tight around himself and had set off in the general direction of the lighthouse. The atmosphere around him had suddenly chilled and he had shivered. A blanket of fine mist had filled the air and an eerie fog had gathered along the shoreline to his right. He had walked on determined to reach the lighthouse before the fog drifted towards him and obscure his way. Finally when he'd reached the lighthouse he'd been bombarded by fine particles of sand blown off the beach by the high winds. Each grain had stung his face like a swarm of angry bees and he'd been forced to close his eyes and cover his face to protect himself. Disoriented and temporarily blinded by the sand he'd lost all sense of direction and had reached out desperately trying to find the lighthouse wall. To his relief he touched something solid and he'd flung himself up against it. There he'd remained, clinging to the lighthouse wall like moss on a stone.

Izward had spent the last twenty minutes like this, his back against the lighthouse recalling the events that had brought him to this predicament. He watched waves crashing on the beach and saw foam forming in the ebb of each wave. The wind sent the foam scurrying across the sand like dandelion seeds in the fury of an autumn wind. Above him another beam of light flashed through the clouds but Izward knew its warning was no longer important. Satellites orbiting the planet high above the earth now directed navigation through the estuary. The lighthouse was a museum piece carefully maintained by the Institute to provide its inmates with high adventure and a taste of reality.

"Zeeman! You old fraud," he shouted convinced his tutor was hiding, "I know you're out there."

There was no reply. Izward had convinced himself that his tutor's disappearance was a hoax. A carefully planned act deliberately executed to test his courage. The Institute's Mentors were always testing him. It was their way of evaluating his potential.

The wind abated and the rain eased. The fog drifted ever nearer creeping towards him like a leopard stalking its prey. Izward stared into the fog hoping to see Zeeman come striding through it but unlike the heroes in his adventure games no one came to his rescue. The fog engulfed him and he became lost in a swirling mist of confusion.

The Creator had been waiting, drifting and whirling in the mists of time for an eternity. Hidden in the fog it approached Izward.

Seafarer's tales tell of ghostly spirits that haunt the fog. The Ancients believed them to be the souls of lost mariners drowned in the oceans of the world. Izward didn't believe such nonsense. He had researched *The Seafaring Legends of the Ancients,* before he had left and *PETE* had reassured him, *"it was superstitious nonsense."* Nevertheless the fog frightened him. It caressed his body like the thermo-blanket on his bed and he felt a strange unnatural presence all around him. He tried to get PETE's reassurance once more but he wasn't there. He frantically pressed and repressed all the buttons on his terminal but there was no response. His Family was offline and he was alone. Izward started to panic. Suddenly a ghostly shape came wailing through the mist and Izward was convinced it was Zeeman. He ran blindly towards it.

Suddenly he felt nothing below his feet and he felt himself falling through the air. For a second he was the hero of a fantasy game flying from danger. But this wasn't a game and he knew he couldn't fly. He thought he heard the thud of his own body strike the ground but he couldn't be sure. All he could remember was a stabbing pain in his back then nothing but blackness.

The fog cleared and the Creator drifted skyward. It would be patient. There would be other opportunities.

Location *The Void*

Time Zone *Unknown*

A New Lease of Life

Once upon a time four and half million millenniums ago an event took place that was to alter creation forever. The *Creator* had thought the universe boring and in need of a new lease of life.

The *Overseer*, an omnipotent apprentice responsible for implementing the Creator's plans for the cosmos had finally finished. He'd been working on a Solar System with eight planets and a sun. Creating galaxies was an architectural nightmare and the Creator's latest designs had been difficult to interpret. However the project was now ready for the final stage and the Overseer was taking a well-earned rest.

The key to its construction would be *The Sphere of Creation*. A mystical rock of immense power created from a life-force spirit at the beginning of time. The Sphere's origins remained a mystery but deep inside its interior held the architectural answers to those unknown secrets of creation. It was a source of energy that could create millions upon millions of universes, or create a host of galaxies and populate them with a million different species. This dull looking lump of stone moulded by the hand of God at the beginning of reality was the most powerful force in the known cosmos.

The Overseer positioned the Sphere and retired to the void to await its secrets.

The Creator of the universe waited, anxious to see his plan become a reality.

Suddenly the Sphere of Creation burst into life.

The Sphere of Creation

The Sphere of Creation turned a fiery red and began to spin. As it spun it increased in size. With every rotation it enlarged itself until it was the size of a planet. The surface of the sphere crackled and exploded with cosmic activity and bolts of red and yellow lightning scurried across its surface spiralling into continuous streaks of rushing light.

From the fiery surface of the raging planet *Birth Stars* formed and were hurled into the emptiness of space. The heavens around the sphere lit up with starlight brilliance. A thousand brightly coloured stars surrounded the sphere like newly born entities waiting for direction. Each star flickered and pulsed with a life-giving nucleus. Suddenly the outer shell of the sphere exploded and a thousand pieces of molten rock were thrown into space. The force of the explosion scattered the waiting stars out into the far reaches of the cosmos.

What remained of the sphere began to glow and expand until it burst into flames. A blazing inferno of fire raced around its surface until the whole planet was ablaze. Gigantic fireballs shot out from its surface spreading heat and light across the galaxy.

Here the *Sun* would remain a burning light of hope in the darkness of space. Its brilliance would reach the far corners of the galaxy and bring about the miracles of creation. It was the star of all stars and a shining example of the Creator's grandeur.

Big Bangs

The Creator hated big bangs. It had witnessed several and had hated them all. Explosions unsettled the order of things and caused disharmony throughout the cosmos. However, galaxies couldn't be made without them so the universe braced itself for a spectacular birth.

A thousand fragments of liquid rock hurled chaotically across the emptiness of space setting the Cosmos on fire. They crashed and collided together with such explosive force they fused together into spinning balls of fire. Each rotating sphere spun wildly in chaotic orbits around a fiery sun. Clouds of gas and red hot metal swirled above the forming planets showering their surfaces with metallic rain.

It would take a million millenniums for the galaxy to evolve so the Creator waited patiently for time to pass. To the Creator time had no meaning. Immortality was forever and therefore the measurement of time insignificant.

A thousand million years later the planets had cooled and were ready for life. For the Birth Stars a thousand million year pilgrimage around the universe was about to end.

The Birth Stars

Travelling through the corridors of time the *Birth Stars* had journeyed the universe in search of a home. Finally their trek across infinity had come to an end and ahead of them had been the galaxy they'd spent an eternity seeking. They had come to a halt and had carefully aligned themselves over their chosen planets. There they hung a universe of stars in a galaxy of planets. Below them the planets had looked dead and lifeless and in need of that spark of life that would give them meaning. They spun slowly in orbit unaware of the mysteries that were about to explode on their surface.

Timed to perfection in a harmonious chorus of movement the first cluster of stars had shot across a thousand miles of space towards the unsuspecting planets. Cluster upon star cluster followed in its trail. A thousand fiery stars blazed through space leaving trails of sparkling light to linger in the blackness over the planet. With their trillion-year journey at an end each burning star crashed down onto the surface of the planets in a hail of fire.

On several of the planets the force of the impact was so great huge pieces of granite broke away from the surface and exploded upwards into outer space. There, in the coldness of space, these lifeless giants of rock would spin in an everlasting orbit around the mother planet forever.

Far below these circling moons, on the surface of several planets, great changes were taking place. The fiery red glow of the sun shone across the galaxy and the planets were blazed in heat and light. The evolutionary forces that had lay dormant within the stars began to take root and grow. From what had once been lifeless planets there now stirred the first signs of life.

The light of day would remain for all time and as the planets spun in their everlasting orbits life would evolve according to the cycle of day and night. So had begun the Creator's experiment. Life had flourished on most planets and the prospects for a livelier universe were well under way.

However all had not gone to plan. The Creator's flawless design lay in ruins. Something had gone terribly wrong. Where the third planet from the sun should have been there was the empty blackness of a *Black Hole*. Instead of counting nine planets the Creator could only count eight. One planet had not been created and that would spoil everything.

An Error in Calculation

The Creator's anger spread itself across the galaxy in an instant. He had wanted nine planets but only eight had materialised. There had been an error in calculation and it summoned the Overseer to discuss the oversight.

Creating a galaxy is a difficult and complex phenomenon and errors do occur. Unfortunately being only an apprentice architect it had misread the Creator's design and had only ordered eight planets instead of nine. The Creator was furious and anger thundered across the heavens again.

The Overseer could only apologise for its mistake and hoped the Supreme Being would forgive it. Being divine and all knowing the Creator knew it had been a genuine mistake and its anger subsided.

The apprentice sensed the Creator's forgiveness and the rumblings of discontent had faded from the heavens and serenity had settled across the cosmos.

However the Creator was still unhappy. The great experiment had sadly come to an unexpected halt and without the full complement of nine planets the universe would remain unfinished. A billion trillion hours of careful planning would be wasted and heaven knows what would happen to those millions of life giving stars, that were at this very moment, waiting patiently, somewhere in space, to fall upon the surface of a not yet created planet.

The Black Hole

Mistakes had to be corrected. Unplanned errors like the loss of a planet would have devastating effects on the galaxy's development and the Creator had to correct it. It grew impatient and summoned the Overseer. The Creator's orders were clear. The shattered fragments of the Sphere of Life were to be found and placed outside the Black Hole.

In an instant the Overseer had travelled the galaxy, picked up the scattered pieces and had returned.

Empty of light and blacker than a hundred nights the Black Hole reached out from a shroud of darkness across a galaxy of light. A thousand pieces of rock, deposited by the Overseer, floated around its perimeter like a captive asteroid belt. Each magical segment was spinning and twisting itself around in a never-ending spiral around the rim. There they drifted waiting for the final element that would turn them into the ninth planet.

The Creator entered the Black Hole. It began to spin and a million pieces of rock began a spiralling journey towards its centre. Faster and faster the vortex spun as wave upon wave of rock fell into the hole. In the centre of the vortex a solid ball of matter began to form. Slowly it began to spin, its speed increasing with every revolution. As it spun it grew in size its gravitation field attracting the orbiting rocks like a magnet. Suddenly the spinning ball burst into flames as the final fragments of the Sphere plunged to their destruction on the planet's surface.

At the centre of the operation had been the Creator directing and orchestrating the birth of the planet with pinpoint accuracy. This time it had left nothing to chance and everything had gone according to plan.

After a thousand million years the planet cooled and it was finally ready for life. One more celestial event was needed and the planet would be complete.

Suddenly the heavens were filled with a billion stars all streaking across the blackness like celestial warriors going into battle. They fell on the planet and the surrounding blackness echoed with the noise and light of a million stars creating life. Then the planet slipped into another dimension and blinked out of existence. On its return great changes had taken place. The planet was awash with blues and greens and great oceans of water covered most of its surface. Where the oceans ended an assortment of islands were exposed. Bathed in heat and light from the sun the planet reflected a bluish haze. White mist swirled above its surface partially hiding the luscious greens of the islands below.

Hidden amongst the mist and clouds was the Creator. Here it would remain an invisible spirit that would nurture the planet through its infancy.

To the life forms that would evolve it would be worshipped and called a God.

Carefully the Creator manoeuvred the planets into position and counted them. It counted nine.

The universe it had planned all those millenniums ago was finally finished.

With the new planet in place the galaxy was finished.

Proudly the new planets spun in an orbit around the sun just as the Creator had originally planned and eagerly awaited the first signs of life.

Location *The Planet Earth*

Time Zone *The Past*

The Island of Tellurian

Like a giant blue ball the third planet from the sun rotated in the blackness of space. White mist gathered above its surface and clouds drifted gently across the heavens. Around its surface a hundred islands floated in a sea of blue.

The creatures that lived on these islands said an invisible spirit with immense power inhabits the misty world above them, observing and guiding their lives with devout understanding.

The Creator, gently stirred by a warm solar wind, began to drift lazily across the sky. It drifted back in time to search for the memories that recalled the planet's birth and the creation of life.

The planet Earth had found itself part of a complex solar system sharing space and time with eight ageing planets.

The life forms on these planets had either become extinct or had moved off to other galaxies. Most of the planets were now empty and infertile and their days of greatness long since departed.

Life on the Earth had begun deep in the oceans of the planet and the waters had teemed with life.

Strange creatures of all shapes and sizes moved beneath the surface and the waters had bubbled with new life forms.

A cold blast of wind brought the Creator back to the present, scattering its memories like seeds in the air.

All that had been a thousand generations ago and the life forms on the planet's surface had evolved into a thousand different species. Creatures of all shapes and sizes now roamed the land and swam in the seas.

The Creator looked down and rejoiced at the planet's splendour. Never had there been such a wonderful place in all of creation.

Surrounded by clouds the tiny *Island of Tellurian* awaited nightfall. A forest grew at its centre and spiralled out in a circular maze across the entire island. Where the trees ended a range of high mountains encircled the forest like walls of a giant fortress. Beyond the mountains gently sloping hills ran down to a shoreline of fine sand and pebbles. Surrounding the island was a vast blue ocean abundant with life.

It was an island of mystery and a place of discovery.

It was the birthplace of legends and the creator of myths.

It was a place of magic and the beginnings of sorcery.

Alternative dimensions existed side by side and *Gateways* of energy linked one world to another. Fragments of the future intermingled with segments of the past.

It was an island of *hope* in a universe of doubt.

The solar wind returned and the Creator continued its journey around the planet.

Below on the island of Tellurian sunlight was fading and a thousand shadows crept across the landscape. Rain began to fall and the forest grew dark.

That night Tellurian slept uneasily and when morning came, the island awoke to another shadow, the shadow of evil.

Vulgor

On the tiny island of Tellurian the forest bubbled in tropical heat. Although the light from the morning sun was struggling to get noticed, its heat had already penetrated the air and was heating up the ground. Mists of hot damp rain rose in the air like smoke from a fire. The overnight rain was still falling and a million rivulets of water ran along the veins of a billion leaves. The island echoed to the sound of dripping water and the creatures of the wood still sheltered in their homes. The early morning bustle of woodland life had come to a brief stop. Patiently the creatures of the forest waited knowing the sun would break through the clouds and the day would return to normal.

Such was the cycle of events on the island. However today would be different and events would be far from normal. An evil would come and threaten the tranquillity of their lives.

The sweet pungent smell of sulphur drifted across the trees and into the nostrils of *Vulgor*. The bird was perched in a large oak tree between the fork of two twisted branches. A yellow mist drifted all round its huge reptilian body hiding it from view. The mist hovered like an evil spirit covering the creature in a cloak of corruption. The giant bird drew breath and inhaled. Two yellow streams of thick putrid smoke flew into its nostrils. The whole of its body grew in size as if the smoke had given it strength. Its large oval shaped eyes turned a menacing red and its black inner pupils became cold and staring. Those satanic eyes now looked out across the tops of the trees at a trail of wispy yellow cloud that had been its flight path from out of *The Dark Zone*.

Vulgor looked to the horizon. From his position at the top of the tree he could see right across the island. On the horizon the creature could see the cloud- barrier that hid the Gateway. The portal still sparked with energy and particles of light flashed across its aperture. But the Gateway was unstable and Vulgor knew it could disappear at any moment.

The portal began to fade. Cloud drifted across the opening and slowly the gateway between the two dimensions was no more.

Vulgor smiled to himself as he put the first part of his dastardly plan into action. Yellow drool dribbled from out of the corners of his mouth and slithered across his jaw onto a leaf. The leaf buckled under the strain and the evil smelling liquid slithered off onto the leaf below. More and more of the vile mixture trickled out of Vulgor's mouth and onto the tree. Globules of yellow pus ran slowly down the bark like maggots searching for food. Having reached the foot of the tree it trickled off onto the ground and into the soil. Vulgor looked down at the poisoned soil and grinned. Once it had soaked into the ground nothing could stop its progress and the balance of nature would become unstable.

Vulgor prepared to leave. His plan was simple. Eventually this pathetic little island would change. The yellow poison would create the *Terrawurms* and they would eat into the island and erode its foundations. Once the island had been corrupted it would be a threat to the rest of the planet. Having been infected with evil Tellurian would be cast into the Dark Zone. He would invade and Tellurian would be his.

Vulgor had tried to capture the island before but had failed, this time it would be different.

The assignment was over and it was time to find the Gateway and return home. The giant bird looked to the rain filled skies and squawked angrily.

He hated rain.

Inside his mouth a row of razor sharp teeth ran along both jaws. They were crooked and stained yellow from the liquid that pooled in his throat. He snapped and snarled angrily at the rain and shuffled uneasily on the wet branch. The tree swayed under the strain and the branches bent and creaked under the weight.

He had nestled himself under a canopy of leaves in an effort to escape the rain. Rain was rare in his dimension and he felt uncomfortable with its touch. Water had run down his back and had made small lakes in the scales that covered his body. Angrily he opened his gigantic wings in an attempt to rid himself of the excess water. A deluge of water fell to the ground.

Having shaken the water from his body he jumped off the branch into the air. Spreading his wings to catch the wind he glided around the tree. It was a large ancient oak many centuries old and it took several seconds to fly all the way around it. The air thumped with the sound of beating wings as he searched the tree for signs of life.

The first rays of the sun had broken through the clouds and shafts of light lit up the forest. The rain eased and a hundred rainbows hung in the trees. It had been several hours since his last meal and the rumblings in his stomach told him it was time to eat. He explored the oak for signs of food. In the centre of the tree half way up from the ground the tree divided into three separate stems. Each trunk was thicker than the original column and grew off at gnarled angles. Branches grew from everywhere and in the centre of each trunk was a large black hole. Thinking these might be the homes of tree dwelling creatures and the source of a good meal he swooped down to investigate.

The wind from his wings whistled through the branches and the leaves rustled in fright. Vulgor looked into the holes but the dwellings were empty, the occupants long since departed. He headed towards the ground and misjudged the landing. He fell awkwardly into a pool of water and splattered the trees with mud. He skidded along the ground until he struck a tree and came to stop. Angrily he struggled to his feet covered in mud.

Suddenly his attention was drawn to movement in the tree behind him. Turning towards the sound he could see a large wooden door carved into the bark. A maze of smaller trees grew around its entrance and twisted around the trunk. These smaller trees snaked themselves up the tree and into the foliage above. Leaves and branches hung down over the entrance making the door behind almost invisible.

Unaware of the danger Mrs. Clutter, Wizard Zardo's housekeeper was busily cleaning the doorstep. Being a *Dactyl* she prided herself on her cleanliness. Rain had never stopped her cleaning the Master's step before and today would be no exception. Dropping onto all fours she picked up her scrubbing brush and dipped it into her bucket of soapy water.

Vulgor looked at her with hunger in his mind.

She noisily scrubbed away at the well-worn stones oblivious of her surroundings.

Vulgor looked at the bird-like quadruped and saw an end to the rumblings in its stomach.

Mrs. Clutter suddenly felt cold and a shiver ran down her back. At first she thought it might be spots of rain running down her neck and she shrugged the feeling away. Then the light faded and a gigantic shadow fell across the doorway. She turned and looked up with horror. A huge bird was coming towards her.

Vulgor opened and closed his jaw, snapping his teeth with terror.

Mrs. Clutter panicked, as daylight became a row of razor sharp teeth bearing down on her. The bird's mouth opened wider and Mrs. Clutter saw yellow slime running across the creature's tongue.

Vulgor's jaws snapped together and he began to chew. As he chewed its teeth clattered against metal and its mouth tasted soapy. Finally having found it too difficult to chew the bird gulped and swallowed his prey whole. Something sharp lodged in his throat and he began to cough and choke. Every breath was a struggle and he felt dizzy.

From her hiding place in the bushes next to the door Mrs. Clutter saw the giant bird flap its wings and fly off into the sky. Only her quick thinking had saved her from certain death. Realising that the bird's elongated beak blocked any clear view of her she had thrown her bucket of soapy water into those hungry jaws before they had snapped shut. The giant bird had eaten the bucket instead of her. With the bird gone Mrs Clutter came out of hiding. She was scared. She had never seen anything like *that* before. Quickly she opened the front door of Wizard Zardo's home and went inside.

Flying home, Vulgor had managed to dislodge and cough up the bucket. The bucket had fallen to earth and down an old well in the centre of the forest. It had nosily clattered down the well shaft until caught on bushes growing halfway down. Inside the bucket was one of Vulgor's teeth embedded in the twisted metal.

Vulgor was angry. His throat hurt and his belly rumbled. His jaw ached and he was missing a tooth. Eagerly he flew towards the mist and the safety of the Dark Zone. Inside the cloud was the doorway that would transport him back to the comforts of his own dimension. As he entered the mist he prayed the *Twins* had prepared the portal correctly.

Inside the cloud Vulgor waited. The mist curled and swirled all around him covering his body in a shroud of white. Suddenly the mist began to spiral and a small circle appeared at its centre. As it spun the circle enlarged. Through the gap he could see the Dark Zone. With one triumphant flap of his mighty wings he flew through the Gateway and entered his domain.

The Dark Zone

The Dark Zone trembled and the sky turned yellow. Bolts of electricity crossed the heavens and thunder rumbled across the mountains. The earth shook and the land cracked open. Mighty monoliths of rock and stone shot up from out of the earth. Pools of molten liquid bubbled and fire exploded a thousand metres high. Rivers of lava flowed down the mountains and across the dry and scorched landscape.

Varen and *Koor* looked up at the giant oval shaped stone and smiled. The shimmering image of Vulgor filled its centre. The Master was almost home and the whole of the Dark Zone awaited his arrival.

The Genesis-stone hovered between two pillars of solidified lava, suspended in the air by an invisible force. Around the outer rim of the stone a series of mystical runes had been etched into the rock. It stood at the centre of Vulgor's castle and towered high above its surrounding walls. The *Eye* was Vulgor's Gateway into Tellurian. Beyond the walls the ground fell away into a furnace of molten lava. A thousand metres below the castle a volcano angrily bubbled and hissed

The Twins, mesmerised by the image in the stone, remained still and silent. A thick green liquid dribbled from the corners of their mouths and onto the ground. The air around them smelt of sulphur and a yellow mist drifted up about their heads.

Varen and Koor were brother and sister and almost identical. They were winged reptilian birds hatched from the same egg. Each stood eight metres tall and had vulture like necks. They had large transparent wings with clawed hands on each wing tip. Their thin skeletal hands contained three large curved talons, which they used to hold and inspect objects. Except for a missing left toe Koor was identical to his sister. They shared the same thoughts and even had the same carnivorous appetites. Even Vulgor could not always tell them apart.

The image in the Eye faded and was replaced by swirling mist. The twins turned and looked at each other, their Lord and Master was ready to enter the Zone and they busily prepared the altar for his arrival. Suddenly the Dark Zone trembled and the ground shook and they found themselves struggling to stay on their feet. Small pieces of lava, loosened by the quake, clattered and tumbled all round them. A blast of hot ash swept across the castle's courtyard showering them with red-hot embers. But the twins remained steadfast their vigil uninterrupted.

Vulgor's castle was an impregnable fortress built from the lava inside the cone of a sleeping volcano. Encircling the castle was a giant wall of lava, which ran along the rim of the volcano's crater. Inside the castle slabs of solidified lava formed the interior walls and inner chambers. Its doors and corridors were the empty lava tunnels left behind after cooling. These ran like giant termite warrens throughout the castle. Holes and caverns of every shape and size lay under the surface forming an underground network of connecting rooms. On the surface the cooling lava had caused trapped air bubbles to burst and create an intricate pattern of craters forming the exterior walkways for the castle's inhabitants.

Vulgor and his cohorts had lived in the Dark Zone for as long as they could remember. The castle was their only shelter against the brutal conditions beyond its walls. They were trapped in a dimension that was doomed. The great circle of life neared its completion and the future would only remember places like the Dark Zone in myths and legends. Vulgor and other creatures like him would soon fade away and exist only in fairy tales and mythology.

But Vulgor and his conspirators had other plans.

Varen and Koor hadn't eaten since Vulgor had departed and their need for food was great. They began to search the castle-grounds for victims. Koor scratched and sniffed, scraped and clawed but failed to find anything worth eating. Finally he spotted a *Vulcan-worm* wriggling its way across the ground. Unable to burrow down into the lava the worm was at the mercy of the bird. Koor pecked at it and picked it up in its beak. The worm wriggled and squirmed unable to free itself from the bird's grip. Tossing it up into the air Koor opened his mouth and the creature tumbled down his throat. In an instant the worm had gone.

Varen had spotted a *Dragon-bird* and with a flick of her tongue she caught the unfortunate creature in mid air and popped it into her mouth. With a grin she swallowed the creature whole.

A flash of lightning streaked across the sky and struck the Eye. The supporting pillars of lava shuddered and began to vibrate. The twins sensing Vulgor's arrival rushed back to the stone.

Below the stone was an altar carved from a block of lava. The block had been hollowed out and now contained a pool of yellow steaming liquid. A circle of small fires had been set around the shrine and the smoke from their flames filled the air with the smell of sulphur. A raised platform encircled the altar that acted as a step.

Varen and Koor approached the shrine.

Stepping onto the platform they plunged their talons under the steaming liquid. The pool swirled and bubbled and thick columns of yellow smoke drifted along their wings. Soon both creatures were covered in a yellow film. The smoke continued to drift upwards creating a thick yellow column of swirling smoke. The smoke thickened and began to form steps between the stone and the altar. More and more steps formed until the yellow mist had created enough steps to reach the centre of the Eye. With the stairway complete the Gateway between the two dimensions began to open.

Standing like a pair of golden statues Varen and Koor silently waited Vulgor's return.

Methuselah

In the forest of Tellurian stood *Methuselah* the oldest living tree in the forest. It was stronger and taller than any other tree in the wood and provided shelter for the Great Wizard Zardo.

The rain had stopped and Methuselah felt the heat drying out its timbers. The morning heat had spread throughout the forest like a blazing inferno and the trees steamed in a wet sticky mist. The mist floated through the branches clinging to the bark like beads of pearls.

Scarred with age and with a lifetime of memories Methuselah searched the inner circles of its life. Thousands of circles ran throughout its ancient body, each circle represented a year in its life. Every ring told a story and held a memory.

Searching long into its past the tree found the rings that recorded the island's history and it drifted back into its past.

The island had provided a fertile environment for the first living creatures that had crawled out of the sea. Life on the island had prospered and had spread across the ocean; soon the entire planet was home to a trillion different species.

Methuselah sensed danger and its thoughts returned to the present. An unpleasant sensation began to seep up from the ground into its roots. Dismissing it as nothing more than a sympton of old age it resumed its recollections.

In those early years things had gone well for the planet and it had flourished, however an evil force had invaded the island and had tried to destroy it.

Methuselah again felt the unpleasant sensation of age. In the thousands of years of its existence the ancient tree had never experienced anything like it before.
Seeking out the rings that chronicled the Dark War's conflict Methuselah recalled the events that led up to the Dark Zone's invasion.

It had started when Gorf discovered the Genesis-Stone and the Gateway that separated The Dark Zone from Tellurian.
The Dark Zone had been a dimension of chaos and disorder and held all the unwanted creatures of creation. It had been designed by the Creator to protect the planet from evil and corruption.
Using the Eye the creatures inside the Zone had escaped.
Led by their leader Vulgor, the monstrosities of the Dark Zone roamed the island plunging it into chaos.
They would have destroyed the whole planet if not for Zardo, a simian being from the future.

Methuselah paused, the light from the sun was fading and another day had passed. Soon the sun would disappear and night would come. The mighty oak groaned as the evening wind whistled through its branches and it shuddered with pain as it felt Vulgor's poison slowly creeping up its trunk.

The Creator had come to Zardo in a dream and had showed him the Dark Zone's invasion. Visons of fearsome creatures and utter destruction had filled the creature's mind with despair.

The images had faded and voices had echoed through his head.

"Zardo," whispered a voice, "we seek your help."

Zardo had daydreamed unaware of the hypnotic request being implanted in his mind.

"Rid us of the evils you have seen."

The voice had become a chorus and then a symphony.

"Only you can save us."

A thousand voices had echoed the message.

"Help us Zardo! Help us all!"

When Zardo awoke he had found himself beside a giant tree in the land of his vision. He was in a forest in the hottest of summers. His own world had gone and he was alone. Whether it was lost in the planets past or in its future he had no way of knowing but he knew he had changed. Physically he'd grown more upright and the hairs around his face had grown. Those around his chin had turned white and almost touched the ground. He had felt different and the hairs all over his body tingled with excitement.

Finding an opening in Methuselah's trunk he had entered the tree, walking upright for the first time in his life. Inside the tree he had found a room and quickly established a home.

It would be from inside this tree that he would organise the fight against the Dark Zone.

In the room he had found several pieces of furniture and a large Grandmasters clock. Inside the clock had been a magical charm, a talisman of great power that would give him the ability to cast spells and perform great feats of magic.

The Dark Zone was eventually defeated and the forces of evil driven back to the Zone. Several creatures had been captured and imprisoned but Vulgor had escaped and had fled back to his own dimension.

The Gateway had been sealed and hidden and Zardo had been hailed a hero and made Wizard of Tellurian.

With its story at an end Methuselah sealed the *Rings of Time* and still feeling unwell drifted into an uneasy slumber.

Nightmares

Inside Methuselah, Mrs. Clutter was banging loudly on Wizard Zardo's inner door. She was worried and very upset. She had narrowly escaped being eaten alive by a monstrous bird that she knew shouldn't exist.

She had heard horror stories about such creatures from her parents and as a child these tales had given her nightmares. The creature shouldn't exist. But she'd seen it. She had fought it off with her bucket of soapy water and it had flown off choking and spluttering. Mrs. Clutter half smiled to herself thinking of how funny the creature had looked flapping its wings and spluttering and coughing at the same time.

Mrs. Clutter continued to thump on the door anxious to tell Wizard Zardo what she had seen.

Slowly the door creaked open and a sleepy eyed Wizard Zardo appeared. His round friendly eyes smiled at her. Hanging from his chin was a long white beard that almost touched the floor. On his head he wore a black pointed hat that flopped and dangled like a broken twig every time he moved his head. On the end of his nose balanced a pair of wire-rimmed glasses. Draped around his body hung a long black cloak that sparkled with a thousand sequins. Around his neck dangled a Talisman.

"Now, now my dear, no need to knock the door down, I was just having forty winks."

He yawned.

"But!"

Zardo held up his hand and Mrs Clutter stopped.

"We wizards get very tired you know, it's not easy being a magician."

"I know sir but!"

Zardo ignored his housekeeper and carried on lecturing her.

"Wizards need lots of sleep."

"Sorry your Wizardship but I've seen…"

"Its all that chanting, shouting and conjuring up words of magic. Its exhausting work making and casting spells. Ordinary creatures just don't know!"

Zardo continued talking unaware of Mrs. Clutter's urgency.

"But your worship this is important," she shouted.

Zardo stopped talking and looked at his housekeeper. She looked worried and frightened. He opened the door wider and invited her into the room. He yawned once more and closed the door behind her. He crossed the room to his favourite chair and sat down.

"Now my dear what's the matter?"

He listened carefully to Mrs. Clutter's story. After she had finished he sat silently in his chair. He looked solemn and worried. He mumbled softly to himself over and over again. Mrs. Clutter saw fear in those warm gentle eyes and knew something dreadful was about to happen.

Outside, unaware of the dangers to come, the forest prepared for nightfall. When the sun re-appeared in the morning things would never be the same again.

Tyrann

Thunder rumbled and the ground shook, Vulgor was returning to the Dark Zone and the elements celebrated his return. Outside the castle gate, *Tyrann*, Vulgor's pet lizard, joined in the festivities. Burdened by a heavy chain around its three necks, it stood up on its two hind legs and roared.

Inside the castle Koor and Varen were oblivious to the giant lizard's revelry. Their attention was on the stone above them. The vortex had stopped spinning and the centre had become translucent.

Suddenly the centre of the stone burst outwards and a thousand sparkling stars lit up the portal. When the stars faded Vulgor flew through the gateway. Koor and Varen fell to their knees fearful of his wrath. They bowed their heads and firmly fixed their eyes on the ground in front of them.

Vulgor landed at the top of the stairway and began his descent. Half way down he slipped, lost his footing and tumbled headfirst down the stairs. He came to rest on his back with his legs kicking aimlessly in the air. He tried to get up but couldn't. The more he struggled the angrier he became. Soon he was spinning around in circles like a dying *Lava-fly*.

The twins started to snigger but remained kneeling.

Vulgor cursed and started flapping his wings against the ground hoping to flip himself over. He failed. The more he tried the more comical he looked.

Finally Koor and Varen were unable to control themselves any longer and they burst out laughing.

"This isn't funny!" exploded Vulgor, "get me up!"

Koor got up, went over to Vulgor and poked him with his foot. Vulgor grumbled loudly and rolled over onto his stomach.

"Ouch! That hurt," complained Vulgor.

"Sorry your Lordship," said Koor smirking, "I was only trying to help."

Varen looked away and sniggered.

"Well don't," shouted Vulgor, "if I thought for one moment you were laughing at me I'd…"

"I wasn't your Darkness, honest," protested Koor trying to keep a straight face. Varen continued to giggle covering her face to hide the laughter.

"Because if you were…" threatened Vulgor still lying face down in the dirt.

"I wasn't your Lordship, ask Varen." said Koor helping Vulgor to his feet. Vulgor pushed the bird away and struggled to his knees unaided.

"I've a good mind to turn you both into Gargoyles," threatened Vulgor as he finally stood up.

Varen angered by the injustice of such a punishment turned towards Vulgor.

"Me? Why me? What have I done?" she squawked. "I never kicked you."

"That's it!" scolded Vulgor, "I warned you."

Vulgor's pupils suddenly turned red and a bolt of energy shot from his eyes and struck Varen in the chest. Her body exploded with pain and she felt herself flying through the air. Her wings caught fire and she smelt the odour of burning feathers. With a thud she landed on the ground several metres away.

"The next time I won't be as lenient," said Vulgor.

Fearing the same Koor fell to his knees and begged for forgiveness. Singed and smelling of roasted chicken Varen picked herself up and joined her brother. Cowering at Vulgor's feet they both pleaded for leniency.

"I'll think about it," teased Vulgor as he hovered above them.

"Find me some food you pair of over bloated maggots," he ordered, "I haven't eaten in hours."

Varen and Koor nodded not daring to protest.

"Meet me at *The Cave of Shadows* when you've caught me something," he concluded and flew off.

By the time Koor and Varen looked up Vulgor had gone. They stood up and breathed a sigh of relief. They could see his outline in the sky far off to the north.

Suddenly, without any warning, Koor clouted Varen across the jaw.

"Ouch! What was that for?" protested Varen.

"For being a bird brain," said Koor, "fancy giggling like that at the Master. You nearly got *me* a roasting too!"

"Well I didn't, so shut your beak!" said Varen.

"Won't! Bird brain!"

"Squawk face!"

"Chicken breath!".

"Drumstick legs,"

The quarrel would have lasted much longer but for the sudden and almost fatal interruption of a volcanic bomb. Its approach had gone unnoticed due to the excessive noise of their argument. It struck Koor on the head and the unsuspecting bird exploded in a puff of smoke. When the smoke cleared Varen could see Koor standing in a large hole surrounded by burning lava. He was scorched and singed and smouldering like a fire doused with water.

Varen smirked and started to laugh.

Meanwhile, at the Cave Of Shadows, Tyrann was howling loudly having been awakened from its dreams by the familiar noise of Vulgor's wings. Tugging hard against its chains the three-headed lizard eagerly awaited its masters arrival.

Vulgor landed awkwardly skidding along the ground like a stick on ice. Tyrann could see the danger and stepped aside allowing his master to slide past him. Suddenly Vulgor came to an immediate halt as Tyrann's chain wrapped itself around his neck. The force of the impact dragged Tyrann off his feet, into the air and onto Vulgor's chest.

Vulgor couldn't move, the lizard's weight was pinning him to the ground and any movement tightened the chain around his throat. Drips of slaver fell on his face as the creature's three scaly heads snarled and snapped.

"Bad lizard," choked Vulgor, "down boy! Get down!"

Tyrann was too angry to respond. He howled louder and shook two of its three heads. The other looked invitingly at Vulgor's throat.

The chain around Vulgor's neck tightened yet again and he struggled for air. He tried to reason with the animal but the words became gargled and unclear.

"Nice Tyra...urg!" said Vulgor as his pet moved its head and the chain gripped tighter around his neck.

"Get... off...me!" Vulgor's words were strangled out of existence as Tyrann looked up and saw Varen and Koor flying towards him.

Koor hated Tyrann; the lizard had once bitten off a toe in an argument over a piece of meat. Since that attack Koor had longed to get even with the brute. But Vulgor had protected it. Tyrann had guarded Vulgor's most sacred of places, the Cave of Shadows and was therefore untouchable.

Koor crashed into Tyrann's stomach knocking the startled creature off Vulgor and onto the ground. Vulgor quickly flipped himself up onto his feet and released the chain from around his throat. Tyrann landed on its back and began kicking the air wildly with its huge back legs. Its smaller forearms waved from side to side as it attempted to roll itself back onto its feet. The chains around its necks entangled and pulled taught turning the creature onto its stomach. Tyrann lay outstretched on the ground panting for breath.

Koor went over to Vulgor with a grin wider than a canyon. Varen, still clinging to a two-headed *Ratadon* she'd caught for Vulgor's dinner, flew down and landed beside them both. She tossed the meal towards Vulgor, who greedily caught it and started to devour it.

Vulgor swallowed the last piece of flesh and belched loudly. It had been very tasty and he belched again.

Across the courtyard Tyrann had returned to the cave's entrance.

"Come with me," screeched Vulgor and flew off to the cave's entrance. Koor and Varen followed.

Vulgor put Tyrann in his cage and Vulgor entered the cave. He paused only to beckon his conspirators to follow and then was gone. Only the sound of his claws clattering down the steps gave a clue to his whereabouts.

Quickly Koor and Varen entered the darkness and followed him into the Cave of Shadows.

The Cave of Shadows

Vulgor had discovered The Cave of Shadows many centuries ago hidden at the end of a long narrow passageway cut into the lava. Its secrets had inspired the Dark Wars and given birth to demons. He needed its inspiration once again.

The tunnel was exactly as he remembered it and he moved quickly down the spiralling steps into the darkness. Half way down it got brighter. Unseen flames flickered around the passageway casting a reddish tint over the walls. Strange drawings of unknown creatures were etched into the walls and Vulgor could see giant reptilian shadows moving all around him. The shadows followed his descent until they faded into the blackness. Finally he came to the end of the steps and paused. Ahead he could see the icy cold waters of *The Lake of Fire*. The lake looked dark and menacing with patches of burning oil floating on its surface. Bubbles of sulphur burst to the surface and filled the air with the smell of rotten eggs. A narrow strip of shingle about three metres wide surrounded the lake making a pathway around the water's edge.

Vulgor flew across the lake remembering how its waters had created the *Gores*. Sculptured by the

Vulgor picked himself up and staggered to his feet. He held his stomach and rubbed his jaw. His missing tooth still ached and the pain in his stomach only added to his agony.

Koor and Varen seeing their master's discomfort scrambled to their feet and went across to him.

"Stay away from me you pair of Dodos."

Vulgor pushed them aside and looked up at the pyramid.

It was covered in carvings. Unknown creatures of all shapes and sizes had been drawn on every side. Some had two heads others three. Some flew and others didn't. One figure towered above them all. It was humanoid and reminded Vulgor of Wizard Zardo. The human figure stood erect and held a large globe shaped object in its hand. Above the figure, eight more globes of differing sizes had been carved in the wall. At the top of the pyramid winged reptiles had been drawn. Their wings outstretched as if in flight. Each flying reptile carried a lizard like creature on its back. Towards the base of the pyramid an army of animals fled in panic from a pack of three headed dogs.

Vulgor moved closer to the pyramid and touched it. Immediately the structure reacted to his touch and a fine yellow mist drifted out from what appeared to be a sealed entrance.

"What is it?" asked Koor," I've never seen anything like it."

Varen shook her head and gazed up at its splendour.

"Its awesome," she whispered, "where did it come from? "

Vulgor ignored them and moved closer to the pyramid. He placed his head against the door and listened. The hidden opening continued to vent gas and Vulgor was engulfed in thick yellow smoke. Suddenly there was a click and part of the wall began to move. Vulgor stepped back.

"Yes!" he squawked with excitement.

The doorway opened and more yellow smoke billowed out.

"Wait for me," ordered Vulgor and entered the pyramid. Immediately the doorway closed and Koor and Varen were left standing alone.

Suddenly the twins felt sleepy.

They found a rock and lazily sat down against it.

Soon they were fast asleep.

Inside The Pyramid

Inside the pyramid *something* flopped in the darkness in front of him.

Slop!

There it was again. It sounded like the noise an egg makes when it breaks on the floor.

Flop! Slop!

This time it was closer. He could hear breathing. He stretched out a claw but felt only darkness.

"Who's there?" whispered Vulgor but there was no response.

Flop! Slop! The *something* moved again. He tried to follow the sound but the darkness camouflaged it.

"What do you want?" said a voice from the blackness. Vulgor turned and stared into yet more darkness. He was sure he recognised the voice. He peered deep into the gloom hoping to confirm his suspicions but saw nothing.

"What do you want?" repeated the voice more firmly.

"Gorf is that you?" said Vulgor.

There was a long pause. The air suddenly chilled and a familiar stench drifted towards him. His nostrils twitched and he smelt the foul odour of stagnant water. Now he was positive, only Gorf had an odour as bad as that.

"But it can't be!" said Vulgor, "you're dead!"

Again there was no reply.

"It's me! Vulgor! Remember me?"

The creature in the darkness said nothing.

Vulgor's mind wandered back to the Dark Wars. Gorf had been one of his Generals. He was a Tellurian who'd been seduced by the evils of the Dark Zone. It had been Gorf who had found and opened the Gateway between the two worlds. Without Gorf the Dark Wars would never had happened.

Vulgor smelt Gorf's unmistakable foulness again. He searched the shadows for his lost comrade but saw no one.

Hidden in the darkness was Gorf. He was puzzled and very confused. A century of imprisonment had made him mindful of Zardo's anger.

Vulgor could be an illusion, a cruel deception created by Zardo.

He would remain silent and wait to see what happens.

Gorf

Gorf had been born on Tellurian in a stream on the outskirts of Amphibia. His father and his father before him had both been kings of the city and tradition ordained he was to follow in their footsteps.

He had hated life as a Tadphib and wished only to grow legs and hop out of the water. Life in the water was harsh and only the strong survived. He had been bottom of the food chain and had needed to be resourceful to survive. He saw the weak devoured and the foolish die. So he grew cruel and callous and sacrificed others in order to survive.

Having finally metamorphosed he had hopped out of the pond and had waited impatiently for his ageing father to die. Decades passed and he grew meaner and more repulsive. He became fat and bloated. His stomach bulged and layers of fat grew around his belly like dried mud. His skin wrinkled and lines of putrefied skin formed around his feet like slices of rotting meat. Warts and carbuncles infested his body and boils spurted yellow pus over his skin. Sores festered and his head grew out of all proportion to his body.

Eventually his father had died and he was proclaimed King of Amphibia and the twin kingdoms of Amphia and Hibila. He was carried (it took twenty young Amphibs to lift him) into the town's shared square and placed upon the great Doat's Stone and ordained king.

But his reign was brief. He abused his situation and used it for personal gain. He did little to improve the lives of his subjects and become obsessed with sorcery and black magic. He read Amphibious, a book about the history of his species and discovered Anura, the city's first king, was a great sorcerer. Anura had written down his secrets in a book called The Anthology of Sorcery. He had wanted that book and had ransacked the city searching for it. Finally he had discovered it hidden under the Doat's Stone.

Attracted to the darker side of the book he had studied the art of black magic and had been seduced by its power. He discovered the mysteries of the Dark Zone and was able to open the Gateway into its domain. He became an evil tyrant governing the Amphibs through fear and threats of supernatural tortures. The Elders and Chief Priests of the city had feared his evil tyran-

ny and had plotted to overthrow him. But before they could imprison him he'd escaped through the Gateway into the Dark Zone.

Inside the Zone he had persuaded Vulgor to invade Tellurian, destroy the Amphibs and conquer the rest of the island.

With the Gateway between the two dimensions open the creatures of the Dark Zone had invaded Tellurian and an epic battle between the two worlds had taken place. But the war had been lost and he and the Gores had been captured by Zardo and imprisoned in the Black Pyramid. There they had remained until now.

Secrets of the Pyramid

The Lord of the Dark Zone grew impatient.

"Show yourself!"

Vulgor's words echoed in the darkness like distant thunder.

Silence.

"Gorf you over bloated amphibian," squawked Vulgor angrily, "where are you?"

The blackness responded with more silence.

Vulgor's pupils grew red with anger and from his eyes a bolt of energy shot out into the darkness. It struck a wall and exploded in a shower of flames. For a few seconds the pyramid was bathed in light and Vulgor thought he saw a large animal standing in front of him. It stood six metres tall and stank of rotting food.

The flames quickly died and the pyramid was plunged into darkness.

"Curse you Gorf! " said Vulgor; "I demand you show yourself immediately."

A shaft of light suddenly broke the darkness and lit up a figure standing on a rock surrounded by a small circular pond.

"Gorf is that you?" said Vulgor. "What have they done to you?"

The figure didn't move.

Vulgor shuffled to the edge of the pond and looked across at Gorf, he'd been turned to stone.

Swish!

In the darkness above him, Vulgor thought he heard movement. He looked up but saw nothing.

Whoosh!

This time it was behind him and he spun to face the intruder, but again there was no one there.

Suddenly they were all around him whispering in his head.

"Set us free! Set us free!" They chanted.

Then the invisible beings were gone and the pyramid fell silent.

"WHAT DO YOU WANT?" boomed Gorf suddenly turning towards Vulgor.

Vulgor was taken by surprise and stepped backwards.

"Gorf! You're alive," shouted Vulgor, "you scared me to death."

Gorf sat down on the rock and gazed across at his long lost General.

"Is *that* really you?" asked Gorf.

"Yes Gorf it's Vulgor."

"I thought you dead," said Gorf.

"And I you," replied Vulgor, "It must be a hundred years since I saw you last."

"Only a hundred," said Gorf, "it seems like a lifetime."

Suddenly a large dragonfly, attracted by the light, flew into view and Gorf flicked out his tongue and ate it.

Vulgor watched as Gorf ate the fly.

"It's my lunch!" said Gorf flicking out his tongue to reveal a two-headed water snake wriggling on the end of it. Vulgor caught the sight of other creatures trapped inside the amphibian's gigantic mouth.

"Sorry," said Gorf swallowing the contents of his mouth with a loud belch.

"Pardon me!"

Gorf belched again and the familiar smell of stagnant water drifted into Vulgor's nostrils.

"Wind," said Gorf, "I always get wind after a meal."

"I thought you were dead!" said Vulgor.

"I might as well be," moaned Gorf, "call this living?"

Gorf lifted his enormous head and raised his huge eyes in disgust.

"How did you know where to find me?" asked Gorf.

"I didn't," said Vulgor. "I wasn't looking for you."

"You weren't?"

" No!"

"So you haven't come to rescue me?"

"Rescue you? I don't understand," continued Vulgor, "I went to the Cave of Shadows to create more Gores, instead I found you and this pyramid."

"Gores?"

"It's taken me nearly a century but I've succeeded in opening the Gateway again," explained Vulgor. "I'm planning to invade Tellurian."

"You're invading Tellurian?" asked Gorf.

Vulgor stopped talking and looked across at Gorf angrily.

"Must you keep repeating everything I say?

"Sorry your Lordship."

Gorf could see Vulgor's eyes turning red and past experiences told him to beware.

"But Vulgor, your Darkship, you don't understand," explained Gorf, "this pyramid has been my prison and has been for nearly a hundred years."

"A prison?"

"Zardo put me here after the Dark Wars."

"Zardo!" muttered Vulgor.

"The Gores are here too, prisoners like me."

"My Gores, alive," squawked Vulgor. "Where are they?"

Gorf hesitated before replying.

"Um! Everywhere and nowhere."

Vulgor looked into the blackness beyond the shaft of light and saw nothing.

"Look you over bloated bladder of spawn, I haven't time for your riddles. Where are they?"

"They're invisible!" croaked Gorf, "spirits of the air."

"Invisible!" screeched Vulgor, "what do you mean?"

"It's this place," said Gorf, "it possesses great power."

Vulgor suddenly remembered the disembodied voices that had flown around him.

"They're not as great as mine," boasted Vulgor bombarding the room with energy bolts. They exploded on the walls lighting up a room without doors.

"You see Sire," said Gorf, "there's no escape. I've tried, its impossible."

Gorf shuffled uncomfortably on his rock.

"Look you timid little *tadloid*," blasted Vulgor, "I got in, so I'll get out!"

The amphibian shook his head.

"I don't think so your Darkness," said Gorf, "you're a prisoner in here too I'm afraid."

Vulgor stared at Gorf and in his anger released an energy bolt at him.

"Nothing keeps ME a prisoner!"

Gorf dodged out of its way but lost his footing and fell into the water.

Splat!

Water splashed everywhere. The energy bolt struck the wall behind Gorf. There was a small explosion and then silence.

"Sorry," spluttered Gorf wondering how Vulgor would react.

Vugor just glared at him and said nothing.

"There's nothing we can do about it," insisted Gorf, "we're trapped."

"Oh are we?" growled Vulgor. "We'll see about that."

Vulgor went silent and stared into the water.

Gorf waited patiently.

The room went silent for several seconds.

"Any ideas yet?" interrupted Gorf after what seemed like an eternity.

"No! Go away and let me think."

"Sorry," whimpered Gorf and he closed his eyes. Immediately the waters around him began to bubble and glow with an eerie red light. A beam of crimson came up from the bottom of the pool and scanned him. Rays of light broke the surface and spiked through his body like arrows of sunlight. The water turned red and then slowly faded into a translucent pink. Finally the light faded and the water cleared.

Vulgor stared at Gorf in disbelief.

"How did you do that?" asked Vulgor with great interest.

"Oh its something I discovered years ago," answered Gorf, "watch!"

Suddenly the water rippled and images of the Dark Zone appeared just under its surface.

"It's the Dark Zone!" shouted Vulgor excitedly.

"I know," said Gorf, "I created it."

"You created it?"

"Yes. I just jump into the pond," continued Gorf, "close my eyes and dream."

Vulgor said nothing.

"Vulgor?" asked Gorf interrupting Vulgor's meditation.

"Shush! I'm thinking."

Gorf went silent.

"And whatever you dream appears in the water," asked Vulgor.

"Um! Yes I suppose it does. I never thought of looking at it like that," said Gorf.

"No I don't imagine you have," said Vulgor, "otherwise you might have discovered a way out of here."

"What!"

"Don't you see," said Vulgor, "the pyramid uses your imagination to create a fantasy. It not only creates your dreams but also your nightmares."

"Sorry your Greatship, but I still don't understand."

"Look, you dream of the Dark Zone and what happens?"

"I see the Dark Zone."

"Correct," said Vulgor.

Gorf swam to the edge of the pond to get closer to Vulgor.

"And your worst nightmare?"

"Being imprisoned in here for all eternity," replied Gorf.

"Precisely! Now do you understand?"

There was a moment's silence before Gorf answered.

"No!"

"Its an illusion," said Vulgor, "a very good illusion I'll grant you, but an illusion nevertheless."

"What is?"

"This prison, that pond, the food you eat," continued Vulgor, "Zardo has found another Gateway and is using it to keep you and the Gores prisoners in your own dimension."

Gorf climbed out of the water and stood next to Vulgor. Water dripped off his body and onto the floor making it wet and shiny.

Gorf looked at the pond and the pool of water at his feet.

"It's not real," insisted Vulgor, "none of it is."

"So I've been wandering around in my own nightmare all these years?"

"Yes," said Vulgor suddenly grabbing Gorf by the throat, "stupid aren't you?"

Gorf nodded.

"But Zardo has made a big mistake," gloated Vulgor letting go of Gorf's throat.

"How?" asked Gorf.

"We turn his own illusion against him," continued Vulgor, "and trick *him* into becoming *our* prisoner."

Vulgor laughed and spun around like a demented *Scorpo-bug* about to sting a victim.

"Come my overbloated friend," encouraged Vulgor, "time to shatter illusions and get revenge."

With that he pushed Gorf into the imaginary pond.

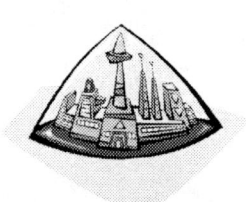

Location   *The Planet Earth*

Time Zone   *The Present*
   – Three Hours Later

Izward

Izward was drifting in a sea of blackness. He dreamt of serpents and sea dragons, of giant squids and monstrous fish. They swam towards him out of the pages of a giant book that floated in front of him. They snapped and snarled, spat and squirted their mouths open ready to devour him. Then they were gone and he was left to dream in timeless oblivion.

He dreamt he was flying in the air and gliding through brightly lit rooms. Swooping along passageways and crashing through doors that split in two and swung apart. He saw himself on an operating table surrounded by nurses and doctors. They held strange metal objects, which they hurriedly inserted into his body.

Screens beeped and monitors flashed. Alarms wailed and sirens shrieked. Suddenly the room vanished in a blaze of light and he felt himself drawn into the centre of its brilliance. For a second his eyes opened and masked faces looked down at him, but they faded into the light and disappeared. He felt cosy and safe and sank into a blissful slumber.

Location   *The Planet Earth*

Time Zone   *The Present*
              —Two Years Later

Coma

Izward's consciousness was travelling along a narrow tunnel towards a bright blue light. How long the journey had taken him was unclear but he knew it was coming to an end. The circle of light was getting bigger and he was racing towards it at great speed. Suddenly the tunnel disappeared and he crashed through the light.

He opened his eyes and looked up into a clear blue sky. The sky looked familiar but he couldn't remember why. He tried to move but some unknown force held him. He could hear bleeps and clicks and the familiar music of Tchaikovsky's Overture '1812' playing somewhere in the background. Tchaikovsky had always been his favourite composer and he closed his eyes to listen to the man's genius. He loved the final movement and as the cannons roared and the bells announced Napoleon's defeat he drifted back into unconsciousness.

Ever since the operation PETE had monitored Izward's recovery. Two years earlier Izward had come back from *The Abandon Zone* with horrific spinal injuries. To save his life the Institute doctors had carried out a series of emergency operations on his damaged spine. They replaced crushed vertebrae with state of the art artificial ones and used Microsurgery techniques to repair sections of his spinal chord. After the operation he had gone into a deep coma and was taken to the Institute's hospital wing for evaluation.

Izward's future at the Institute looked bleak. His injuries would prevent him from achieving his potential and therefore no longer a viable investment. However his expertise in VTR programming was outstanding and the Institute could not afford to lose him. The Mentors elected to keep him on *Schedule* and provided him with the medical facilities to aid his recovery. He was wired up to a Holographic Brain-Imager and PETE was left to monitor his progress. Various therapeutic interventions were introduced and PETE conducted brief sessions of sensory stimulation.

Over the next two years PETE stimulated Izward's subconscious with voices of his *Family* and music from his favourite composers.

Suddenly the Midi-Alarms around Izward's bed sounded again. Machines bleeped and equipment buzzed, bells rang and T.V. monitors flashed.

PATIENT EMERGING FROM COMA

Areas on the rotating holographic image above Izward's bed turned green indicating electrical activity in the Brainstem and the Cerebellum. More and more sections turned green as the EEG and C-T scanners showed Izward struggling for consciousness.

PETE's two-year vigil was about to be rewarded. His patient was waking up.

Location   *The Planet Earth*

Time Zone   *The Past*

Captain Hoot

High up on the mountains of Tellurian the overnight rain had filled the *Lake of Eternity* to overflowing. When morning came it was wet and grey and a howling wind blew across the lake making its waters difficult to navigate.

On the lake a single boat struggled against the wind. Captain Barnacle Hoot, the pilot and owner of the vessel *Eternity* was in danger of capsizing. He should never have ventured out on such a morning but he had a service to provide.

He sat alone desperately trying to steady the rocking boat. The wind howled through his feathers and his large round eyes stung with the force of the rain. Water bombarded the fragile vessel and the boat rose and fell with the swell of the water.

The bottom of the rowing boat was awash with water and Hoot was convinced the vessel was in danger. It had taken on too much water and was perilously close to sinking.

He regretted not learning to swim.

Wet and very tired from the effort of keeping the boat afloat, Hoot prayed for a miracle.

A lifetime of memories flooded his mind and he remembered the day he became a hero.

During the Dark Wars he'd been Wizard Zardo's Wing Commander. In those days he'd been a gifted young owl responsible for Aerial Strikes and Skyward Strategies.

In the final days of the Dark Wars Vulgor had been facing defeat and had ordered the Gores to find Zardo and destroy him. The battle had taken place over the Forest of Tellurian and he'd taken command of the Terrodacs and had led them against the Gores. Attacking in triangular groups of nine they'd swooped down on the unsuspecting Gores and had surprised them. The Gores had panicked and had fled in confusion.

From their location on the ground Zardo and the Tellurians had bombarded the bewildered Gores with wooden spears and makeshift javelins and victory had been Zardo's.

However, one of the Gores had avoided detection and had broken through their defences. It had tried to kill Zardo but he'd attacked it and it had fled. But as the Gore had retreated it had bit into his wing and snapped a bone. He had plummeted to earth like a stone and had hit the ground with a thud. He had known the instant he hit the ground he would never fly again.

He'd been proclaimed a hero and Zardo himself had presented him with a medal for his bravery.

After the war he had bought himself a small boat and now ferried the good creatures of Tellurian across the Lake of Eternity.

The wind eased slightly and for the first time since daybreak the sky began to brighten. The rain stopped and a hazy yellow sun penetrated the clouds. Suddenly the sky was full of screeching seabirds and Hoot's mind returned to the present.

They dipped and dived, swooped and hovered around the little boat as if it were a shoal of fish. Several had landed on the boat and were now perched along its sides unaware they were upsetting the stability of the vessel.

"Shoo! Yer pesky scavengers," hooted Captain Hoot, "be off with yer!"

The *Seadacts* ignored him.

"Clear the decks yer flock of flying fish bellies," bellowed the owl, "yer sinking me boat!"

Fearing the boat would finally capsize Captain Hoot prepared to abandon ship. His life ring, a hollowed out log with the words *H.M.S. Eternity* etched around the rim, was his only hope, but that now floated out of reach at the front of the boat. He cursed himself for not wearing it. Suddenly the boat started spinning out of control.

Lake Eternity

Lake Eternity has a number of underwater currents that run like invisible rivers under the surface of the water. They leave the lake through a labyrinth of holes and tunnels that flow unnoticed under the ground. Like the roots of an ancient tree these tunnels connect in a maze of watery highways deep under the island.

On the surface of the lake Hoot's boat was spinning hopelessly out of control. His vessel had been caught in a whirlpool and was being sucked under. The boat was swamped with water and he knew it was going to sink. He took a deep breath and filled his lungs with air. The boat suddenly disintegrated and he found himself being dragged under.

The water felt cold and frightening and his lungs burst for air. He kicked out wildly hoping to escape the current and find the surface but it was far too strong. He panicked and lost all sense of direction and he knew he was going to drown.

Then he saw the Mermaid.

She glided towards him like a watery spirit bathed in an aurora of blue light. She had the face of a young girl and a thousand strands of golden hair floated about her head like sheaves of corn in a summer breeze. She hovered in front of him swishing her tail for balance. She looked at him and all his fears melted like snow on a hot winter's day. He stared in disbelief. Captivated by the creature's beauty he could only stare and wonder at the meaning of such a vision.

She smiled and started to sing and he suddenly felt warm and secure. The creature's voice soothed away his fears and he no longer felt afraid. He closed his eyes and drifted into blackness.

The angelic singing stopped and Captain Hoot opened his eyes. He knew he should be in heaven and about to spend eternity in paradise. But the landscape around him was not what he'd expected. He'd expected heaven to be a wondrous place full of fun and excitement. Instead it looked dull and uneventful. There were no angels to greet him and he felt cold and wet. Instead of flying through the clouds with cherubs he was bobbing up and down like a cork in water. Suddenly his confused mind realised he wasn't dead and by some miracle he was still alive. Around his waist was the wooden lifebelt from his boat. It was keeping him afloat and safe from drowning. How it had got there he had no way of knowing.

Then he remembered the girl and he knew his guardian angel had been watching over him.

A Great Danger

Wizard Zardo had listened to his housekeeper's story with utter amazement. Her description of the bird was that of Vulgor, a creature he thought he would never see again. Her sighting of Vulgor could mean only one thing he'd found a way to re-open the Gateway into Tellurian.

To avoid panic he'd convinced Mrs. Clutter she'd seen a seadact enlarged by the curvature of her bucket. To demonstrate how she'd been fooled he had taken a spare pail from his broom cupboard and had shown her what might have happened. He had put his face in the bucket and she had seen his reflected image twist and bend around the inside of the pail. She had started to laugh and soon both of them were chuckling and giggling as the wizard's distorted face danced around the bucket.

She had gone home happily convinced she'd seen a seadact and not some creature from her nightmares. Zardo had smiled at her in that reassuring way all wizards have and closed the door quietly behind her. After she had left he had sat down to analyse her discovery.

If Vulgor had returned it meant Tellurian was in great danger. The thought of another war terrified him. He was getting too old for conflict and needed time to organise his thoughts and consult his books.

He spent the last remaining hours of the day searching for the knowledge that would save Tellurian from the evils to come. Finally he stopped reading and rubbed his tired eyes. The book offered no solution and he would have to consult others. He put it down and went towards his bookcase.

Next to the bookcase was his astrological chart. Carved into the wall were twelve mystical signs each representing a different phase of the planet's orbit around the sun. Against each symbol a series of runes and numerals had been added. A large red circle had been drawn around an etching of two fish and the numeral X. He put his finger on the symbol and smiled.

"Why its my birthday," he said softly to himself, "today's my birthday."

Feeling very old he selected another book from the bookcase and returned to his chair.

The Orb of Fire

Outside the pyramid Varen and Koor snored loudly, their heads resting on each other's shoulders. The moment Vulgor had entered the pyramid a strange tiredness had come over them and they had fallen fast asleep. There they had remained unaware of the events that were taking place inside the pyramid.

Inside Vulgor was making plans. Finding Gorf and the pyramid had been an unexpected bonus. The pyramid was a Gateway to Tellurian and Gorf's pond a window to Zardo. He would use both to bring about Zardo's capture. Having formulated his plans he summoned Gorf.

"Gorf?"

"Yes Sire?"

"I want you to do something for me."

"And what is that your Lordship?" said Gorf swimming towards the edge of the pond.

"Find Zardo," said Vulgor.

"What!"

Gorf looked terrified and Vulgor threw him one of his thunderbolt glares.

"But, Sire," said Gorf weakly.

"That's an order!"

"Yes your Darkness," said Gorf reluctantly.

"That's the spirit," beamed Vulgor, "spoken like a true Darkling!"

Vulgor quickly prepared the magic that would send Gorf through the Gateway.

He produced a large silver sphere and started to roll it around in his claws. It started to hum and make strange whistling sounds. The more he rolled it the louder it hummed. It crackled with energy and bolts of lightning arched arounds its surface.

"What's that?" enquired Gorf reaching out with an inquisitive hand.

"Don't touch that," shouted Vulgor hiding it from view, "it's the *Orb of Fire*."

Gorf retracted his hand immediately.

"It's a magical metal sphere forged from the volcanic fires of the Dark Zone," he shouted, "its power will reverse the energy flow from the Gateway."

He held the orb high above his head and began to chant strange words. Rivers of energy meandered across its surface and it began to glow.

Vulgor's chanting continued until the orb became a bright blue ball glowing in his claws. A blue aurora surrounded his body and fire flickered in the pupil's of his eyes.

There he stood, on the edge of the pond, waiting for the Orb to perform its magic.

Unfamiliar Water

Lake Eternity is at its prettiest at sunset. It is a canvas of spectacular beauty for all to see. The sky deepens to a blood red and the sun hangs in the heavens like a yellow ball. The waters of the lake turn a cold orange and a rippling image of the sun dances across its surface. The horizon turns a fiery red and the outline of mountains silhouette against the sky. But this evening, the lake had only one observer, Captain Hoot.

The owl had drifted in the lake most of the day and had been carried along with the current. It had taken him far and he now floated in unfamiliar water.

He was wet and tired but thankful to be alive.

Soon the sun would set and he would face darkness. He looked around hoping to see some familiar landmark but there was nothing he recognised. The lake had narrowed into a river that now flowed through a rocky canyon. Granite cliffs towered high above him and between the cliff tops he could see the sky.

Then like the blowing out of a candle the day ended and an eerie half-light lit up the sky.

The current became much stronger and he felt himself being swept along with its flow. With each new bend in the river there came a different obstacle. He encountered rapids and underwater currents, eddies and whirlpools. But as he rounded the next bend he heard the roar of water and knew he was about to face his greatest challenge yet.

Another Dimension

The Orb had become transparent and from out of Vulgor's claws came a shaft of blue light. It swirled across the surface of the water like a morning mist.

"Gorf, are you ready?"

"I think so," said Gorf unconvincingly.

"You'd better be," thundered Vulgor, "my invasion rests on your success."

"I know," replied Gorf, "that's what worries me."

Vulgor had explained what would happen to him but the thought of being split into a thousand atoms and then hopefully be reassembled in another dimension worried him.

"There's nothing to worry about," coaxed Vulgor, "trust me there's no danger."

"If you say so Sire."

Gorf tried to remember what he had to do once in the other dimension but Vulgor's instructions seemed all of a muddle.

"Don't be such a tadpole! There's nothing to it. Trust me! Ready?"

"Yes your Lordship." said Gorf.

Gorf closed his eyes and Vulgor looked deep into the Orb. The fire in Vulgor's eyes passed into the orb, down the shaft of light and into the pond.

The water began to bubble and an eerie red glow engulfed Gorf's body. Rays of light broke the surface and spiked through his flesh like spears. Then they dimmed and slid back into the water. The redness faded into pink and the waters cleared. From the surface of the pool a watery image of Wizard Zardo appeared.

The Mysteries of the Universe

Wizard Zardo yawned and closed the book. With a sigh he placed it on the floor beside his chair. Its contents gave him nothing. He would have to search others. The log fire had burnt low and the clock on the mantelpiece ticked noisily to the hour.

Tick! Tock! Tick! Tock!

The pendulum swung freely counting out the seconds that would herald another hour.

Tick! Tock! Tick! Tock!

Round and round turned the cogs locking together in perfect harmony.

Tick! Tock! Tick! Tock!

Whirled the wheels and levers in a never-ending circle of time.

Anticipating the striking of the hour Wizard Zardo put his hands over his ears and waited for the clock to chime. The clock clicked and whirled as a small door in the clock's face flew open. From out of the door a small wooden gnome sitting on a toadstool popped out. The figure had been carved out of wood and painted a bright yellow. A large blue pointed hat sat on its head and it held a large cudgel in its hands.

As the hands of the clock approached the hour the wizard squeezed his hands tighter to his ears. He looked at the clock and waited for the hour to strike. As the big hand touched twelve another door in the clock's face clicked open and a large trout like fish jumped out. Immediately the gnome hit the fish on the snout with its cudgel. As the club hit the fish the clock struck the hour.

Bong!

The whole room shook. A teacup fell off the mantelpiece and several of the wizard's books slid off the bookcase onto the floor.

Bong!

The doors rattled and the timbers vibrated. The whole of the inside of the tree rattled as the grandmaster clock informed Zardo it was two o'clock.

Then silence!

Having delivered the time as accurately as it knew it returned to normal.

Tick! Tock! Tick! Tock!

The fish jumped backwards through its door and the gnome hurried home to wait patiently for another opportunity to whack the fish.

Tick! Tock! Tick! Tock!

Wizard Zardo took his hands away from his ears and stood up. He went over to the fire and bent down to examine the teacup. It was broken beyond repair. He carefully picked up the pieces and placed them back on the mantelpiece. He waved his forefinger at the broken pieces and magically they floated back together.

Zardo crossed the room to his bookcase and examined his priceless library. Written somewhere amongst these books must be the information he so desperately needed. Hundreds of books lay in untidy piles on top of each other. Books about magic and sorcery, about spells and incantations.

Several lay open on the bare wooden shelving disclosing chapters on powders and potions, herbs and spices. He gently ran his finger across each manuscript for tell-tale signs of dust but there was none. He inwardly congratulated Mrs. Clutter for her devotion to her work, she was a fine housekeeper and he trusted her judgement.

He bent down and rummaged through the books on the bottom shelf. The books here were much older. Some were very old, older than time itself and their pages were aged and crumbly. He handled these carefully, fearful of obliterating their fragile contents. He searched on lifting up each book in turn and reading out loud its title.

Spells of the Ancient Ones
How to Become a Magician
A Practical Study in Magic for Wizards
The Wizard's Guidebook
The Anthology of Sorcery

He had several more practical magic type books but these were not what he was looking for. He explored his bookcase further and to his delight found his own book hidden amongst the others. He picked up the manuscript and lovingly read its title.

The Mysteries of the Universe by Wizard Zardo

The book was unfinished and he flicked through the pages eager to read his own words. He marvelled at its contents and knew he'd written the greatest book on magic ever written. He'd meant to bring it up to date but time and old age had got in the way. Suddenly he remembered the chapter he'd written on The Dark Zone. He cursed himself for not having remembered it earlier. He took the book and sat down. He flicked through the pages and found the chapter he was looking for. Quickly he read its contents and to his great delight found the relevant information.

It would take careful planning but he knew he could defeat Vulgor.

Out of Existence

The earth shuddered as Vulgor's castle trembled in the aftershock of another earthquake.

Between the shaking towers of lava the Genesis-stone swung wildly out of control held in place by its invisible cradle.

The altar below the stone rumbled and two blinding yellow lights blasted out from either side of the shrine and up the towers. Spiralling around each of the columns the light-beams headed towards the Eye.

Having reached the top they shot towards each other and crashed together in a clash of light. There was a blinding flash and a beam of white light struck the centre of the stone. The beam reflected off the Eye towards the Cave of Shadows.

Travelling faster than the eye could follow a single beam of light entered the cave, down the passage and into the pyramid.

Once inside, the beam struck the Orb of Fire and passed through it down into the pool. The orb went yellow and flames raced around its surface and Vulgor still clutching the orb, was bathed in a halo of yellow light.

Varen and Koor who were still fast asleep in the cave saw nothing. The hypnotic effects of the pyramid still held them captive. However a beam of light now lit up the cave like a beacon. It buzzed and droned like a hive of angry bees drowning out the noise of their snoring.

Inside the pyramid the beam of light spread across the pool like melting candle wax. The water clouded and a rainbow of colour slowly covered the surface. Zardo's image faded and Gorf was alone once more.

"Remember my overgrown Wartface," reminded Vulgor, "you have to get Zardo into the Gateway."

The amphibian nodded. He felt strange. The effect of the orb had already begun and he felt light-headed. His hands and feet had become transparent and he could see the waters of the pool through them.

"Remember," shouted Vulgor, but before Vulgor could give him his final instructions Gorf faded out of existence.

The Mirror

Wizard Zardo stopped reading and rubbed his eyes. His chapter on the Dark Zone was, as he had feared, incomplete and needed to be finished. He stood up and began to search for his quill.

The room had chilled and he felt cold. He shivered slightly as he put more logs onto the fire. They burst into flames immediately and he stood in front of the fireplace warming himself.

Above the fireplace was a large upright mirror. He looked into it and saw his own troubled eyes staring back. They looked tired and sad. Dark rings of worry hung in folds under each pupil and he looked old and ancient.

He gently tapped the mirror, knowing it kept a dark secret.

He looked again at his ageing features and ran a bony finger along the wrinkles on his face. But he shouldn't worry he told himself, his secret was safe and the Gateway was sealed forever.

Having abandoned his search for the quill he returned to his chair. He would use a more reliable method for finding his pen. He sat down and picked up his book. He uttered a few words and a feather-pen and inkbottle suddenly appeared and floated in front of him. Taking the pen in his right hand he dipped it into the inkbottle and he started to write. He wrote quickly pausing only to gather his thoughts. He knew time was against him and he needed to finish the chapter.

However in his eagerness to finish he failed to see a very familiar figure materialise in the mirror.

The Lord Of The Dark Zone

Gorf had had the most terrifying experience of his worthless life. Passing from one dimension to another had not been a pleasant experience and he never wished to do it again.

"Where are you?"

Vulgor's voice echoed inside Gorf's head like the sound of the sea inside a shell.

"I don't know, but I can see the wizard, he's writing something in a big book," said Gorf.

"Good," said Vulgor's voice, *"it worked."*

But Gorf wasn't so sure. Unable to move or even see himself he began to question his state of being.

"Where exactly am I?" he asked.

"You know where you are," answered the voice inside his head, *"we discussed it before you left. You're at the other side of the Gateway."*

"But I can't see myself," said Gorf, "it's as if I don't exist."

"Um...you don't!" said Vulgor.

"What! I don't exist?"

"Correct!"

"You mean I'm not an *Amphib* anymore?"

"In a manner of speaking, yes!" stated Vulgor with great authority.

"Then what am I?" said Gorf getting very concerned.

"Well…Um… How can I explain this? You are your own mind without your body."

"What?"

"Don't worry your body's safe. It's floating around somewhere. No harm will come to it. You'll get it back when you pass through the Gateway."

"But!"

"Look, its all to do with the magic in the Orb," explained Vulgor impatiently.

"But I need my body, " demanded Gorf.

"It's far too complicated to explain," lectured Vulgor, *"you'll get it back!"*

"When." asked Gorf?

"Soon! Trust me I'm the Lord Of The Dark Zone, I know these things."

Gorf said nothing. He missed his body and his mind felt lonely and detached. It wasn't a very nice body, he knew that, but it was all he had.

"Remember get Zardo through the Gateway and the Orb will do the rest."

"And how am I going to do that," asked Gorf?

But there was no reply.

As he watched Zardo writing he suddenly had an idea. The Gateway was disguised as a mirror. If he used its illusionary powers to become Zardo's reflection he could trick the wizard into the mirror.

The Wizard in the Mirror

Wizard Zardo stood up, placed his book on his chair and walked over to the mirror. He looked again at his ageing image and stroked his long white beard. He ran his fingers through the matted strands hoping to untangle the knotted whiskers.

The image in the mirror copied his every move.

"Oh witches whiskers," he cursed out loud as the unruly whiskers curled back to their original positions.

"Warlocks!" he swore at his reflection.

"There's no need for that! " scolded a familiar voice from inside the mirror, "we mustn't swear."

Zardo recognised the voice it was his own. He turned back to the mirror and saw his own reflection had taken on a life of its own. No longer did it mimic his every move but spoke and moved independently.

Zardo looked at the image inside the mirror with utter amazement. It was an exact copy of himself.

Slowly he walked towards it and stared straight into the eyes of his double. The wizard in the mirror copied his every move.

"Its rude to stare," said the image.

Thinking something must have had gone wrong with an earlier spell he cursed again.

"Oh! Warlocks!"

"Don't swear," said Gorf mimicking Zardo's voice to perfection.

"This is silly," said the wizard out loud, "how did this happen?"

Zardo grew angry with himself. He must be getting forgetful in his old age. How could he not remember creating that! He looked at the other Zardo and it waved at him. He ignored the temptation to wave back and stood silent for a second or two. His mind went blank and he shook his head from side to side. He was getting far too old for all this silliness and decided to get rid of the apparition. He pointed his finger at the mirror and started to cast a spell. The reflection pointed back.

"This should do the trick."

The magician cast his spell but the image remained. Enraged at his failure he tried again.

"Be gone false spirit, out of sight. Take to the air, go take flight."

Nothing happened.

"Oh! Bother and bog warts!" said the wizard.

"It must be the Gateway playing tricks on me again."

Reluctantly Zardo looked into the mirror. His reflection waved and smiled at him. Zardo half returned the smile and decided to go along with the charade.

"What do you want?" said Zardo.

Gorf was pleased with himself. His plan was going well. Zardo didn't suspect a thing.

"Well I've noticed it's our birthday," said the disguised voice of Gorf, "I've come to wish us a happy birthday."

"Great!" said Zardo unimpressed. He hated birthdays and if this was a true copy of himself it should have known it.

Gorf sensed Zardo's unease. He had to be careful. He didn't want Zardo becoming suspicious.

"Look I've got us a cake," said Gorf.

From the shadows of the mirror a birthday cake appeared. It floated forward and squeezed through the mirror leaving ripples on the surface of the glass. It hovered in front of Zardo and waited. The wizard stared at the cake and then at his double.

The image in the mirror smiled reassuringly.

"There's something missing," said the figure in the mirror, "how old are we now?"

"Three hundred and fifty five," whispered Zardo, "but surely you should have known that?"

Zardo was growing more and more suspicious and Gorf knew it. He would have to act soon otherwise the wizard would see through his deception.

"Candles! We've got no candles on our birthday cake."

Suddenly two candles came gliding through the mirror and came to rest on top of the cake.

"Perfect," said the reflection, and immediately burst into several verses of happy birthday.

Happy birthday to me,
Happy birthday to you,
Happy birthday to both of me,
Happy birthday to us!

After several embarrassing minutes his double finally finished with,

For we are jolly good fellows,
We are jolly good fellows
For we are jolly good fellows
And so say all of us.

"Thank you, thank you. I think I've got the message," said the wizard holding his hands over his ears.

"But there's more," coaxed the image, "come closer I've a very special present for you as well."

Gorf was ready to spring the trap. Just a little bit nearer and he would have him. Zardo ventured forward.

"Oh to hex with this! This is ridiculous, " said Zardo and stopped.

Silently Gorf cursed his bad luck.

"You're a fake! A spell gone wrong!" said the wizard shaking his finger at the reflection of himself in the mirror. He turned away from the mirror and sat down.

"Don't go," but Zardo had sat down and picked up his book before Gorf could persuade him to collect his surprise.

But Gorf would be patient he would try again later.

A Wall of White Water

Captain Barnacle Hoot was tired. He had spent what seemed like an eternity in the water. He was wet and cold and his legs were numb. His feathers drooped and his eyes hurt. His head ached and his stomach throbbed where the wooden life belt was wedged around his waist. He felt sick and ill and wished only for a swift end to this nightmarish journey. He had long forgotten how many hours he'd drifted or how far he'd travelled. Ahead he could hear the pounding sound of water crashing on rocks.

The roar of the waterfall grew louder as the river swept him nearer to the river's end. Ahead of him he could see a row of grey pillars spanning the river like stone stalagmites. They stood a hundred metres tall and towered high into the evening sky. A rickety wooden walkway had been built along the tops of pillars to provide a path across the river. As the river carried him nearer he could see parts of the walkway had rotted and large holes had appeared. At the centre of the bridge the two supporting pillars had split and sections of the columns had fallen away. Here the wooded path had gone completely leaving a large gaping hole.

Beyond the bridge the river plunged over the edge of a deep ravine and disappeared into uncharted waters. Behind the waterfall stood a towering cliff just visible through the hazy mist. Trees and bushes, vines and creepers hung to its face like the whiskers on a giant.

Twisting and turning with the current the river carried him under the bridge towards the edge of the waterfall. A wall of white water swirled all around him and a barrage of noise thundered in his ears. Mist and spray filled the air and waves of water crashed all around him.

Suddenly he was swept over the edge and he fell into oblivion.

Happy Birthday

Zardo tried to write but found it impossible to concentrate. He sensed he was being watched and turned towards the mirror.

"Hi!" said Gorf in Zardo's voice, "Happy Birthday!"

His double held up a large parcel about half a metre square. It shone like morning sunbeams and was wrapped in shiny rainbow coloured paper. It had been carefully tied up with yellow string with a large label attached to it. "Happy Birthday Wizard Zardo," read the label.

"It's our birthday present," said the impostor, "come over here and open it."

"Leave me alone," mumbled Zardo angrily, "can't you see I'm busy?"

"Very well," said the image, "I'll leave it here. You can open it later."

The likeness of Zardo faded from view.

"Don't forget to open your present," echoed a voice from somewhere inside the mirror.

The wizard gave a sigh of relief and returned to his writing. He tried to write but found it impossible. Finally his curiosity got the better of him and he turned towards the mirror.

Something was floating in its centre. He put down his pen and approached it. In the mirror he saw a large box. It was spinning around a central axis and he could see letters had been printed on each of its six faces. As it spun it spelt out a word.

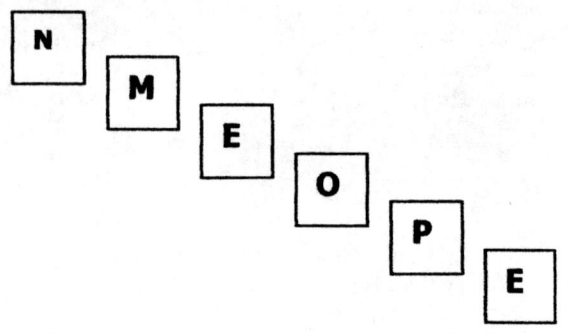

N M E O P E

"Oh! Dragon droppings," he uttered, "I've no time for silly games."

He ignored the message and returned to the book. He wrote on and on until his task was completed and the chapter was finished. He blew on the inky wet pages to dry them and closed the book. He sat back to admire his work and smiled with satisfaction. He had discovered a way to defeat the Dark Zone and it was safely hidden in his book.

However he would need to protect those secrets. He turned to the back of the book and tore out a blank page. He closed it and using the book as a rest wrote on the torn out page.

The mysteries of the universe are many
Open its eye to understanding

Seek out its darkest secret
And good shall always triumph over evil.

He went across to his bookcase and selected *How To Become A Magician*. He opened the book, placed the torn out page at its centre and closed it. He put the book back and returned to his chair. He removed the talisman from around his neck and placed it on the cover of the book.

Immediately the amulet started to glow and burn into the cover. Waves of green smoke rose from the smouldering leather as an imprint of the talisman was scorched onto the cover. When the smoke cleared he put the amulet back around his neck.

In the centre of the book a large EYE now looked back at him.

Three hundred and fifty today

Suddenly the box in the mirror began to sing.

Three hundred and fifty today
He's got presents galore
Never been three hundred and fifty before.
Three hundred and fifty today
Three hundred and fifty today
He's got a surprise in store
Open the box for a whole lot more.

At his age Zardo hated birthdays and songs like this only reminded him of how old he really was. He would have to put a stop to all this birthday nonsense once and for all. Placing his book firmly under his arm he stood up and marched over to the mirror.

Three hundred and fifty today
Three hundred and fifty today
He's got a surprise in store
Open the box for a whole lot more.

The box was still slowly turning and spelling out its message.

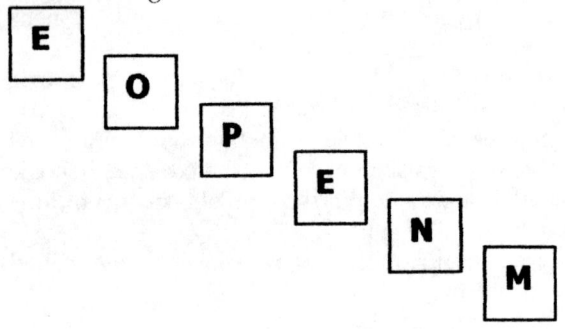

E O P E N M

As it rotated it continued to sing. On and on it droned.

Angrily Zardo shouted at the mirror,

"Yes I've got the message. I'm three hundred and fifty five years old today. Thank you for reminding me, now will you please go away."

The singing box ignored him and started a new tune.

I am a present
A jolly jolly present
I am a present
So open me to day
Don't hesitate my friend
A birthday wish I send
So open me and find out what I am.

Zardo could stand it no more. The continuous singing was driving him crazy. If the only way to stop this insanity were to open the box then that's what he'd do. He stretched out his arm and put his hand onto the mirror. Where his hand touched the surface the mirror rippled like the waters on a lake and began to melt around his fingers. He was then able to push his hand inside and touch the box. The parcel stopped singing and he took hold of the string and tried to pull the parcel through the mirror. The box wouldn't budge it just silently hung there.

"May a cauldron of bat droppings fall on your head, " damned Zardo as he tugged and pulled at the string.

It wouldn't move. Angrily he thrust his other arm through the glass and his book fell unnoticed onto the floor. He grabbed the cord with his other hand and pulled hard on the string with both hands. Still the box refused to move. His fingers hurt where the string dug into the joints and beads of sweat ran down his forehead. He pulled and tugged, heaved and strained but the parcel could not be shifted.

"A Warlock's curse on you!" condemned Zardo and gave up the struggle.

"Who wants a silly old present anyway? Keep it!"

He tried to let go of the string but to his horror found he couldn't. Somehow his fingers were frozen around the cord and he couldn't move them.

"By the Black Arts of Hell what magic have we here?" he mumbled struggling in vain to escape the clutches of the mirror. He tried to move his hands but they too were stuck.

What was this stupid *Gateway* doing he thought?

"Release me at once," ordered Zardo, "or else!"

Zardo struggled to free himself but the unknown force holding him only gripped his wrists tighter.

His fingers throbbed and his hands ached.

He tried again to free himself but it was impossible. The more he struggled the more frustrated he became.

There had to be some logical reason why the Gateway was acting like this. Dimensional magic was very complex. It was part spiritual and part biological and there were lots of complicated procedures that could go wrong. The Inter-dimensional Relay System may need updating or the Time-Portal Controls adjusting. He would have to investigate. Like himself the Gateway was getting old and in need of a complete overhaul. However before he could do any of that he had to free himself.

He tried one more time to release himself but he couldn't.

"Ha! Ha! Ha! Ha!"

Suddenly he heard laughter inside his head. It wasn't the happy kind of laughter that fills you full of joy but the evil kind that freezes the soul.

"Ha! Ha! Ha! Ha!"

There it was again. He felt the cold tingle of fear run down his spine and struggled desperately to free himself.

"Vulgor!" whispered Zardo.

"Yes Vulgor!" said the voice.

Zardo's heart sank.

"I've waited a long time for this moment," boasted the Lord of the Dark Zone, *"and now I have you!"*

Vulgor laughed again.

"Go to Hell," cursed Zardo.

"Temper! Temper!" said Gorf suddenly reappearing in the mirror as Zardo's double.

"You're not me! You're an impostor," said Zardo angry. "Who are you?"

"An old friend," said Gorf, "don't you remember, you imprisoned me in here."

"Gorf!"

"Yes Gorf!" said his own image, "and I'm about to be set free."

Zardo knew escape was hopeless. He'd been out manoeuvred and he cursed himself for not reacting sooner. He had made a grave error and was about to pay for his mistake.

Under The Mountain

Captain Barnacle Hoot was flying.

He soared high in a moonlit sky counting stars and hunting food.

He hovered silently on a midnight breeze searching the ground below for signs of life.

Then suddenly he began to fall and his dream ended.

Instinct told him to fly out of danger but that was impossible and down he plummeted.

He fell through a mist of white water that thundered in his ears and took his breath away. Several hundred metres below he could see the bottom of the ravine. Water gurgled into a large hole and disappeared under the mountain.

Escape was impossible.

He quickly wrapped himself into a ball and took a deep breath.

Whoosh!

He was plunged into total darkness. He fell for several more seconds with the sound of crashing water all around him.

Splash!

He hit the water with a *splat* and sank. Icy cold water slid over him like a blanket of snow and he shivered. He kicked and thrashed but the underwater currents were too strong and he was swept deep under the mountain.

Plop!

He surfaced. It was pitch black and the noise of rushing water was everywhere. He quickly gulped in air and filled his lungs with oxygen. He'd swallowed a lot of water and he felt sick. It sloshed in his stomach and he began to cough and retch.

Ugh!

Being sick made his stomach feel better and he took another deep breath to clear his head. The air was damp and cold but very refreshing. Gradually his eyes grew accustomed to the dark and he was able to see his surroundings. He found himself floating along a narrow channel cut into the rock. Ahead he could see the twists and turns of the river as it meandered its way under the mountain. The walls were wet and slimy and water trickled from large cracks cut into the stone.

Attached to the walls were blobs of yellow slime. He'd never seen anything like them before and curiosity made him stretch out and examine one. Suddenly it moved and he withdrew his claw quickly.

On closer inspection he saw they were all moving. They throbbed and pulsed together as if one entity. Thin spidery tentacles grew from each pulsating mass creating a network of veins across the ceiling of the tunnel. Above his head they had joined together to create what appeared to be perfectly formed stalactites.

Thousands of these yellow needle type structures hung from the roof of the cave like the fingers of a thousand skeletons. They shone a fluorescent yellow and cast an eerie light across the cave.

Suddenly he felt a cold splash of liquid on his face and he froze with fright. It felt wet and unpleasantly sticky and it smelt horribly of rotten eggs. He panicked for a moment as the yellow liquid ran down his cheek and he frantically clawed at his face in a desperate attempt to remove it.

The river carried him further into the passageways and he could see the yellow sludge had spread everywhere. Most of the walls were covered with it and above him it continuously dripped into the river. The water had turned sickly yellow and thick clumps of yellow goo drifted on top of its surface. The floating piles of slime looked very similar to the entities growing on the walls but were much smaller and didn't have tentacles. There were hundreds and hundreds of them floating on the water. He scooped some of it into his claw and examined it more closely. They were tiny egg sacs with what appeared to be creatures growing inside. At the centre of each shape he could see a small green eye. To his horror one of the eyes blinked at him and he reared back in surprise. He dropped the slime back into the river and watched as it floated back to join the rest of its brood.

The river meandered on carrying him even deeper under the island. The yellow sludge was everywhere. It covered every tunnel and clung to every wall. It hung from every ceiling and floated on every river.

Suddenly he was swept into a cavern with a large underground lake and came to a standstill. Around him drifted millions and millions of egg sacs floating on the surface of the lake like unwanted seaweed. The cave was over two hundred metres long and towered high above his head. Growing down from the ceiling were the roots of hundreds of trees. They covered the entire roof and hung down like forgotten vines in a lost jungle. He pictured the forest swaying gently in the breeze high above him and wished he were there.

He'd been in the watery labyrinth for a very long time and the waters were beginning to take its effect. His feathers had become waterlogged and he was beginning to go numb with the cold. He frantically searched the dangling roots above him looking for one he could climb but he found none. They were all to short. Suddenly the yellow sludge around him began to move and pulsate. Strange clicking noises filled the cavern and Hoot knew something unpleasant was about to happen. Frantically he flapped the water trying to disperse the gathering slime but the more he flapped the thicker it grew. He knew escape was impossible and waited uneasily for the slime to hatch.

The Corridors of Time

Wizard Zardo fought against the grip of the mirror but was unable to escape. The power of the Orb was too great and its magic held him firm. Vulgor had easily defeated him and he cursed his lack of foresight.

He'd failed and the good creatures of Tellurian would suffer for his mistake.

He felt sad and unhappy. Soon the evils of the Dark Zone would invade and he would be powerless to prevent it.

Inside the pyramid Vulgor laughed out loud. His plan was working. He had one more task to perform and Zardo would be imprisoned forever. He held the Orb of Fire high above his head and began chanting.

Zardo's mind was suddenly filled with ancient spells and forgotten magic. The spells spun around his head like messages of doom. He tried to struggle free but it was impossible.

Without warning, the mirror started to vibrate. It bulged and buckled and began to throb like a heartbeat. The box exploded and a greenish fog poured out of its centre and into his room. It drifted across the floor in waves slowly filling the room with a ghostly green fog.

A green mist hovered everywhere.

Suddenly the mirror started to rumble and he felt a tug on his wrists. There was a loud hissing sound and the green mist was sucked back into the mirror. He felt another pull on his arms and noticed the centre of the mirror had gone green. The mist was gathering at its centre and was slowly spinning around like a whirlpool. His legs left the floor and for several seconds he hung suspended in mid air with his hands trapped inside the swirling mist.

The mirror was changing and its surface rippled like the wind over the waters of a lake. Zardo could feel the power of the orb sucking him into the Gateway and he was powerless to stop it.

He heard movement and twisted his head to get a better view of the chaos that was going on around him. All the objects in his room were flying through the air in utter confusion.

Cups and saucers danced across the mantelpiece while the grandmaster's clock struck the hour repeatedly.

His table and chairs hung upside down on the ceiling and his bookcase spun hopelessly out of control. Books were crashing against the wall and paper scattered everywhere

His magic carpet had somehow rolled itself up and was now cowering on the floor up against the wall.

His own book had been caught up in the hub-bub and was now doing cartwheels in the air. Its pages were flapping like the wings of a frightened bird as it flew around the room.

He had but one chance to send the book into hiding and keep Vulgor from getting his claws on it. He cast a spell. It worked and the book headed towards the inner door. It flew down the corridor and out into the wood and vanished in the forest.

Inside the mirror Gorf had undergone a startling transformation. He'd re-appeared as a solid ball of green slime without arms or legs. Two large bulbous eyes had been placed on top of his body, which enabled him to see his surroundings. Everything was green and a mist swirled all around him. His new form frightened him and he panicked.

Back inside his room Zardo was about to enter the Gateway.

His legs stretched and his knees bent, his ankles expanded and his toes snaked, and together they all slithered into the mirror.

Then piece-by-piece Zardo's body melted and poured into the mirror until only his head remained.

Suddenly there was a tug on his chin and his beard vanished. His lips kissed the mirror and disappeared without trace. His eyes bulged and his nose stretched. Then suddenly they too went out of existence through the mirror.

Only the top of Zardo's head remained and he felt it being sucked and squeezed, squashed and pulled all at the same time. Then both ears popped and he saw them stretch towards the mirror and disappear into the green mist.

Finally his head became the shape of a hard-boiled egg and squeezed itself gently through the mirror.

Nothing remained of the wizard except his hat, which fell off his head and floated to the floor.

The room went silent and the floating objects fell to the floor. Cups smashed and saucers cracked. Books ripped and chairs splintered. Wood snapped and paper ripped.

The clock toppled and hit the fireplace scattering its mechanism across the floor.

Suddenly the mirror cracked scattering pieces of glass all over the room. Out through the shattered mirror came Gorf. He paused briefly to make a hole in the door and went through it into the corridor. He made a second in the outer door and disappeared into the forest. Zardo's talisman came next. It crashed through the broken mirror and hurled itself through the holes in doors into the forest. There it hid itself amongst the trees waiting discovery.

Slivers of glass lay everywhere reflecting a hundred crazy scenes of destruction. Then, as if by magic, they turned into liquid pools of silver and slowly slithered together to form one large silvery puddle. It solidified and changed shape becoming a large silver finger ring. In its centre was a large blue crystal and etched around its outer rim were strange mystical runes.

It rolled across the room and hid amongst the broken pieces of the clock.

There it would wait until a new Wizard Master could be found.

The New Wizard Master

Tellurian was on the brink of extinction and the Creator feared for Earth's future.

He drifted high above the planet's surface knowing without the help of a Wizard Master the planet was doomed.

His own *Law of Creation* prevented his direct intervention and he would need to recruit a *Superhero*.

Scattered across time and space were The Time Warriors, unknown heroes and heroines who lived out their lives unaware of their destiny. Zardo had been the first now he needed another.

The Creator left, his search for a second Time Warrior had begun.

Terraworms

Captain Hoot was cold.

He closed his eyes and imagined himself sitting by a large blazing fire. He felt warm and safe. The imaginary fire crackled and spat out fiery splinters of heat while a large pot of fish soup boiled and simmered at its centre. He took a deep breath, expecting to smell the sweet aroma of boiled fish instead he smelt rotting eggs.

He opened his eyes to the sound of yellow sludge bubbling on the surface of the water. The gooey liquid was plopping like hot tar in a pit. As it spluttered the egg sacs burst open and small worm-like creatures were thrown up into the air.

He looked in horror as the worms grew wings and flew off into the cave. Some flew across the cavern and attached themselves to the walls while others settled on the roots of the trees. He imagined this scene in all of the underground passageways and knew he had to inform Zardo of his discovery.

But first he had to escape this nightmare.

Climbing up a tree root and digging his way to the surface looked his best option but all the roots were far too high.

He would need to find roots much lower.

Using his wings as oars he steered himself out of the cavern and into a nearby passage. Here an underwater current caught hold of him and swept him along the tunnel.

The tunnel was long and thin and the walls were etched with yellow tentacles and slime. The ceiling was covered in worms and he could see these had lost their wings.

At the end of the passageway he could see a cave. In the centre of the cave dangled hundreds of root like creepers about five centimetres thick. They hung above the water dripping a slimy green liquid into the yellow sludge below.

Methuselah had taken a lifetime to grow these roots.

A million years of growth had twisted and moulded together thousands of rootlets to create them. They had provided this most ancient of trees with food and life giving nourishment. They had given Methuselah its strength. They now looked dead and lifeless, bathed in a deadly shade of green.

The current caught hold of Hoot again and he was swept into the cave towards Methuselah.

A Visitor

Zardo felt confused and disjointed.

Every part of his body seemed to have a mind of its own.

His feet raced after his toes and his legs chased after his feet. His arms followed his hands and his knuckles pursued his fingers. His torso was stretched beyond the bounds of possibility and expanded as far as his eyes could see.

He felt bewildered and detached.

His neck stretched towards his shoulders, pulling his reluctant head with it. His eyes popped out of his head and would have overtaken his toes but for the attached sinews that held them in place.

Wrapped around him, like the silver threads of a cocoon, stretched his beard constantly tugging and pulling him towards the unknown blackness ahead of him.

On the other side of the Gateway, Vulgor celebrated, the Dark Zone was about to entertain a very special visitor.

Talon

A harvest moon lit up the sky and a mist drifted through the forest like smoke from a dying fire. Sunrise was several hours away and the creatures of Tellurian slept unaware of the abduction of Wizard Zardo and the arrival of Gorf.

Gorf had arrived as a large green ball bouncing along the forest floor. He had eventually rolled to a stop besides the ruins of a building.

Then he'd started to regenerate.

First his legs had grown then his arms. His head took much longer and he'd stood there looking like a deformed *Slugadon* waiting for the rest of his body to emerge. Eventually his head had popped out and the rest had followed.

Immediately he'd recognised his surroundings. He was back home in Amphibia.

The place was deserted and the twin cities of Ampha and Hibila lay in ruins. On either side of the riverbank stood the remains of hundreds of houses. The whole city had been razed to the ground.

Beyond the ruined city Gorf saw the lake where he had been born. The moon hovered over its surface casting a rippling beam of light across its waters.

At the end of the lake he could see the twin windmills that once produced food for the community. The circular buildings were bathed in moonlight and appeared to be undamaged. However the sails were ripped and hung in tatters.

"Where are you?" said a voice inside his head.

It was Vulgor.

"Amphibia," said Gorf, "outside the old windmills.

Gorf looked at the deserted buildings and suddenly had an idea.

"Why not start the invasion from here Sire?" suggested Gorf. "Use the windmills as a Command Centre."

For a second there was silence while Vulgor considered Gorf's suggestion.

"Very well! Amphibia it is! The Gores and I will meet you inside the windmills within the hour. Make sure no Tellurian sees you."

"They won't," said Gorf. "What about Zardo?"

"Safely with us in the Dark Zone," gloated Vulgor, *"I'm preparing a little surprise for him."*

Night was nearly at its end and Gorf needed to get inside before daylight came. Leaving Amphibia behind him he set off for the windmill.

High on one of the windmill's twin sails, perched *Talon*, Tellurian's only *Eagle*. He was fast asleep. It had been a terrible stormy day and he'd caught nothing for supper. He'd fallen asleep hungry with an empty rumbling in his stomach. As he dreamed of big juicy mice his slumbers were disturbed by a strange smell. It drifted in and out of his dreams and awakened the hunger in his belly. He blinked open an eye thinking the smell might be food. Far below he saw a huge figure walking across the grass. The smell drifted up towards him and he recognised it to be a mixture of rotting vegetables and dead fish. Neither of the smells suggested a tasty meal so he closed his eye and returned to his dreams.

Gorf entered the windmill and set about his preparation unaware his activities were being observed.

The Gores

Vulgor held the Orb of Fire over the pool and waited.

A beam of light penetrated the ball passing right through it and into the pool. The orb vibrated and he felt the orb's energy enter his body. His bones shook and his nerves tingled. His blood boiled and his heart raced. He felt strong and invincible.

Zardo's capture was nearly complete.

High above him in the sparkling darkness of the pyramid, he could hear the cries and wailings of the invisible Gores. Soon they would be free and the planned invasion of Tellurian could begin.

Outside the pyramid Koor and Varen were still asleep unaware of the changing events inside the pyramid. Soon their nightmarish dreams would be over and they would awaken.

Vulgor waited, patiently keeping a watchful eye on the pool. The beam of light went deep into the water and created an underwater glow that made the waters of the pool crystal clear. The pool shone and sparkled like raindrops in a stream.

Vulgor gazed deep into its depths seeking the moment that would herald Zardo's arrival. Suddenly the pool exploded in a fury of noise sending a funnel of water high into the air. The column remained, suspended in mid air defying gravity and flowing upwards from the surface of the pool.

The Orb of Fire flew out of Vulgor's hands and hovered over the column. It started to spin about its axis gradually increasing in momentum until it was a silvery blur spinning above the column. A single beam of light shot up from the surface of the pool through the orb and into the ceiling of the pyramid.

For the moment Vulgor was drained of energy and was unable to support the weight of his body. He fell to his knees and balanced unsteadily at the edge of the pool.

Suddenly Zardo floated to the surface and began spinning and spiralling around the edge of the pool. Like an elongated eel Zardo coiled himself around the pool in one continuous loop, unable to see where he began or where he ended.

Vugor watched with fascination as the swirling waters spun his enemy towards the column of water. Then like a chord of twine wrapping around a spindle Zardo went up and around the outside of the column. His feet reached the top and were sucked into the orb. The rest of him quickly followed and the funnel of water fell back into the pool.

Vulgor got to his feet and saw the orb hovering over the pool. As it spun it started to increase in size. Larger and larger it grew until the outer shell fractured and splintered into a thousand cracks. The cracks widened, spread apart by the expanding surface.

Vulgur could see Zardo coiled up inside. Suddenly a beam of light spiralled out of the orb taking Zardo with it. It shot through the top of the pyramid and disappeared into the blackness.

The orb continued to expand, getting bigger with every revolution. Each crack grew wider until only the thinnest of strands held it together. Realising the orb was going to explode Vulgor began a slow and careful retreat. Finally the orb burst and the pyramid shattered into a thousand pieces.

Vulgor closed his eyes expecting to be hit by flying debris but to his surprise the expected bombardment never came. When he opened his eyes the pyramid was gone and he was standing on the shingle near the lake. Floating in the air above him were hundreds of transparent triangles, each with its own special brilliance. One by one the lights went out until only six triangles remained. The light inside these intensified and they started to expand. Larger and larger they grew until Vugor could see deformed creatures crawling around inside them.

Suddenly they all exploded at the same time and out flew the Gores.

A Gaggle of Gores

Koor was inside a pyramid drowning in a sea of flames. Yellow smoke drifted around him and he gasped for breath. An invisible force was pulling him down into a fiery pit of liquid fire. He struggled to escape but sank until only his head remained above the surface.

He felt no pain and began to wonder why.

Varen was inside a pyramid drowning in an ocean of flames. Yellow choking smoke drifted all around her and she couldn't breathe. An invisible force was pulling her down into a furnace of liquid fire. She struggled to escape but sank until only her head remained above the surface.

She felt no pain and began to wonder why.

Simultaneously the pyramids in both their dreams exploded and they awoke to the sound of creatures flying around them. The pyramid was gone and hovering over the lake were six flying skeletons.

They each had reptilian skulls and apart from their size looked the same. They had little or no outer skin and their bodies were transparent. Their necks were stripped of flesh and attached to crooked shoulder blades. They had curved and deformed backbones that tapered into long pointed tails. Every bone was bent and crooked. Stretching along either side of the backbone was a transparent membrane of skin. These, when fully opened, were the creatures wings. Thin spindly arms jutted out from under the wings to give them support. On the end of these limbs were small claws. Two lumps of bone attached to either side of the backbone provided additional legs and dangling off them were skeletal feet with crooked claws.

Growing under the creatures' backbones in transparent sacs were the reptiles' heart and organs. The sac contained hundreds of tiny veins and arteries that pumped red liquid into the heart.

Koor and Varen could see the creature's hearts beating as they hovered above them.

Protruding out of their skulls were crocodilian-like jaws containing rotting and mishapen teeth. Two blood red eyes blindly glared from deep black sockets on either side of the head.

Then they were gone flying across the lake into the semi-darkness. The cave fell into an eerie silence and only the occasional crackle of burning oil on the surface of the lake broke the tranquility.

The pyramid had gone and Koor and Varen were left alone in the Cave of Shadows to wonder what had happened to Vulgor.

After several more seconds of silence they heard the familiar flapping of wings. The sound grew in strength until every corner of the cave echoed with its noise. Then from out of the blackness came Vulgor.

Around him flew the skeletal reptiles they had seen earlier flying in perfect formation around their leader. They flew up to them and hovered above their heads like predators over a dying carcass.

"It is time!" bellowed Vulgor, "join us."

Vulgor turned and flew off across the cave quickly followed by his Gaggle of Gores.

Koor and Varen took to the air and followed.

The Ogres Of Destruction

The Wizard's journey to Vulgor's castle had been a nightmare. He'd been pulled and pushed, squeezed and stretched across two dimensions and now felt weak and confused.

He was floating on his back unable to move staring up at a blood red sky. All around him towered strange black walls and crooked pinnacles of lava. They formed a circular barrier between him and a frightening world.

The land beyond the fortress was ablaze with violence. Rivers of lightning forked across a sky full of black volcanic ash and streams of burning lava spewed down mountainsides. Volcanoes erupted and fireballs of molten rock flew through the air. Fissures in the ground cracked open and gigantic flames of fire burst to the surface. Everywhere he looked he saw chaos and destruction. Thunder rumbled in the distance and flashes of yellow lightning crackled through the air.

He felt hot and lonely and wanted to escape. Above him he could see two large towers and below on the ground a stone altar. Yellow smoke drifted up from the ground and into the centre of a large circular stone suspended between the towers.

He struggled for a second or two then gave up. The Dark Zone held him in its grip and there was no escape.

In the distance he heard the rumble of an earthquake and within seconds the impact hit the castle. The ground split open and huge cracks appeared. Fire and steam drifted up from the fissures and mingled with the yellow smoke from the altar.

The air became thick and pungent and he couldn't breathe. His throat burnt and he began to gasp for air. He felt dizzy and fell into unconsciousness.

The earthquake ended leaving most of the castle intact. The fissures sealed and the Dark Zone returned to a relative calm.

Vulgor flew out of the Cave of Shadows and waited. The others quickly followed and hovered next to him.

"Come my ogres of destruction let us meet with Zardo and take our revenge."

Tyrann recognised the voice of its master and poked one of its heads through the bars of its cage and howled for attention. The creature was hungry and it wanted feeding. The lizard's two other heads quickly followed the first and all three roared in chorus.

"Silence! Be patient!" yelled Vulgor aware of the animal's needs, "soon you shall have all you can eat!"

Vulgor flew down and released the lizard. Tyrann walked over to the cave's entrance and flopped down on its hind legs. Its tail rested on the ground behind him. The chain around its necks pulled tight and the lizard shuffled backwards to loosen its grip. The chain sank to the ground with a thud.

"That's a good lizard," said Vulgor patting one of the heads.

The other two turned and growled at him. Vulgor knew the old dragon could be very disagreeable when it was hungry. He searched under his wing and brought out the remains of the ratadon he'd half eaten earlier. He threw the rotting flesh into one of Tyrann's mouths and it gobbled it up in seconds. The lizard wanted more but Vulgor shook his head and flew up to join his colleagues. The creature growled disapprovingly.

"Come, Zardo awaits us!" squawked Vulgor and led the Gores over the castle walls and into the castle.

Koor and Varen followed several metres behind.

Twilight Time

Morning was an hour away and like every other morning for the past twenty years Talon's biological clock told him it was time to rise. He opened his eyes, stretched out his wings and gave them a couple of flaps. This had been his morning ritual ever since he could remember. Nothing ever changed. He yawned, preened himself then prepared to look for breakfast. It was still dark and he felt very hungry, yesterdays search for food had been a failure.

From his perch on top of the windmill he looked out across the early morning landscape. Nothing moved. It was far too early for other creatures to be up. The *Nocturnes* would just be going to bed and the *Day-timers* not yet awake. This was *Twilight Time* and the whole of Tellurian was sleeping.

He would have to wait for breakfast.

While he waited for dawn to arrive and the hunt for breakfast to begin he suddenly remembered the creature in the night. He began to wonder who the mysterious visitor was and what it was doing. He decided to investigate and jumped off his perch and flew through a rip in the windmill's sails. He glided down through a hole in the roof and began to search the inside of the buildings for the smell of dead fish and rotting cabbages.

Gorf was asleep, propped up against a pile of rotting beams in a large room.

He snored loudly and his immense body wobbled and rippled as he breathed.

The room was circular in shape and had a large wooden door that led to the outside world. The door was old and the early morning twilight crept through the holes around its edges. An arched walkway cut into the wall led to an identical room.

Centuries of dust and grime blackened the walls and cobwebs clung to the surface like broken cartwheels. Stone steps had been built into the wall that led to an upper room. The floor had long since rotted away and broken floorboards lay scattered around the downstairs floor.

In the centre of the room were two large wooden cogwheels full of woodworm. They were mounted on a large wooden trestle that was bolted to the floor. Four rusty metal bolts held the bench in place. The larger wheel stood at right angles to the smaller one and several smaller wheels and sprockets held the machine upright. A giant wooded spindle ran from the centre cog up to the top of the windmill. The top half of the spindle had broken away and lay discarded on the floor in the corner of the room.

Talon came to rest on top of the broken spindle.

He looked down at the sleeping figure and caught the familiar smell of dead fish and rotting cabbages. The enormous creature slept, unaware he was being observed.

Gorf's dream was cold and uncaring.

He'd been inside the grinding-room of a large windmill hovering above hundreds of amphibians laughing and croaking orders at them.

They'd been terrified of him and had frantically tried to leave the room, but the doors had been locked and there had been no escape for them.

They'd panicked and had hidden amongst the cogs and wheels that turned the giant grinding-stones and he had laughed at their foolishness.

As he neared the end of his dream Gorf pulled the lever that would activate the machine.

He woke to the sound of his own laughter and the distant screams of his unfortunate victims.

Gorf yawned and Talon caught the stench of decaying fish.

The creature below stood up and stretched. Rolls of fat rippled up and down its body like waves on the ocean. Once on its feet it plodded around exploring the windmill

It kicked at the door and Talon wondered what it was doing.

Talon knew something was wrong and instinct told him the creature below was up to mischief. He knew it to be an amphibian but he had never seen one that size before. He thought them extinct destroyed in the Dark Wars.

He quietly flew nearer and settled on a wooden beam above the intruder's head.

Gorf sensed movement and looked up into the rafters. Talon shuffled into the shadow and Gorf saw nothing.

Gorf returned to his investigations and summoned Vulgor.

"Vulgor are you there?"

"What?" said Vulgor after some considerable time.

Talon looked for a second creature but saw nothing.

"Our invasion?"

"What about it?"

"Invasion!" thought Talon almost falling off his perch. "It's planning to invade."

"When did you say you were arriving?"

"As soon as I've dealt with Zardo," replied Vulgor, *"expect us within the hour."*

"Within the hour, thank you Sire, everything will be ready."

Talon was stunned. This oversized amphibian and its unseen conspirators were planning to invade the island. They must be stopped and Wizard Zardo must be informed immediately.

Outside it was raining and storm clouds were gathering over the mountains. Thunder rumbled in the distance and the sky-looked grey and threatening. Ignoring the danger Talon took to the air and flew off to find Zardo.

An Exchange of Power

Wizard Zardo awoke and was immediately surrounded by noise. It swirled around him like an angry wind on a stormy day. He could hear the sound of wings beating the air and the constant chatter of voices. He wished he could stop this madness, but the Zone had rendered him useless.

Zardo couldn't see his assailants. They hovered somewhere beyond his vision but he could hear them laughing. Suddenly a bolt of energy arced from the Genesis-stone and into his body. He felt it draining away his powers.

"See how the wizard's life-force feeds the Eye."

Zardo recognised the voice it was Vulgor's.

Zardo shook and twitched as the Genesis-stone drained more of his power into the Eye above him. He could do nothing to stop it, only watch his own immortality slipping away.

"Look! The Gateway opens," squawked Vulgor, "the Eye shows us the way."

Weak and barely able to move Zardo focused what little strength he had on the stone above him. Its centre had become translucent and on its surface clouds swirled together to form a thick grey mist. The mist spiralled and at its vortex a tunnel of light appeared. Through the tunnel Zardo could see the ruined city of Amphibia.

"Go my Ogres of the Dark the Gateway is open."

Zardo heard the pounding of wings.

Whoosh!

The first creature flew past him. A wave of heat buffeted his body and Zardo was rocked from side to side.

Whoosh!

There was another blast of hot air and two more thundered past. Zardo recognised them immediately and he cursed his frailty. His feebleminded attempts to rid the world of such monstrosities had failed. They had escaped their exile and were once again united with Vulgor.

Two more flew into view and Zardo caught a passing glimpse of their skeletal like bodies. As planned prison had changed them, a few more centuries and the pyramid would have devoured them completely. But they'd escaped before the process was complete and these tyrants from hell were once again free to unleash their evil.

Frail, weak and drained of all magical power, Zardo watched the creatures fly up to the portal. There they waited and hurled abuse at him.

"Look how the pathetic old crone withers," mocked *Stulgore* the oldest and meanest of the resurrected monstrosities,"I spit on your patheticness."

The rest of them laughed and took it in turns to copy their comrade.

"That's for a century of misery," spat *Vengorey* the youngest. Green drool hit Zardo's forehead and the rest of the Gores burst out laughing.

"Take that!" shouted *Degoreger* flying down and giving Zardo a slap across his cheek with its shrivelled wing.

"And that!" squawked *Aerogeth* following closely behind his comrade and giving Zardo a hefty kick with its deformed foot.

"Look at us!" howled *Predigore* his skin hanging off his bones like meat on a partially eaten carcass, "this is your doing!"

Pheogore, said nothing, it waited by the portal for the others to join it.

Suddenly waves of energy sparked up from Zardo's body and entered the Eye.

"Now!" shouted Vulgor, "we must go now!"

The Gores turned towards the Eye and flew through its Gateway. Instantly they disappeared in a flash of light.

Koor and Varen followed leaving Vulgor alone with Zardo.

"Fear me Zardo," said Vulgor hovering over the helpless Zardo, "I shall have my revenge."

Zardo stirred and half opened his eyes but he was too weak to remain conscious. An overwhelming urge to sleep washed over him and he closed his eyes and fell into a deep coma.

Leaving the unconscious Zardo to the evils of the Dark Zone Vulgor flew into the Eye. There was a blinding flash and he disappeared.

The image on the Genesis-stone faded and the stone returned to normal.

In The Old Well

Morning had yet to waken the forest and most of Tellurian's inhabitants were still asleep unaware of the tragic events of the night. Twilight had faded but daybreak still lingered in the darkness. A strange poison had invaded the forest and the infection was spreading.

Immediately below Methuselah was Captain Barnacle Hoot. He felt sick and dizzy. He was trapped in an underground river being carried towards the roots of a large tree. Hopefully he could grab hold of them and escape the water.

Around him the tunnel was alive with worms. They slithered and crawled everywhere.

He loathed them.

He had observed their tactics and knew they were using the underground river system to spread themselves under the island. Once in position they had started to eat themselves to the surface. They attacked anything solid. Wherever they gorged holes had appeared. The holes were irregular in shape and varied in size. Inside the holes a green fungus had formed. This had quickly grown until the hole had been filled to overflowing and the fungus had dribbled out onto the surrounding areas. The worms were also attacking the roots of the trees and were slowly eating their way up inside them.

Hoot approached Methuselah's roots. Here the river flowed much faster and he could hear the sound of water falling onto rocks beyond the cavern. If he failed the river would sweep him into the blackness.

A single root about half a metre wide dangled just above the water line. It hung down from the base of the tree and would be his only chance of escape. As he neared the root he saw it was covered with worms. The thought of touching these monstrous creatures repulsed him.

Suddenly he was under the tree and it was now or never. He jumped up and grabbed the infested root and pulled himself clear of the water. The root began to swing and he felt himself swaying backwards and forwards like a pendulum on a grandmaster's clock. Lumps of earth fell from the tree stump above him and he was showered with mud and soil.

He hung on fearing he would lose his grip and fall back into the water. His grip held and gradually the swinging motion eased and he came to a standstill.

He could feel the creatures wriggling against his chest and he smelt the sour odour of decaying grass. He hung on despite the urge to let go and rid himself of these repulsive parasites. He looked up and saw several of the creatures had crawled up the root and were attacking the base of the tree. They looked like giant green earthworms but these were much plumper and he couldn't tell where the heads of the creatures began or where their tails finished. Both ends were identical and they moved like giant caterpillars pulling and sliding themselves along with the underbelly of their bodies. Occasionally one of them would stop and raise itself up into the air. There it would hover swaying backwards and forwards like a snake ready to strike.

He suddenly felt movement around his waist and feared the worse. His stomach was covered with worms. The thought of being eaten alive by these sea serpents from hell was more than a seafaring bird could endure. He screamed and shouted abuse at them and tried to dislodge them.

"A seaman's curse on yer..." he hooted jumping and pulling on the root at the same time.

"Let go of me!" he screeched.

The louder he shouted the more he swayed. The greater the swing the weaker the tree's foundations became. Finally the worms fell back into the river and he stopped swinging. He looked down at his waist and gave a sigh of relief. The worms had been eating the life belt attached to his waist and not him.

Wrapping his wings tighter around the root and gripping it tightly with his feet he pushed himself up the root. Claw over claw he pulled himself upwards. Mud and debris fell from the exposed tree above and the root creaked and groaned under the strain.

As he climbed he saw the worms had eaten away large areas of the tree. Fungus spilled out of the holes and dribbled down the roots. Realising the root he was climbing could break at anytime he quickened his ascent. He encountered more worms and took great delight in knocking them off into the water below. As they fell he could see a small circular hole in the centre of their bellies. It opened and closed and he assumed this was the creature's mouth. He couldn't explain how the creatures were able to eat the things they did but he knew they were destroying the balance of nature.

He had almost reached the top and had come to the area where the tree grew through the ceiling. He would be able to dig through the soil and find his way to the surface.

He noticed worms ahead of him. They had reached the base of the tree and were crawling all over it. One had burrowed itself deep into the tree's core and was devouring the sappy sinews of its bark.

Crack!

Suddenly the root broke and he found himself falling. As he fell he twisted in the air and the detached root wrapped itself around his body. He fell towards the water struggling to free him self.

Swish!

Something shot through the air and wrapped itself around his body. It was thin, wet and slimy and stank of fish. It was reddish in colour and rough to the touch. For a second he dangled in the air like a hooked fish on the end of a line then suddenly found himself flying through the air. Up he flew towards the roof of the cave and straight through a hole in the ceiling. It was pitch dark and he felt the wind rushing passed him. Up and up he went until suddenly he stopped in mid air and began to fall. He fell only for a second before he felt a sideways tug and he came to rest on something solid. The slithery slimy fish-smelling object unwrapped itself from around his body and he was left staring into darkness. He could hear water falling somewhere in the blackness. He untangled himself from the root vines and stood up.

He could see nothing.

"A vast yea landlubber," he shouted, "who be there?"

Only his echo answered.

At the back of the cave, hidden in the darkness, eyes watched him.

Gradually a shaft of light filtered down from a hole somewhere above him and he could see his surroundings. He was in a large cavern. The cave floor was wet and pools of water stood everywhere. The ground sloped and a fast flowing stream ran along it. He watched the water swirl and gurgle its way towards a small waterfall at the end of the cave. Beyond the waterfall he could see a pool. The light source was coming from a shaft cut into the rock above the pool. He smiled to himself.

Fate had been kind.

He had stumbled into the old well shaft in the centre of the forest.

The walls of the shaft were wet and slippery and large creepers clung to its walls like giant strands of hair. Half way up he spotted an old bucket lodged against the wall. Growing out it was a long transparent tube. It grew down the wall and into the cave. He followed it into the shadows behind him. He peered deep into the darkness but saw nothing. He was about to turn away when he thought he heard a hissing noise.

"Barnacles!" he cursed and turned towards the well.

Two red eyes appeared in the shadows behind him. They floated ten metres off the floor swaying from side to side. Slowly the eyes moved forward and a shadowy figure came out of the darkness.

Vulgorite

Vulgorite came out of the shadows and slithered across the cave towards the unsuspecting owl. It approached Hoot from behind and silently hovered behind him ready to strike. The bird sensed danger and slowly turned around. He looked up and came face to face with a monstrous creature with red bulging eyes. It towered high above him hissing and swaying from side to side.

Its head and neck resembled that of a vulture and it had the body of a giant snake. Its skin was covered in green scales that oozed slime. He was unable to determine its length as most of it was still hidden in the shadows of the cave.

Vulgorite lowered its head and opened its jaw. It hissed loudly and Hoot could see inside the creature's mouth. It had two fang-like teeth that oozed a greenish slime. As it swayed the liquid sloshed around in its mouth spilling out over its jaw and onto the ground. He recognised the slithery object that had wrapped itself around him earlier. It was the creature's tongue. It now lay coiled inside the animal's mouth.

Suddenly the tongue moved and slithered towards him.

It began exploring his head.

He could feel the creature's tongue sliding and slithering over his feathers. He felt it slither down his face and across his mouth. Finally it wrapped itself around his neck and he felt the tongue tighten around his throat.

The reptile hissed and lowered its head. It arched its snake-like body just below the neck to position itself in front of his face. The creature shuffled and a ripple ran down the full length of its body. Vulgorite stared into the owl's eyes and he began rocking its head from side to side.

Hoot stared hypnotically at the beast unable to break away from those red glaring eyes. They stole into his soul and took away his resistance. His mind was no longer his to control and he began imitating the creature's every move. He swayed backwards and forwards copying the actions of his captor.

He felt the tongue around his neck slacken and saw it slither back inside the animal's mouth. The creature hissed and opened its mouth. Wider and wider it expanded until he could see right down its throat. He could smell and taste rancid fish. A slimy liquid splashed over his cheeks as the beast's jaws opened to swallow him.

Crack!

The creature stopped.

Rumble!

Something in the darkness had distracted it.

Crash!

The creature turned towards the noise.

Crunch!

It howled in pain.

It's wailing echoed around the cave like the desperate cries of a snared animal. It hissed and howled and started lashing and whipping its body in anger. It tugged and pulled but couldn't free itself from the unknown force that gripped its tail. After several more futile attempts to free itself it left the owl uneaten and slithered off towards its tail.

With those hypnotic eyes gone Hoot was able to move again. Quickly he ran towards the waterfall and leapt over it. For a second it felt like he was flying again and he directed himself towards a bush growing on the opposite side of the well.

With a thud he hit the wall and clung onto the bush. The bush held and he began to climb up the shaft.

The well was covered with plant growth. Vines hung everywhere and a network of bushes and trees meandered up its walls. The shaft was wet and damp and water dripped off everything.

He could see the top of the well and the storm clouds gathering in the skies above. He continued to scramble up the wall using the trees and bushes as footholds. Half way up they came to an end and he would need to use one of the dangling vines to finish his climb. He took hold of the nearest and tugged at it. It held firm and he started to climb.

Ahead of him he could see a metal bucket and climbed towards it.

Water dripped down relentlessly. It ran along every nook and cranny and down every crack and crevice. He was soaking wet and it took all his strength to drag himself up to the bucket. He looked in and to his horror found it full of worms.

They had attached themselves to a large tooth and were injecting it with a yellow liquid. Growing out of the tooth was a tube that ran down into the cave below. The tube was translucent and he could see a reddish liquid flowing along it. He suddenly realised the worms were feeding the creature that attacked him. He quickly ripped them away from the tooth and threw them down the shaft. He watched them fall and heard them splash into the water below.

Suddenly he saw a long snake-like shadow slither across the water and knew the beast was still alive and looking for him.

He had to escape the shaft.

He looked for an alternative route and spotted a large hole in the side of the well.

Suddenly he had an idea.

He tore the feeding cord away from the tooth and tied it to the handle of the bucket. He put the bucket in the hole and filled it with stones from the wall. He placed the rotting tooth under his wing and started climbing again.

Vulgorite's tail had been buried under kilos of fallen rock. It had pulled and tugged, wriggled and squirmed until the rocks had crumbled and its tail was free. It had resumed its pursuit of the owl searching every centimetre of the cave. Suddenly the sound of movement in the well shaft had attracted its attention and it had quickly slithered across the cave to investigate it.

The top of the well shaft was visible.
A couple more good pushes and he would be safe. Above he could see the handle that moved the bucket up and down the well and he stretched out a hand to grab it. Suddenly something wrapped itself around his leg and pulled him.
He looked down the well and panicked. The creature's tongue had wrapped itself around his foot and the rest of it was slithering up the shaft towards him.
He held onto the handle tightening his grip.
Frantically he tried to shake the tongue loose but it stayed firmly wrapped around his foot. He looked down and could see its eyes getting larger as it crashed and collided its way towards him.
The reptile was almost on him. Its jaws were fully open and he could no longer see its eyes only its gaping mouth.
Quickly he took the tooth from under his wing and threw it at the bucket. The tooth hit the bucket and the pail fell through the hole. Down it fell taking the umbilical chord with it. Vulgorite's tail quickly followed dragging the rest of the creature with it. Its tongue still wrapped around his foot stretched and snapped. The last he saw of the creature was its severed tongue disappearing down the shaft.
He quickly climbed the last few metres of the shaft and using the old timbers across its entrance swung out of the well and into the forest.

Location   *The Planet Earth*

Time Zone   *The Present*

—*Three Years Later*

Play the Game and Save the Universe

Izward was falling through a foggy white mist that twirled and swirled all around him. Strange humanoid shapes with grey featureless faces hovered around him. Spindly arms and legs floated from their elongated bodies like the legs of a giant spider. Grotesque hands with long bony fingers were pushing and shoving him down into the grey mist. He struggled to free himself pulling and prising at the fingers that were all over his body, but their grip was too strong and he continued to fall. Suddenly out of the grey mist came the ground and he screamed.

Izward awoke and his reoccurring nightmare was over. He issued an order to his *ambulator* and the machine took him across the floor to his work desk. A row of TV monitors attached to computer keyboards and CPUs burst into life as he approached. The ambulator adjusted his body shape and he sat down. He picked up the VRT visor and plugged it into the VRT OPS Box and placed the visor over his eyes. He switched on the machine and began to perfect his invention.

It had been three years since his accident and Izward had learnt to live with the recurring nightmares. The fall at the lighthouse had left him in a coma and he had slept for almost two years. When he finally did awake, thanks to PETE's vigilance, Izward discovered he'd damaged his spine and was unable to walk. However the Institute had valued his expertise and had commissioned the development of the ambulator, an experimental orthopaedic device designed to help the physically challenged.

The device gave Izward the ability to move freely about the institute and carry out his experiments on VRT. The appliance was a thin flexible contraption that was moulded to the contours of his back and legs. Bionic circuitry stimulated the material enabling it to mimic the movement of the lower back and legs. When fitted next to the skin it was virtually impossible to detect. It was voice activated and apart from the slightly mechanical movements it created when in use the User was unaware of its presence.

Izward removed the visor and placed it back on his workstation. He rubbed his eyes and stared out of the window at the artificially created horizon. The dome shaped roof of the Institute's protective shield reflected a tranquil blue sky. Synthetic clouds drifted around the dome in precise patterns creating the perfect day. Soon the day would fade into night and the same projected images would create the ideal night. This twenty-four hour cycle of day and night provided the Institute's residents with the perfect environment in which to live and work.

The Institute stood on two man-made islands built by the Ancients to protect the coastline during times of conflict. Each island had the same hexagonal shaped building constructed from concrete and steel. According to PETE the original buildings were military fortresses armed with guns and weapons. The Institute's Mentors had decided these abandoned forts would make ideal research establishments and the forts had been modernised. Three centuries later they were the most sophisticated laboratories in the whole of the New World.

The islands were situated three kilometres from the shore and were about a kilometre apart. A transparent tube had been constructed between the two buildings and inside the tube was a walkway and monorail.

Izward could see the other building from his window. It had been expertly restored. A metal skin had been welded around the building with steel shutters and windows to provide light. Two large rectangular balconies with cone shaped roofs and floors jutted out from its side. Izward had researched the original use of these balconies and PETE had told him that the military had put their weapons of war in them. They were now used as recreation and observation areas. On top of the building was a metal clad box that according to PETE once housed the soldiers who looked after the forts. It now contained the satellite control systems that enabled the Institute to communicate with the rest of the world. On top of this building turned a large satellite dish.

Izward returned to his workbench and picked up the visor. He put it over his eyes and immediately the holographic adventure he'd been designing resumed. Izward hit the computer keyboard with speed and expertise. On the monitor in front of him lines and lines of computer programming raced across the screen. In his visor the action continued and the characters in front of his eyes ran or jumped, lived or died according to the program lines being tapped out on his keyboard.

Whole landscapes changed at the tap of a key.

Finally Izward removed the visor and switched off the VRT OPS CPU that stored and converted the lines of programming into VR Images. The system worked. The technology behind it was simple. By using bio-connectors hidden in the visor the Users brainstem could be stimulated and electrical impulses sent to any part of the brain. Different areas of the brain could be activated and the desired effect created. If you wanted the user to experience the illusion of walking and talking you stimulated the Cerebellum, to see colours and organise shapes the Occipital Lobe. His new VRT OPS CPU did all this and a lot more too.

He pressed the keypad on PETE's new look computer screen and a holographic image of a young woman appeared. She was about his age and had long blond hair.

"This is Samantha," said a soft voice, "can I help you?"

Izward liked the new *family members* he'd been allocated. They reflected his maturing attitude.

"Get me VR Main Frame," said Izward.

"Very well sir."

A holographic keyboard floated above his wrist and Izward gently touched the keys and wrote…Register…VRT OPS CPU 1…Prototype… Virtual Reality System… Product Slogan… LIFE IS A GAME AND REALITY IS THE NAME… Inventor…IZWARD W. ALLEN.

Suddenly a message flashed up on every screen.

> TIME WARRIOR
> YOU ARE THE CHOSEN ONE
> PLAY THE GAME AND SAVE THE
> UNIVERSE
> GAME REQUIRES
> VRT OPS CPU 1 SYSTEM
>
> TO CONTINUE PRESS ENTER

The Game

Izward looked at the screen in front of him and shook his head. This wasn't possible. He struck the side of the monitor with the palm of his hand. For a second the screen went blank and all the monitors in the room hissed static. Suddenly they burst back into light flashing a different message,

> TIME WARRIOR IZWARD
> SUCH VIOLENCE IS NOT NECESSARY
> THERE IS NOTHING WRONG WITH YOUR
> EQUIPMENT
> TRUST ME!
>
> TO CONTINUE PLEASE PRESS ENTER

The keyboard faded and Samantha's imag[e] returned.

"May I add my congratulations," said Samanth[a] smiling.

"You may, Thank you," said Izward.

"Do you need anything else sir," enquire[d] Samantha.

"No Sam," he'd already shortened her nam[e] "that'll be all for now."

He touched PETE gently and the SERIES [?] computer switched itself off. He ordered the a[m]bulator to take him across his room to his sofa a[nd] the machine gently sat him down.

"Music!" he shouted and the room respond[ed] with Beethoven's Symphony Number Nine [?] second movement. Izward closed his eyes [and] went to sleep.

The Creator, having waited for Izward's recover[y] turned to the future to summon Izward into the pla[nned?] past.

Outside on top of the Institute's roof the [satel]lite dish swung towards the eastern skies. It [had] picked up a strange signal from the far rea[ches] of space and had moved into position to re[ceive] a message.

Izward's TV monitors suddenly burst int[o life] and filled his room with static and flashing [lights]. He woke up and thinking there had been [some] sort of electrical surge ordered the ambula[tor to] take him to his workstation. Quickly the ma[chine] positioned him over his chair and he sat dow[n. He] was just about to throw the main switch an[d turn] everything off when the static stopped and [the] TV monitors went blank.

For a moment Izward was taken by surprise, then realising it must be a joke, looked around the room expecting to see Beth hiding somewhere. Beth was his assistant and this looked like one of her pranks. Although the Institute's Mentors frowned upon Personal Relationships they had allowed Izward and Beth to work together. Beth was a whiz with computers and she'd helped him construct the hardware for the OPS CPU. The success of his new Virtual Reality console had been down to her expertise. Over the last three years they'd become the best of friends. She had helped him overcome the trauma of his disability and had given him the strength to carry on with his *Schedule*.

Secretly Beth had reprogrammed PETE to receive direct input from her own computer in order for them both to communicate secretly to each other. She had installed minute cameras in each of their wrist computers to create real holographic images of themselves. Now at the touch of a button they could see and talk to each other.

He looked at the screen in front of him and reread the message. This had to be Beth messing him about. Earlier Beth had gone to her room leaving him to finish off the programme routines. He had promised to tell her the minute the OPS CPU and VTR visor were operational and together they would register their findings with the Institute's Computer. In his haste he had registered without telling her.

He switched on PETE and asked for BETH 1. Immediately a pre-recorded holographic image of Beth appeared above his wrist. The face of a thirteen-year-old girl with long blond hair informed him that she was not available; she was asleep and did not want to be disturbed. The image faded and Izward instructed PETE to turn itself off.

If it wasn't Beth, then WHO had invaded his programme?

Izward inspected the hardware for signs of interference. He could see none. He examined the visor and opened the OPS CPU. Nothing had been tampered with. Finally he switched off the power and rebooted the system. The screens flashed a new message.

TIME WARRIOR IZWARD
AS I HAVE TOLD YOU
THERE IS NOTHING WRONG WITH YOUR
EQUIPMENT
TRUST ME

TO CONTINUE PLEASE PRESS ENTER

Thinking there must still be a glitch in the system he hit the monitor again. The screens flickered and another message appeared.

TUT! TUT! IZWARD!
I'VE TOLD YOU NOT TO DO THAT!

TO CONTINUE PLEASE PRESS ENTER

Amazed at what he was seeing, and thinking the OPS CPU must have developed its own intelligence, he pressed ENTER.

Suddenly the monitor screens around the room burst into colour and the room was filled with flashing lights. Each screen displayed a sequence of different colours that lit up the walls and shone onto Izward's face. Izward stared hypnotically into the screen his face reflecting the changing colours on his monitor. Suddenly all the screens in the room burst into red and Izward could see a ball of fire appearing in the centre of his screen. The fireball grew until it filled the entire screen. Around him all the other screens in the room mimicked his own. Soon the laboratory was filled with miniature fires as each screen displayed a blazing ball of fire. An eerie red glow settled across the room making Izward appear like a demon in the depths of Hell.

Suddenly words appeared on the screen. They began at the bottom of the screen and scrolled slowly upwards. From out of the monitors a young girl's voice read the scrolling words.

I AM THE CREATOR
MASTER OF THE GAME
AND GUARDIAN OF TELLURIAN

The words scrolled up the screen and disappeared off the top of it.

THIS IS MY STORY

FROM OUT OF THE SPHERE CAME THE
ESSENCE
OF LIFE AND A GALAXY WAS CREATED

Suddenly all the screens in the room went black. At the bottom of the screen more words appeared and slowly moved upwards.

A SUN WAS BORN AND THE PLANETS
EVOLVED
CREATING LIFE THROUGHOUT THE
UNIVERSE

In the blackness of each screen a different sphere suddenly appeared. Each globe spun and rotated in the centre of the screen. Each ball had its own unique colour and surrounding cloud formations. Izward recognised them immediately, they were the planets in his own solar system.

The words moved on and up the screen as the voice continued its story.

BUT THE GALAXY LAY UNFINISHED
A PLANET HAD FAILED TO APPEAR
AND WOULD BRING DISORDER AMONGST
THE STARS

On all the screens a single planet appeared. Izward recognised it immediately. Its blues and greens, its swirling clouds of white. He was looking at his own planet, the planet Earth.

The words scrolled on as the story unfolded.

BUT I THE CREATOR CORRECTED THAT
MISTAKE
AND CONSTRUCTED A WORLD SO PURE
ITS PERFECTION WAS THE ENVY OF THE
UNIVERSE

Izward stared at the screen admiring the skill and ingenuity of the graphics.

The words moved on and up as the voice continued its narrative.

ORDER RETURNED AND THE UNIVERSE
WAS SAFE.

The screen continued to scroll the words upwards as the Creator's story slowly unfolded.

BUT AN EVIL THREATENS TO DESTROY
THAT HARMONY
AND BRING ABOUT ITS DESTRUCTION

On all the monitors the planet Earth exploded and the screens returned to the balls of fire that introduced Izward to the game. From out of the flames more words appeared.

Tellurian needs the help of a time warrior.
YOU are that warrior.

The words stopped in the centre of the screen and started to flash.

Izward looked unbelievably at the screen and wondered how the Game knew his INTERNET name. Whoever had designed the programme was a genius. He continued to stare at the screen hypnotised by the flashing words. Finally unable to resist the mystery any longer he pressed ENTER.

Izward watched the screens as the words slowly rearranged themselves to display a new message.

THE GAME
OF
WIZARD MASTER
TIME WARRIOR OF TELLURIAN
IS
READY
TO
PLAY

This time there was no voice and Izward watched as the words on the screen faded into others.

ARE YOU BRAVE ENOUGH TO ENTER THE
WORLD OF TELLURIAN
AND BECOME A WIZARD MASTER?

Gradually the words dissolved and were replaced by others.

DARE YOU FIGHT THE EVILS OF THE DARK
ZONE
AND CONFRONT CREATURES BEYOND
YOUR IMAGINATION?

"Yes!" shouted Izward completely carried away by the lure of the game.

YOU DARE!
GOOD!
THEN PRESS ENTER
AND
LET THE GAME BEGIN!

Izward pressed enter and a figure of a young girl appeared on the screen. Izward stared at her unable to believe his eyes. It was Beth, or someone who looked like her.

"Beth?" questioned Izward.

The girl turned towards him and smiled. She certainly looked like his Beth but the young girl on his screen was different somehow. Her facial features were similar but her blond hair was much longer and she looked older and a little taller. She was wearing a long white shimmering gown that covered her entire body. The gown came to rest just above her ankles and she wore open leather sandals. The imagery was perfection far beyond anything he thought possible. Whoever had written and designed *this* game had skills far greater than his.

The beauty on the screen stretched out her arms and held them just below her head.

"Welcome Time Warrior," she said.

Izward looked at the screen. The figure looked like an angel. Her gown shone like translucent gossamer, and hung down at the sleeves like wings.

"I am the Guardian of Tellurian," she informed,*" and I shall be your Mentor and accompany you on your Quest."*

Izward was astounded. How could a game re-create such reality? Somehow it had reproduced a character that resembled someone who was very dear to him.

"Listen to my council and be guided by my wisdom," she explained.

Izward was intrigued and waited for the girl to continue.

"You are about to enter a world of interactive characters and real time environments. Once inside the game you live its reality. Your future will be the illusion and Tellurian's past your reality."

Iwzard grew impatient. He fiddled with the VTR visor eager to put it on.

"I am the Creator of the Game, this is my symbol."

A strange symbol appeared on the screen.

♌

"Follow its path and be guided by its light."

Then she faded from the screen leaving the rune to deliver its message.

Izward waited and waited. Nothing happened. The rune continued to flash and Izward grew impatient. He looked at the symbol on the screen wondering if this was a clue to the next phase of the game. It must be he reasoned and tried to remember what she had said.

'Follow its path and be guided by its light,' she had instructed.

He stared at the symbol. The longer he studied the more familiar it became. Finally he remembered where he had seen it before. It was part of an old computer FONT used in the twenty-first century. Computer keyboards no longer carried such FONTS. However he recalled he had an old CD disc somewhere with it on. He searched his workstation and found it. He inserted the disc into the OPS CPU CD drive and loaded the FONT into its memory banks.

He removed the disc and loaded up the WINGDINGS FONT. He searched its file, found the ♌ key and pressed it. Suddenly a crescendo of noise came out of the monitors and Izward was bombarded with the choral climax of Beethoven's Ninth Symphony. Across his monitor more words appeared.

CONGRATULATIONS WIZARD MASTER

YOU HAVE SUCCESSFULLY PASSED THE
TEST
YOU ARE INDEED A TRUE TIME WARRIOR
YOU HAVE PROVED YOURSELF WORTHY
OF THE TASKS AHEAD

The girl glided back onto his screen and Izward watched as the creature gently turned towards him. She smiled and her angelic face filled the screen. Her face was slim and smooth and her long blond hair fell across her face like rivers of gold. She reminded him of a painting of the mythical goddess *Venus,* he once had had the privilege of viewing whilst visiting the ruins of a *real time* museum.

"Your game reality is the ancient island of Tellurian," said the girl, *"your quest to rescue Wizard Zardo, a fellow Time Warrior, and together destroy the evil forces of the Dark Zone."*

Her voice drifted around the room like the ancient song of a nightingale.

"I offer you the following hints," she continued, *"remember them well, they will be of great value."*

The girl faded from the screen and an island appeared.

"This is the island of Tellurian," explained the voice of the girl, *"it is an island full of magic and mystery, myth and legend. Its resources are many, so become a wizard and use them wisely,"*

Izward looked at the screen and was taken on a bird's eye journey around the island. He darted through trees and over the tops of mountains. He swooped along rivers and flew over lakes. He dived into caves and through dark underground tunnels. Finally he flew high into the air and hovered above the island looking down at the surrounding ocean. Suddenly the island faded and the girl returned.

"First find the Ring of Genesis," said the girl, *"summon its power and I shall be there to guide you."*

On the screen a large circular ring appeared. Its three-dimensional image began to slowly rotate allowing Izward to study the object more closely. It was silver in colour and looked like metal. In its centre a large cube shaped stone had been set which reflected a deep sea blue. Around the stone, etched into the ring's circular perimeter, were several symbols. Izward looked at them carefully trying to determine their meanings.

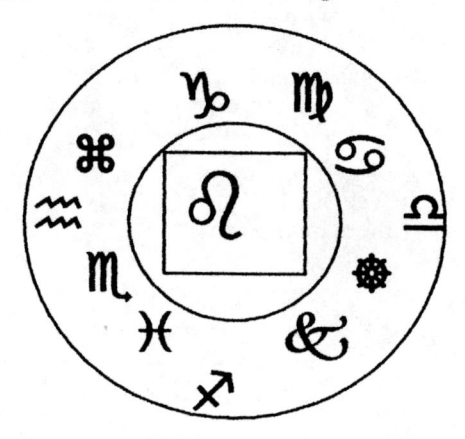

Izward watched as the girl placed the ring on her finger and pressed one of the symbols. The blue stone in the centre of the ring began to spin. Slowly at first but gathering more and more momentum with every turn. Finally the image of a strange bird appeared hovering over the spinning stone.

"*The Ring,*" said the girl, "*is your greatest weapon. Its magic allows you to eavesdrop on your enemies or make contact with your allies.*"

Izward watched as she pressed another symbol and the image above the stone changed to a wriggling worm.

"*Each symbol,*" continued the girl, "*represents a player in the game. To make contact or observe its progress press its symbol and all will be revealed.*"

The ring on the girl's finger dissolved.

Izward watched as the girl moved closer to the screen.

"*Izward,*" she whispered, "*come closer I have something important to tell you.*"

Izward moved closer to the screen. He could see Beth's deep blue eyes staring back at him.

"*I must warn you! The events you are about to experience are real,*" cautioned the girl, "*you have but one life do not waste it.*"

The girl vanished from the screen and was replaced by more instructions.

PUT ON YOUR VRT VISOR NOW!

Location *The Planet Earth*

Time Zone *A Long Time Ago*

Into The Past

Izward picked up the visor.

He was pleased with its design. It was semicircular in shape and only six centimetres wide. It was moulded from toughened *Technoplastic* and was virtually indestructible. He held it in the palm of his hand admiring its shape and style. It was light and comfortable weighing little more than a few grams. It was worn over the eyes and ears and gripped the User's temples. It had been constructed using the latest *Plasto-technology* techniques, a manufacturing process known only to the Institute. This technique enabled objects to be designed with internal energy sources making external wiring obsolete. Izward examined the OPS CPU. It too had been designed using *Plasto-*technology. The unit was slim and less than twelve centimetres long. Shaped like a computer keyboard with a holographic touch sense keypad it provided the User with the latest technological advancements in the field of Virtual Reality.

Izward read the screen again. Instinct told him the unit was malfunctioning and should be investigated before being used.

Ignoring his own warning Izward slipped the visor over his eyes and entered the game.

A Technological Miracle

Izward found himself standing in the centre of an enormous circular chamber.

The room had been ransacked.

Torn up books, pieces of broken furniture and the remains of a clock were scattered all over the floor. Tree roots grew down from an unseen ceiling and a large wooden door gave access to an unknown world beyond.

Izward looked around the room amazed by the complexity of the illusion. He stretched out a hand and touched the wall. He half expected his fingers to go through it but instead it was solid and rough to the touch. The projected images around him were faultless, perfect in every detail. This indeed was VR technology far beyond his experience and it was difficult to believe it had been created through electronic chips and bio-stimulators.

Izward explored the scene.

He was in a room built inside the trunk of a large tree. The room was a mess. Books and debris littered the floor and the mechanical remains of a large clock lay in pieces across the hearth of a stone fireplace. The twisted face of the timepiece rested in the fire its hands bent beyond repair. Above the fireplace a single beam of wood acted as a mantelpiece. On the beam stood a single cup and saucer, its contents hot and steaming, waiting to be drunk.

Izward couldn't believe his senses. Here was a programme that defied reality. Interaction of this intensity was impossible. But here he was experiencing the greatest VR experience of a lifetime. Whoever had created this masterpiece had accomplished a technological miracle.

He walked over to the centre of the room, bent down and picked up one of the books. It was old and covered with dust. He could smell the leather binding around its spine. He blew away the dust and read its title: *How To Become A Magician*. He opened the book and began to flick through its pages browsing at the chapter headings: *The Art of Spell Casting* read one of the chapters: *Incantations* read another. The whole book, if the *Introduction* were to be believed, would make you a Wizard in ten easy lessons.

Izward smiled to himself and was about to put it back on the floor when a single page glided out of the book and floated gently to the floor. Izward put the book on the mantelpiece and went to retrieve the page. He bent down and picked it up. The page had writing on it. The ink was faded in places but he could just make out the name of the person who had written it.

Wizard Zardo

There was more writing but Izward found it difficult deciphering the wizard's spider like scrawl. Eventually he succeeded and read the message out loud.

The mysteries of the universe are many
Open its eyes to understanding.
Seek out its darkest secret
And good shall always triumph over evil.

He was about to place the note in his pocket when he realised he no longer wore his cyber-suit. With all the excitement of the game he had failed to notice the programme had given him different clothing. He now wore a one-piece black leather suit with large turned down lapels. Each lapel had a circular sequence of symbols similar to the ones he saw on the ring. Around his waist hung a red leather belt with a large silver buckle. On his feet he wore large black leather boots that stopped just below his knees. His suit sparkled as if a thousand stars had been sewn into the cloth.

Suddenly he felt a pain shoot across his forehead.

Whilst developing the system Izward had discovered that over exposure to VRT stimulus gave you a headache. Also wearing the VRT visor for long periods of time created identity confusion when the User returned to normality. Therefore until he had perfected the system he had limited the visor's use to periods of fifteen minutes.

He went to remove the visor but to his horror found it wasn't there.

The Passageway

Izward suddenly felt trapped and confused.

His heart raced and his stomach churned. Unbelievably his visor was missing and he knew that was not possible. The visor, although invisible during VR experiences, was always there, worn over the eyes, projecting and directing the action.

You removed it and the game ended.

Without the visor the game should have returned him to the present. It hadn't and he knew something was terribly wrong.

He looked about the room beginning to realise what he was experiencing was no illusion. It would be impossible for his brain to receive the appropriate signals without the visor.

The room, the scattered books and broken furniture, everything he saw and touched, was genuine. This wasn't deception, this was reality and somehow he'd been transported to another dimension. Where exactly in time and space he'd gone was still a mystery. However two things were certain, this was NO GAME and if the girl was to be believed, REAL.

He tried to remember what the girl had said.

> *I must warn you!*
> *The events you are about to experience are real!*
> *You have but one life.*
> *Do not waste it!*

But before he had time to worry about her warning a loud thumping noise shattered the silence and half frightened him to death.

THUD! THUD! THUD!

Izward looked towards the door.

THUD! THUMP! THUD!

There it was again. The banging was coming from somewhere beyond the door.

THUMP! THUD! THUMP!

Whoever was knocking was getting desperate. Izward carefully manoeuvred his way through the debris and went over to the door. On closer inspection he noticed a small circular hole had been burnt through it.

THUD! THUMP! THUD!

He stood on tiptoe and peered through the hole. He could see a narrow passageway about ten metres long. Along each side of the corridor roots had grown up the walls and over the ceiling, twisting around each other to create a row of arches. At the end of the chamber stood another large door similar to the one he was looking through.

THUMP! THUD! THUMP!

The door at the other end of the passage shook.

Izward stepped away from the hole and tried to open the door. It was much heavier than he'd expected and he needed two hands to pull it open. As he pulled the door squeaked and creaked against rusting hinges. Finally it opened and he walked into the passage.

THUD! THUMP! THUMP! THUD!

The unseen caller was getting more and more impatient.

"I'm coming," shouted Izward.

Izward shivered as he entered the passage. Whether it was from fear or the dampness in the air, he wasn't quite sure. The corridor was dank and smelt of decaying leaves. He walked slowly towards the door listening to the sound of twigs snapping under his feet. His heart raced and the hairs on the back of his neck prickled icy cold.

When he reached the door he stopped afraid to open it. If all this *was real*, and he suspected it was, he couldn't afford to be careless. This was no longer a game one wrong decision could be fatal.

He wished PETE was here to help but he knew that wasn't possible. He was alone and must rely on his own judgement.

He stood, staring at the door, thinking about the young girl's warning, *'you have but one life, do not waste it!'"*

CRUNCH!

Suddenly there was a loud splintering sound and the door almost flew off its hinges. Izward stepped back startled by the sudden noise and almost tripped over a log.

CRACK!

Parts of the door flew off into the corridor.

Fearing the door would be forced off its hinges Izward stepped forward and placed his hands firmly against the door. He pushed hard against it hoping to prevent further damage.

"I'm here! I'm here. Stop your hammering!" shouted Izward angrily," you're breaking down the door!"

The banging stopped and Izward stepped away from the door. He examined it for further signs of damage. Apart from a few additional cracks around the hinges the door had survived the poundings. He also noticed, like the other door, this too had a circular hole burnt through it. Realising it would make the perfect spy-hole he carefully lifted himself up and looked through it. To his horror a large round eye looked back at him and blinked.

"Open the door," said the eye, "I've something very important to tell you."

Behind The Door

Izward struggled to open the door. It scraped along the ground gouging a furrow into the floor. Suddenly it jammed and came to a stop less than a quarter open. A cold icy wind blew through the gap and Izward shivered.

"Let me help you," said the eye.

And before Izward knew what was happening three large claws came around the door and it flew open. Izward was swept behind it and pinned against the wall.

Something entered the passage.

"Zardo!" shouted a voice, "I must speak to you."

Izward couldn't see his visitor; he was trapped behind the door.

"Where are you?"

Izward said nothing fearing his unknown visitor might harm him.

"Look yer old sea-wizard," continued the voice, "this 'ant no time for one of yer little tricks. I have bad news. Our caves are infested with *aliens*."

"Aaaaaa...tishooo!" sneezed Izward unable to stop himself. The unknown creature stopped shouting.

"Zardo, be that you?"

Izward said nothing fearing discovery.

Suddenly a large claw gripped the bottom of the door and it was flung back. It slammed shut and the howling from the wind stopped.

In front of him stood the largest bird he had ever seen. It lowered its head and came towards him. Izward cowered against the wall fearing the game was about to end before it had began. Two large round eyes blinked at him through a mountain of feathers.

"What be this?" uttered the bird picking Izward up by the scruff of his neck.

With the bird's beak firmly around his neck Izward was carried back into the room and dropped on the floor.

Wizard Napping

"Where's Zardo?" questioned the bird.

"I don't know!" stuttered Izward frightened by the creature's unusual size. The bird blinked and turned its head in a complete circle.

"Idiot," hooted the bird in disgust and continued to search the room for Zardo.

The wizard couldn't be found and the owl turned to Izward for further interrogation.

"Who are yer?" ordered the bird, "what creature might yer be?"

"I'm Izward," said the boy lifting himself to a sitting position.

"An Izward! What sort of creature is an Izward?" asked Hoot.

"It's not a creature," said Izward, "it's a name."

"Never heard of an Izward," interrupted Hoot, "where yer from?"

Izward looked at the owl.

It was huge and magnificent.

In his own time owls were never seen and were rumoured to be extinct. He had only experienced them through *Vista-books* and VR adventures. However this one was real and twenty times bigger.

It even talked.

"What yer cockling at?" enquired Hoot. "Never seen an owl before?"

"Actually no!" said Izward.

"What be yer island," asked Hoot?

"My island?"

"Yes! Where yer come from? What place be yer home?"

"I'm not quite sure," said Izward, "its all getting rather complicated."

"Well yer not from around here I be sure," explained the owl looking at Izward suspiciously, "and we don't take to strangers. Especially ones who don't know where their island is."

Izward wished he could stop the game and plan his next move, but real adventures don't have pause buttons.

"I've been sent from the...*Future*," said Izward not knowing how the giant bird would react.

"Don't know any place called the Future," said Hoot, "why yer come here?"

But before Izward could answer there was a rapping on the outside door.

"Who be that?" said the bird directing his question at Izward.

"How should I know," said Izward, "I'm a stranger here, remember."

There was more banging on the door but this time louder.

"You come with me!" said Hoot pushing him towards the door.

Izward sensed the giant owl didn't trust him.

"The door," said Hoot, "I'll be spying yer, so don't try any of yer shinanigins."

Izward opened the inner door and they walked down the passage to the other door. The giant bird pushed Izward aside and looked through the hole in the door.

"Well I'll be a sea-serpent's dinner!" uttered the owl, "what brings yer to this part of the forest?"

The bird opened the door and bright sunlight filled the passage. For a moment Izward was temporarily blinded and all he could see was a vague shape hovering in the doorway.

"Come in," said the owl, "welcome me old shipmate, its good to see you again. It's been too long a voyage since we last met."

"Hoot!" said the creature somewhat surprised, "what are you doing here? Where's Zardo, I must speak to him?"

Izward heard the flapping of wings and then something fly past him.

"Missing!" said Hoot, "and his room's a disaster, I fear he's been abducted."

Izward rubbed his eyes trying to adjust to the brightness.

When his sight returned Hoot and his companion had gone. He could hear them talking in the room at the end of the corridor. He couldn't tell what they were saying but he sensed something was very wrong. He decided he must make friends with the owl and his companion and seek their assistance.

He went to the open door and for the first time since he started this crazy adventure looked outside. He was standing in a doorway cut into the largest tree he had ever seen. It towered high above all the others and from where he was standing, looked as though it touched the sky. Around him was a forest with a pathway that spiralled away into the distance. He could see the forest was dying. The grass was brown and lifeless and the plants were dead and decaying. A sickly green slime had seeped up from the ground and was spreading up the trees.

As quickly as the sun had appeared it disappeared and he heard the rumblings of a storm in the distance. The weather was changing and he feared the game was becoming a little more sinister. He felt a cold chill run down his spine and knew there was something evil out there.

He closed the door and walked down the passage towards the room. Hoot and his visitor were still talking.

As he walked down the corridor Izward thought of Beth and the Institute and how they must be reacting to his disappearance. Beth would be worried sick and desperately lonely. She was a shy girl who found making friends difficult. She would miss him terribly. He wished he could somehow contact her and tell her he was safe but he didn't know how.

His Mentors on the other hand would be furious. They would have assumed he'd defected to another corporation and taken all their secrets with him. He visualised the Institute's Internet Police frantically searching Cyberspace for his whereabouts.

He reached the end of the passage and stopped. He smiled to himself. Another thought had crossed his mind. If he did get back to his own time he had a great idea for a game.

"Izward!" boomed Hoot putting his head around the door.

Izward stopped, fearing they would clash heads.

"Oh there yer be!" said Hoot menacingly, "thought you'd scampered."

"No I'm still here," said Izward, "why should I leave?"

"Thought yer might be wanting to escape like before we ran yer through for the demon you are!"

Before Izward had time to react a large bird flew through the door and landed on his shoulders. Its claws gripped him tight and lifted him off the floor and through the door.

"Got you!" squawked the bird as it carried Izward through the door into the room. Hoot followed and slammed the door shut.

"Now yer wizard napping Darkling what have yer done with Wizard Zardo?" thundered Hoot.

Izward the Wizard

Izward found himself back in the room of books. He dangled in the air held in position by the claws of a large bird. Less than a metre in front of him stood the owl.

"Well," said the owl, "where's the wizard?"

"What wizard?" asked Izward.

"The wizard who lives here," said Hoot, "Wizard Zardo!"

"Oh! Is this where Zardo lives," said Izward with an element of surprise.

Izward looked about the room. It looked slightly different from up at this angle.

"Look, you rotting sea-crab, what have you done with him?" shouted Hoot.

The owl stepped forward and Izward could see anger in its large brown eyes.

"I'm warning yer," said Hoot, "by all the sea gods of Tellurian, if you don't tell us what yer done with Zardo, we'll drop yer in the lake, and let the fishes feed on yer eye balls. Won't we Talon?"

"With pleasure, Captain Hoot, and if he escapes the fishes then the sea-serpents will get him."

"Ever seen a sea-serpent eating?" said Hoot looking into Izward's eyes.

Izward shook his head.

"Not a pretty sight," said Hoot, "is it Talon?"

"Horrible, it is Captain, it's just horrible."

Talon took Izward for a flight around the room.

"It don't bear thinking about," threatened Hoot as he watched Talon manoeuvring around the room with the terrified Izward dangling beneath him. Izward hated heights. Ever since his accident he had avoided high places.

He was beginning to feel sick and a little giddy.

Talon returned Izward to Hoot and dropped him at the Captain's feet. Hoot picked Izward up by the scruff of the neck and looked him straight in the eye.

"So, Izward from the Island of Future, are you going to tell me what yer done with Zardo or are yer going swimming?"

Talon had flown over to the fireplace and was perched on the mantelpiece listening and watching.

"I don't know where he is," pleaded Izward, "the room was empty when I arrived."

"And I suppose yer weren't responsible for all this 'ere wreckage either?" said Hoot picking up one of the books and waving it in front of Izward's face.

"No!" said Izward, "it was like this when I appeared."

"Appeared?" said Hoot letting go of Izward and looking across the room at Talon.

"He says he just appeared?" said Hoot suspiciously.

Talon's eyes stared accusingly at Izward.

"Look lobster-legs, in Tellurian only Warlocks and Wizards *appear*," said Hoot, "so what are you?"

"...Er, I don't know," said Izward, "is there a difference?"

"He's an evil Warlock," squawked Talon in panic, "he's going to kill us!"

The eagle flew across the room and grabbed hold of Izward again and lifted him off the floor.

"No I'm not," shouted Izward, "put me down!"

"You are! I've seen your *accomplice*," said Talon.

Talon turned to Hoot and told him about his mysterious visitor at the windmill.

"They were *mind-talking*," said Talon, "that's why I came to see the Wizard, to tell him about it."

Hoot told Talon about the worms and the snake like creature that nearly ate him and that he too was looking for Zardo.

"Zardo must be told of these events," said Hoot, "and of this Izward from the Island of Future."

Talon shook the suspended Izward making his legs look like two wriggling worms.

"But where is Zardo?" said Talon.

Hoot shook his head. The owl stared at Izward dangling from Talon's claws. Talon swung around and positioned Izward in front of him.

"He knows," continued Talon.

"No I don't! Please put me down!" shouted Izward, "I'm not a Warlock and I'm certainly not planning to kill you."

"Let's torture him," said Talon, "that'll get the truth out of him."

Talon flew to the ceiling.

"Where is he? Tell me or I'll drop you!"

"Stop it!" shouted Hoot, "bring him back down."

"But!"

"Talon, we're Tellurian's, we don't resort to torture," said Hoot, "now bring the creature to me and release it."

Talon lowered Izward to the floor and let him drop the last two metres. Izward landed safely on his feet. The eaglet flew back to the fireplace and sat down sulking.

"Yer say yer here to help?" questioned Hoot. "Prove it!"

"Um!" said Izward unclear as to how to explain what had happened to him.

"It's a game," said Izward, "well sort of, but it's in *real-time* and its actually happening."

"Yer be rattling in riddles," said Hoot utterly confused.

"Sorry," said Izward realising his mistake. He would have to explain in Tellurian terms.

"The Guardian of your island has asked for my help in finding Wizard Zardo," said Izward.

"It has, how?" asked Talon still unsure as to Izward's motives.

"That's difficult to explain," said Izward trying to think of a simple explanation.

"Let's call it through *mind-talking*," continued Izward, "it came to me in a vision and said you needed my help."

"A vision?" said Talon suspiciously.

Talon flew off the fireplace and landed in front of Izward.

"And what did The Guardian tell you in this vision?" quizzed Talon.

"That Zardo was missing and your island was in danger," said Izward.

"How did you get here?" asked Talon. "Where do you come from?"

This was going to be even more difficult to explain thought Izward.

"From the future," said Izward, "through the magic of technology."

"Never heard of either," said Talon.

"Trust me!" said Izward, "they exist."

Izward walked around the room examining the torn up books and broken objects.

"You say this is Zardo's room?" said Izward quizzically.

"Yer, this tree has been Zardo's home for as long as I can remember," said Hoot.

"We call it Methuselah, *the old one*," said Talon, "it's been growing on our island since time began."

"Its strength has been the island's inspiration," said Hoot.

"Until now!" said Izward looking up at the ceiling. A large blob of yellow slime fell from the ceiling and splattered on the floor.

"Look!" said Izward, "it's already started."

"What do you mean?" said Talon looking at the slime stained floor.

"It's decaying," said Izward, "the tree is dying and so is the rest of your island."

"Nonsense!" said Talon.

"Its true," said Izward, "you must believe me."

"How do you know all this?" asked Hoot.

"I've seen it on my computer!" said Izward, "your island is doomed unless we defeat the evil that is invading it."

Another slime ball hit the floor and splattered across several books.

"You've already encountered that evil," continued Izward, "the worms, the snake, the creature at the mill."

"So what we're going to do?" asked Talon.

"Stop them before it's too late," said Hoot.

"It probably is already," said Talon reluctantly.

"Maybe not," said Izward fumbling inside his tunic for the torn out page he'd found earlier.

He held it up for both of them to see.

"A message from Zardo in his own handwriting," replied Izward.

"What does it say?" asked Hoot.

Izward read out the message.

The mysteries of the universe are many
Open its eyes to understanding.
Seek out its darkest secret
And good shall always triumph over evil.

"What does it mean?" asked Talon.

"Its a clue," said Izward, "all adventure games have clues."

"What," asked Talon?

"Never mind," said Izward realising the bird knew nothing of his world of virtual reality games and computers. Izward looked carefully at the piece of writing he held in his hand and looked around the room at all the books.

"I wonder?" he said out loud.

"What," asked Hoot?

"The Mysteries of the Universe," said Izward, "that could be the title of a book?"

"It could," said Hoot looking at the piles of discarded manuscripts scattered around the room.

"And *open its eyes to understanding,* simply means to open the book and read it," continued Izward.

"What's the next line?" asked Talon eagerly.

"Seek out its darkest secret and good shall always triumph over evil," read Izward.

"Seek means find," said Hoot eager to help.

"And *darkest secret* could mean the Dark Zone," interrupted Talon.

"Well done!" said Izward, "I think we've solved it."

"So we're looking for a book called, The Mysteries of the Universe," said Izward, "and a chapter about the Dark Zone, agreed?"

"Agreed!" said Hoot and Talon together.

They began searching the room.

Izward looked in the broken bookcase whilst Hoot and Talon examined the books on the floor. As they searched they dodged drips of yellow slime that fell from the ceiling. It splashed on the floor and on the books making the floor slippery and the books sticky.

"Its not here," said Hoot, "either we're wrong or the book isn't in the room."

"It's got to be here," said Izward, "we're just not looking in the right places."

"Maybe you've got to be a wizard to find it," muttered Talon disappointedly.

"That's it!" shouted Izward, "I'd forgotten I had to do that."

Izward suddenly remembered the game's introduction and the advice he'd been given.

"Forgotten what?" enquired Talon.

"The Guardian's instructions," said Izward.

"And what be they?" asked Hoot.

Izward beckoned Hoot and Talon to come closer. They came and stood either side of him. They lowered their heads so Izward could whisper in their ears.

"I have to become a wizard," whispered Izward.

"A wizard!" shouted Talon and Hoot together.

"A wizard!" repeated Talon utterly amazed at Izward's statement, "and how are you going to do that?"

"I don't know," replied Izward, "I'd hoped you knew?"

Hoot and Talon looked at each and slowly shook their heads.

Suddenly a gust of wind blew open the door and Zardo's message leapt out of Izward's hand and into the air. It fluttered around the room like a butterfly caught in the wind.

Izward chased after it but slipped on a patch of slime and went sprawling along the floor.

Talon tried to grab it but the wind kept sweeping it out of reach. Finally Hoot went over to the door and forced it shut. The wind stopped and Zardo's message floated gently to the floor and landed on top of Izward's chest. Izward quickly snatched it and stood up.

"Got you!" he shouted and looked again at the message. This time it was different.

"Cool!" he uttered. "Wow! This is real cool!"

Hoot crossed the room and looked at the paper. It was the same torn out page he'd seen earlier but the message was indeed different.

"What does it say?" asked Talon joining them.

"I'm not sure," said Izward, "its difficult to read."

Izward tried to read the first line of the new message.

sdraziw lla fo tsetaerg eht odraZ ma I

"It doesn't make sense," said Izward disappointedly.

"Try the next line," encouraged Talon.

srewop lacigam dna egdelwonk ym lla uoy evig I sterces ym reffo I drawzl uoy oT

"You're right! It don't make sense," said Talon.

Hoot took the page from Izward.

"They could be Wizard Runes?" said Hoot examining the words more carefully.

"Wizard Runes?" asked Talon.

"Yes," said Hoot, "a forgotten form of writing known only to wizards."

"So what does it say?" asked Izward excitedly.

"I don't know," answered Hoot, "maybe only wizards can understand them."

"Then why send them to us?" puzzled Izward.

Hoot and Talon looked at each other and shrugged their shoulders.

"Maybe Zardo's books will tell us?" said Talon. The bird flew across the room and landed on a pile of books in the centre of the floor. He searched through them reading out their titles.

A Practical Study in Magic for Wizards Witches and Warlocks

Spells and Incantations
Old Spells With New Ideas

"Now that's interesting," mumbled Hoot pointing to one of the runes in the message.

"What is?" questioned Izward.

"That!" said Hoot pointing to the word *drawzl*.

Izward took the paper and read the word out loud.

"drawzl"

"Drawzl! No! I don't understand," admitted Izward, "what's drawzl?"

"Isn't that your name spelt backwards?" asked Hoot.

"What? Let me see," said Izward.

Izward slowly read out each letter.

"D r a w z l spelt the other way is *Izward*, by all the gods of Tellurian! Well done Hoot," congratulated Izward.

Talon flew back carrying several books in his claws. He dropped them on the floor at Izward's feet.

"Look!" said Izward to the bird," Hoot's solved the riddle of the Wizard's Runes."

"He has? How?"

"You have to read the message backwards," shouted Izward excitedly.

Izward read the next line of the message and translated it.

"draziW a emoceb lliw uoy dna sterces rieht nrael dna skoob ym ot kool"

"Look to my books and learn their secrets and you will become a wizard," translated Izward slowly.

"It works," shouted Hoot.

"What about the first part of the message," encouraged Talon," what does that say?"

Izward studied the document carefully.

"sdraziw lla fo tsetaerg eht odraZ ma I"

"I am Zardo, the greatest of all wizards," he read out loud.

"sterces ym reffo I drawzI uoy oT"

"To you, Izward, I offer my secrets," he continued.

"That's you," interrupted Hoot.

"Shush!" hissed Talon.

Hoot threw Talon an angry glare. He hated his authority being questioned.

"What! Now look here!" mumbled Hoot.

Talon shuffled closer to Izward ignoring his comrade's comments.

"Zardo knew you would be coming," said Talon.

"It looks that way, doesn't it?" agreed Izward.

"He'd planned for you to become a wizard," said Talon pointing to the paper, "and this will tell us how to do it."

Hoot pecked Izward on the shoulder.

"And I've just worked something else out too," said Hoot.

"You have," said Izward, " what's that?"

"Your name," said Hoot.

"I thought you knew his name?" said Talon.

"I do! Fish breath!" scolded Hoot.

"What about my name?" asked Izward trying to stop a very silly argument getting out of control.

"It has the same letters in it as the word wizard," hooted the owl with satisfaction.

Izward mentally re-arranged the letters in his name and indeed made the word wizard.

"Cool!" said Izward,

"Coincidence?" questioned Talon.

"Destiny!" answered Hoot.

"What else does the message say," urged Talon.

"srewop lacigam dna egdelwonk ym lla uoy evig I"

"I give you all my knowledge and magical powers," translated Hoot looking over Izward's shoulders.

"snoitcurtsni eseeht wollof draziw a emoceb oT"

"To become a wizard follow these instructions," finished Izward.

At the bottom of the page a sequence of numbers and runes were written.

A PRAL STDY IN MAIC FOR WIDS CH VII
THE WIDS GUOK CH III
THE ANGY OF SORY CHXI
SP OF THE ANNT ONE CH IX

Izward tried to read them but couldn't.

"The last runes are different," said Izward, "they don't follow the same pattern."

Together they tried to decode the final section of the message but couldn't. No matter how they arranged and rearranged the runes they failed.

A large blob of slime dripped off the ceiling and narrowly missed Hoot. It splattered across the cover of a book.

"Curse this stuff," shouted Hoot stepping out of the way of another blob of falling slime. It too hit the book and splattered across the floor.

"What is this stuff?" questioned Talon lifting his foot to inspect a gluey substance sticking to his claws.

"I suspect it's a poison," informed Izward, "and it's destroying the forest."

Izward knew all good *game-programmers* programmed such disasters. It helped boost excitement levels and gave the players additional problems to solve.

"How do we stop it?" asked Talon.

"I'm working on it," assured Izward.

"What about those," said Talon pointing to the books he'd fetched, "will they help?"

"I don't know." replied Izward, "they might."

Izward knelt down and began looking through the books. He picked one up and examined it. Slime had stuck to its cover blocking out parts of its title.

THE ANGY OF SRY

There was something about the book that looked familiar. He'd seen something like this before. For a moment Izward was silent then suddenly he jumped up and punched the air with excitement.

"Yes!" said Izward, "that's it! I think I've solved it."

Izward handed the book to Hoot.

Look!" said Izward, "recognise that?"

Hoot took the book and looked at it.

"Can't say I do," admitted Hoot shaking his head, "parts of the title are missing."

"Precisely!" said Izward triumphantly, "that's my point!"

Talon took the book from Hoot.

"Here let me have a look," said Talon not wishing to be left out.

He looked at the cover then turned it over. He turned it over again and shook his head.

"Sorry!" said Talon, "what exactly am I looking for?"

"Look at the letters that are left in the title," encouraged Izward, "have you seen them before?"

Both Hoot and Talon looked and shook their heads.

"Look," said Izward showing them Zardo's message, "they're the same!"

THE ANGY OF SORY CHXI

Hoot took the page from Izward and held it against the cover of the book. The same combination of letters appeared on both.

"Well I'll be a sea-squids uncle," muttered Hoot, "they're the same."

"They're titles of books!" squawked Talon with great excitement.

"What about *CHXI?*" asked Izward, "have you guessed what that means yet?"

Hoot and Talon stood silent for a moment.

"Chapter headings!" shouted Talon.

"Correct!" praised Izward.

Suddenly all three were rummaging through the hundreds of books that covered the floor.

"Found one!" shouted Hoot having thrown several unwanted books into a heap in the corner of the room.

"Which?" enquired Izward.

"*A Practical Study in Magic for Wizards*," shouted Hoot.

"Good! I've found *Spells of the Ancient Ones*," said Izward, "that only leaves *The Wizard's Guidebook* to find."

They continued the search. Talon flew around the room picking up books while Hoot read out their titles. Unwanted books were thrown into a corner. The pile grew higher and higher as more books were rejected.

"The Sorceror's Apprentice!" shouted Hoot.

"No!" said Izward.

Talon hurled the book across the room into the corner. It landed on top of the pile and slipped down.

"Next!"

"Witchcraft for Warlocks!"

"No!" repeated Izward.

The book joined the others.

"The Wizard's Guidebook!" read Hoot.

"No!"

"What? Oh! Sorry! Yes, "said Izward.

"Too late!" said Talon as the book flew through the air and landed on top of the others. It slithered down the pile and buried itself inside the mound.

"Oh! Crustaceans," swore Hoot as he hurried across the room towards the pile of books. The others quickly joined him. Together they searched the heap carefully removing one book at a time. Gradually a hole emerged at the top of the pile where they had taken books.

"Found it!" shouted Hoot looking into the hole.

"Well done!" said Izward.

Izward removed the book and stood up. He helped the owl to its feet and together they went to the fireplace. Talon flew across the room and collected the other three books and took them back to his comrades.

All three sat beside the fireplace searching through the books that would make Izward a Wizard.

The River Of Magic

Izward spent the next few hours discovering Zardo's secrets.

He read about magic and the art of illusion, of spells and potions, charms and incantations.

He had practised casting spells and chanting charms, mixing potions and creating illusions. He had practised and practised until he was perfect. Hoot and Talon watched with growing excitement as the room was filled with magic.

A multicoloured beam of light suddenly appeared and raced around the room bouncing off the walls and the faces of the startled onlookers. The room was ablaze with colour.

Inside the beam Hoot and Talon could see an assortment of magical objects. Wizards' cloaks and sorcerers' hats, magicians' wands and witches' cauldrons, bottles and jars, bowls and flasks all spun and twisted around inside the beam. Bottles poured and jars drained, liquids bubbled and powders mixed. All fused together to form a meandering river of magic. Books rose off the floor and opened. Pages flicked and turned as if read by invisible readers. Candles appeared and floated around the room casting flickering shadows on the walls.

In the centre of all this confusion stood Izward.

His face glowed and his suit sparkled. Hoot and Talon stared in amazement, as the beam of light grew longer. They watched as it crossed the room and began to spiral around their newly found comrade. Round and round it spun engulfing the young lad in a cloak of colour. Hoot and Talon ducked as the end of the beam went over their heads and into Izward's mouth. He took a deep breath and inhaled. There was a whoosh of air as the river of magic flowed into his body. Hoot and Talon stood transfixed as the beam of light unwound itself from around Izward and vanished into the young lad's body.

The room went silent.

In the centre of the room Hoot and Talon could see Izward. He stood amongst a pile of books smiling back at them. He still wore the same tunic but a long black cloak had mysteriously been added. It hung from his shoulders like the wings of a bat. On his head he wore a large black magician's hat. He looked about the room and shook his head.

"We can't leave it like this, lets see what I can do."

Izward cast a spell and the room began to change.

Zardo's chair repaired itself and the bookcase reassembled. One by one the books arranged themselves back on the shelves in alphabetical order.

The grandmaster's clock rose out of the fireplace and began to put itself together. Slowly the outer-casing of the clock formed a tower and the mechanics clattered inside.

Its face rolled across the hearth and up the outer frame. It positioned itself on top of the clock with its hands at a quarter to two.

Finally the fish and the gnome went inside and closed the doors.

Cogs whirled and wheels turned, levers jumped and spindles spun.

The pendulum began to swing and the clock started ticking.

Zardo's magic carpet, which had been buried under a pile of books, rolled open and shook itself. Dust flew everywhere. It flew across the room and gently lowered itself on the floor in front of the door.

Finally the chairs and tables, cups and saucers, candles and brooms took to the air and raced across the room, narrowly missing each other in a mad scramble to reposition themselves. They flew around the room and came to rest in the places they'd occupied before the wizard's abduction. The fireplace burst into flames and the room was filled with warmth and light. The slime reversed its flow and slithered back up the walls and disappeared.

Suddenly there was a compelling urge to sit in the chair near the fire. He went over to the chair and sat down. It felt warm and comfortable and a strange feeling came over him. He closed his eyes and dreamed.

A wizard hovered in front of a large mirror and the room was in chaos. Books and furniture flew around the room whilst the wizard disappeared slowly into the mirror.

A large book floated in front of him and he read its title. 'The Mysteries of the Universe'

The room went silent and a green mist filled the air. From out of the haze came a wizard's charm spinning on the end of a chain. It glided gently towards him turning slowly in the air.

It landed on the cover of the book and disappeared into its binding. Suddenly the book flew open revealing a large picture of Wizard Zardo. The image spoke.

"I am Zardo the greatest of all wizards. I bequeath you all my knowledge and mystical powers. I give you the Mysteries of the Universe."

The book closed and headed towards the door. From inside the book Izward heard Zardo's voice again.

"Find me!"

The door swung open and the book flew out into the forest.

"Izward!" said a voice somewhere inside his head, "wake up!"

Izward opened his eyes. Hoot and Talon were gently shaking him.

"Are you all right?" asked Talon.

Izward stood up and nodded. He walked over to the fire and stared into the flames.

"You had us worried there for a second me old shipmate" continued Hoot, "we thought you were…"

"No I'm fine," said Izward.

Izward stared into the glowing embers recalling his vision. Zardo had given him more clues. He turned and looked at his colleagues.

"Tell me about Tellurian and its inhabitants," ordered Izward, "if we're going to save the island I need to know more about your world."

Talon quickly outlined the island's history and the lives of its creatures. He talked about the Creator and the magic of Zardo.

After Talon had finished Hoot talked about the Dark Wars and the evil Vulgor. He recalled the myths surrounding the Dark Zone and Zardo's campaign against its evil.

Izward listened with great interest and after they'd finished returned to his chair.

"Zardo has sent me another message," said Izward.

Hoot and Talon went over to the fire and sat beside Izward.

"I know where he's hidden the *Mysteries of the Universe*."

"The book that tells us how to destroy the Dark Zone?" asked Talon eagerly.

"Yes that one," answered Izward.

Hoot and Talon listened as Izward recalled his dream.

"…And it flew out the door," said Talon, "into the forest?"

"Yes," confirmed Izward, "all we have to do is find it."

Hoot and Talon looked at each other.

"Its rather a large forest..." insisted Talon.

"...To find one little book," finished Hoot.

"Don't worry my friends," said Izward, "remember, I'm a wizard and we have Zardo's magic to help us."

Izward waved his fingers at the bookcase and a piece of paper slid out from inside one of the books. It floated across the room and dropped to the floor at his feet. It unfolded itself into a map of the forest. On it a large X had been drawn.

"There!" pointed Izward, "that's where the book's hidden. All you have to do is follow the map and get it."

Hoot looked at the map and shook his head. He wasn't very good at reading maps and began turning it around to face different directions.

"Now let me see," mumbled Hoot, "I think that way is North and that South!"

"No!" cawed Talon.

The bird took to the air and hovered over the map.

"The other way round," he suggested from above Hoot's shoulders.

"Never mind that now," interrupted Izward "you can sort that out later."

We also need to find Zardo's charm, the Talisman he wore around his neck."

Hoot folded up the map and tucked it under his wing.

"Yes," said Izward, "it opens the book."

"And where's that hidden?" asked Talon.

"I'm not sure, with the book I think," said Izward.

"You think?" questioned Hoot. "Well let's hope you're right. We've no time to search for it if it isn't."

"It will be," insisted Izward, "trust me I'm a wizard."

But before they had time to discuss it further the clock struck the hour.

The whole room shook. The recently mended teacup fell off the mantelpiece and broke while several books slid off the bookcase and onto the floor.

They all turned and looked at the clock. Under the clock's face they could see a fish and a carved wooden gnome sitting on a toadstool. In the gnome's hand was a cudgel and hanging from the cudgel was a *ring*.

Izward stared in disbelief. It was the same ring the girl had shown him at the beginning of the game. She had called it *The Genesis Ring* and she had said it would be his greatest weapon.

"It's the ring!" shouted Izward, "I…"

But before he could finish the sentence the gnome hit the fish on its snout with the end of the cudgel and the ring flew off.

Hoot and Talon shielded their ears from the noise as the inside of the tree shook again. When it was over Hoot and Talon uncovered their ears and looked angrily at the clock.

"A sea-witch curse on yer!" hooted the owl, "what a hullabaloo!"

"Me too!" added Talon not knowing any good seafaring curses to aim at the offending clock.

Having finished its hourly duty the gnome went home and the fish jumped backwards through its door. The clock returned to normal and maintained a more sedate ticking.

Izward had been unaffected by the noise having been too involved with recovering the ring. Fearing it might get broken he had managed to catch it before it hit the floor. He now wore it on the middle finger of his left hand.

He gazed at it moving his finger from side to side. It shone a deep blue and its aurora reflected in his face. He smiled to himself, the last piece of the puzzle had been found and he was ready to finish the game.

The Genesis Ring

Izward stared hypnotically into the ring and thought he saw the face of his beloved Beth. She smiled lovingly at him. He gently touched the ring with the tip of his finger and blew her a kiss. He knew she'd be worried and wanted to tell her he was safe. Back at the Institute his unexplained disappearance would be a major breach of security. By now they would know he hadn't defected. He could visualise the *'CyBoSens'* trundling around the Institute looking for him, accessing his computer files and trying to decode his passwords. The *Cybotic Sentinels* were the Institutes' security guards and if VIPs like himself went missing they would go into action to protect the Institute's secrets. It would be assumed he'd been kidnapped by *Techno-Terrorists* and plans for his rescue would already be in place. *Techno-Espionage* cost the Institute millions of *Uni-Dolls* every year so every effort was made to find the perpetrators and bring them to justice. If only they knew the truth thought Izward.

Izward's thoughts returned to the girl in the ring. As he gazed into the cube, he realised it wasn't Beth.

"Izward?" spoke the girl softly, *"you must act swiftly, summon the power of the ring."*

Curious as to what Izward was doing Hoot moved closer and stood behind him. Talon hovered above him looking down. They both saw the ring and spoke simultaneously

"What's that?" they said in chorus.

Izward quickly explained the purpose of the ring and showed them the symbols around its rim.

"So by pressing one of those runes you can see what's happening anywhere on the island?" asked Hoot excitedly.

"Yes" answered Izward, "watch!"

Izward pressed one of the symbols and the girl's face faded. Hoot's image appeared on the face of the cube and in the background Talon could see Izward and himself.

"That's me!" shouted Hoot.

"And me," said Talon pointing at an image of himself hovering in the room.

Izward touched the ring and the scene above the cube enlarged and filled half the room. The trio watched in utter amazement as they saw an exact copy of the room and themselves.

"Well I'll be a crab's claw," exclaimed Hoot utterly amazed.

"There's two of everything, "said Talon.

Izward touched the symbol again and the scene faded from the ring. The girl's face returned and smiled at him.

"How do you know which symbols to select?" asked Talon.

Talon flew down and stood next to Izward.

"I don't, I get help," said Izward,

Hoot and Talon looked puzzled.

"You see, each game character has a symbol," said Izward.

"*Game?*" questioned Hoot "what is a *game?*"

Talon and Hoot looked at him questioningly.

"Um...Yes! Well never mind that now," said Izward wishing he'd not mentioned it, "you wouldn't understand."

"Try us?" suggested Hoot.

Talon flew across the room and landed unsteadily on top of the clock. He kept flapping his wings to balance himself.

"We're waiting!" said Talon tapping his claws on the clock's face.

"It's a... spell word for protection," lied Izward, knowing his comrades would never understand the truth, "to make you brave and fearless against the forces of evil."

Izward hated lying but sometimes little white lies were necessary.

"You are *Game Player Hoot*," said Izward, "the gallant protector of Tellurian."

Hoot smiled he liked the sound of that.

"And you *Young Game Player Talon*," continued Izward, "you are the heroic protector of Tellurian skies."

Talon flew off the clock and landed besides Hoot. Owl and eagle looked at each other and smiled proudly.

"*Izward*" said the girl in the ring urgently, "*look, the evil ones are here.*"

Izward looked at the ring. The girl faded from view and a ✗ symbol appeared. Izward quickly pressed the corrosponding symbol on the outside rim of the ring and suddenly Vulgor and the Gores appeared in the room.

Hoot and Talon panicked.

"By all the Gods of Darkness!" swore the owl, "it's them!"

"Demons from Hell," squawked Talon.

Hoot and Talon began running around the room dodging the flying serpents.

"They're not here!" shouted Izward trying to calm his colleagues down. "It's the ring, remember?"

Hoot and Talon ignored Izward's cries for calm.

"We have to defend ourselves," shouted Hoot.

"Every Tellurian for itself," squawked Talon.

They ran to the bookcase and began hurling books at the flying monstrosities. Like ghosts through solid walls the books passed through the intruders and struck the wall on the opposite side of the room. They landed with a chorus of thuds on the floor. A misaimed throw by Talon sent a book hurling in Izward's direction. The unfortunate wizard had no time to duck and the book struck his hat and sent it flying through the air.

"Watch it," scolded Izward picking up the hat and stuffing it into his belt. He stood in the centre of the room and glared at Hoot and Talon.

"Stop!" shouted Izward, "look they're not real."

Vulgor's image passed through him.

"See! they're not here, it's the ring."

Izward pointed to the ring on his finger as the rest of Vulgor's brood flew through him.

Hoot stopped in mid throw. He watched as Vulgor and his flying squadron of misfits flew out of a cloud and down towards an island.

"See he's approaching our island right now," said Izward, "we must make plans to stop him."

Hoot dropped the book, which landed on Talon's claw. The bird squawked with pain.

"Sorry!" said Hoot as he watched Vulgor and his army of reptiles swoop down through the trees and into the forest.

Suddenly the room was filled with noise as Vulgor and the Gores attacked several panic-stricken creatures in the forest.

"Tellurians," said Hoot anticipating Izward's question.

Like uninvited guests, Izward and his friends could only watch, unable to help their doomed colleagues.

Around them creatures were running for their lives. For the first time since entering the game Izward saw a Tellurian. They were flightless bird-like creatures that ran upright on two legs. They reminded him of *Pterodactyls* huge bird-like characters from his game *Terror-Saurus*. However these creatures were much smaller and stood upright like humans. Instead of wings, long spider like claws hung down either side of their bodies like the withered arms of old men. They had tough leathery skin covered in hairs that seemed to give some protection against Vulgor's fireballs. Although having bird-like bills their facial features gave them an ape like appearance.

Ahead of him Izward watched as the Tellurians scrambled out of the forest and along a path that led into the mountains. They pushed and shoved, bumped and jostled each other in a desperate attempt to escape the terror from the skies. Suddenly the view changed and the trio found themselves flying over the hills beyond the forest. Below them the Tellurians were still running, heading towards a bridge. Hoot recognised the bridge. It was the one he was swept under before he was taken under the island.

Around him the Gores were grabbing and snatching the Tellurians as they tried to cross the bridge. He watched as Vulgor swooped low and grabbed hold of a Tellurian by its head. The terrified creature struggled and wriggled like a fish caught on a hook. Vulgor took it high into the air and let it fall. It fell like a discarded stone into the open jaws of a passing Gore and was carried away screaming. The rest of Vulgor's men soon followed devouring those unfortunate creatures too slow to get out of their way. Those that did escape found themselves falling through the rotting timbers and into the river below.

Izward knew the Tellurians desperately needed his help and he tried to think of some magic spell that would save them. He raised his hands high in the air and began chanting. Nothing happened and the slaughter around him continued.

Suddenly the scene changed and the trio of watchers were airborne again following the invaders above the road that led towards an abandoned city. In the distance Talon could see the windmills where he'd encountered the amphibian, but before he could inform his colleagues the scene collapsed and Vulgor was sucked back into the ring like a Genie in a bottle.

A Magic Carpet Ride

Vulgor and the Gores disappeared and the room fell into an uneasy silence. Izward stared across the room thankful he could no longer see the plight of the Tellurians. He felt sad and dejected. He had failed them and it had cost them their lives.

"What happened?" enquired Talon breaking the silence.

The eagle flew across the room and landed beside Izward. Izward was staring into the ashes of the fire ashamed to look at his friend.

"Its cold in here!" replied Izward still shocked from the massacre he'd failed to prevent.

He cast a spell on the fire and it burst into life. The fire crackled loudly as if responding to Izward's anger. Hoot plodded across the room to join them and they all stood over the fire staring into the flames.

"The one throwing the fireballs was Vulgor," said Hoot.

"And I did nothing to stop him," said Izward sadly.

"It wasn't your fault," said Hoot gently, "there was nothing you could have done."

"Izward," whispered the ring, *"I must speak to you urgently."*

Izward stepped away from the fire quickly followed by Hoot and Talon. They moved to the centre of the room and looked into the ring. The girl who looked like Beth smiled up at them. Her image was faint and distorted.

"I need recharging," she urged, *"the ring's energy has almost gone."*

Her voice drifted in and out and her image faded and flickered.

"Without the power," she continued, *"the ring is blind and will be useless to you."*

"So that's why Vulgor disappeared," said Izward loudly.

"Yes," said the girl weakly, *"and that's why you need to find the Power Stones that will restore the ring's energy."*

"Power stones?" shouted Hoot, "never heard of em!"

"Me neither," squawked Talon.

"Shush! The both of you" interrupted Izward, "this is important."

Izward sensed the girl had little time left. Her voice was becoming weak and her image almost transparent.

"Where can we find the Stones?" asked Izward urgently.

"Scattered…"

The voice faded.

"…Earth!"

"What did she say?" interrupted Talon.

"Shush!" said Hoot putting a claw over Talon's mouth, "listen!"

Hoot moved nearer to Izward and put his ear close to the ring.

"The ring will know…"

"What was that?" asked Izward who was finding it difficult listening through Hoot's large head.

"… And the Stone will contact…"

Behind them Talon was struggling for breath. His face was getting redder and his eyes were getting wider. Hoot's claws gripped his mouth like the tentacles of an angry squid stopping him from breathing. Talon flapped furiously trying to get Hoot's attention.

" …The stone will glow…" continued the girl.

Talon went limp.

"…The ring will…"

Hoot had been too engrossed with the girl's narrative and had forgotten all about Talon. Finally he took his claw away and the bird fell to the ground gulping in air.

"Sorry" said Hoot apologetically, "forgot you were there."

"Uh…" coughed Talon not quite sure if Hoot was telling him the truth.

" ...Put them together and the ring will be replenished."

The image of the girl faded and the ring went silent.

"Did you get all that?" said Hoot to Izward.

Hoot turned to help Talon on to his feet.

"Here me old shipmate," said Hoot, "let me help ye, it's the least I can do."

"No! I'm fine," said Talon pushing Hoot away, "no harm done."

Izward returned to the fireplace. Suddenly the tree began shaking and Izward held onto the mantlepiece. Hoot and Talon grabbed each other and waited for the shaking to stop. When the tree stopped shaking they crossed over to Izward and began discussing tactics. After several minutes of discussion they stopped talking.

"So it's agreed then," shouted Izward.

"Agreed!" said the others.

"Hoot you go into the forest and find Zardo's book," said Izward, "and I'll find the Power Stones."

"I'll contact the Terrodacs and tell the Tellurians about the invasion," said Talon.

"And we'll all meet back here within the hour and assemble our forces." concluded Izward.

A good plan they all agreed.

Before Izward could utter another word Hoot and Talon had disappeared down the corridor into the forest.

Izward watched his *Game Players* disappear into the mist and wondered how much of the game he'd completed. He'd solved many clues and no doubt was TODAYS HIGHEST-SCORER. But this wasn't the kind of game where you were rewarded with points. Staying alive and being one step ahead of your enemy was the only objective.

This was the true reality of the game and Izward knew he had to defeat Vulgor in order to stay alive. The game plans were simple. First find the Power Stones and recharge the ring. The rest was up to Hoot and Talon.

He returned to the room and found the magic carpet hidden under the chair. He chanted a few magic words and it came to him. He carefully stepped on and was suddenly whisked forward through the door. He toppled backwards and landed on his back. It flew down the corridor and out into the forest. He clung on for several more heart-stopping seconds before he managed to clamber unsteadily to his feet and make his first magic carpet ride.

The Power Stones

Terrifying shapes hid in the mist and flashed past him in an instant.

The carpet pitched and dipped, twisted and turned as it manoeuvred its way through the unseen forest. He was flying blind moving his feet from side to side trying to steer the carpet in and out of the trees.

Finally after several more terrifying near misses he manoeuvred the carpet through the mist and out of the forest. He flew up into the sky and brought the carpet to a standstill.

Below he could see the island.

The forest was hidden in a thick yellow fog and a river of mist, about half a kilometre wide, snaked away from its centre and up to the sky. It meandered far into the horizon and disappeared inside a large dark cloud. The rest of the island was unaffected and was bathed in a sickly yellow light.

He gently pressed the carpet with the sole of his left foot and it slowly moved forward. More pressure and the carpet went faster. Soon Izward had mastered the carpet's control and rode it with all the expertise of a *Jetpack Jockey*.

Riding the carpet reminded him of a VR Space Simulation he designed for WASA the World Aeronautical Space Agency.

He had spent months on its research. *Jetpack* was the latest tool in Space Station construction and the Industry had wanted to train its workers in its use. He had designed a programme that allowed the *User* to gain the experience of manoeuvring *Jetpack Vehicles* through space before ever blasting off. Mind and body control had been an essential part of its mastery and Izward found piloting the carpet similar.

Izward dug his toes into the carpet and the carpet moved forward. He guided it down towards the edge of the forest where the foothills began and started to search for the Stones.

The ring remained lifeless and he moved on.

He flew down a valley, over the bridge where the Tellurians had been attacked and on towards what appeared to be the ruins of a city. It looked deserted and most of the dwellings had been destroyed by fire. Its streets were overgrown with weeds and hundreds of trees had grown up through the rubble. A river ran through its centre fed by water from a large lake high up on a nearby mountain.

At the edge of the city stood two large windmills. To the left of them stood a small oxbow lake, overgrown with reeds.

Suddenly he detected a faint glow coming from the ring and knew it was reacting to the Power Stones. He found the position where the ring shone its brightest and knew the Power Stones lay in that direction. The Stones were making contact and the ring was responding.

With one eye on the ring he set off towards the lake.

A Gathering Storm

The nearer he came to the Stones the brighter the ring.

He was gliding over the lake heading towards four columns of dazzling blue light coming out of the water.

He brought the carpet to a standstill and looked at the beams of light.

At the base of each column the lake hissed and bubbled. A transparent blue dome had formed over the columns creating a pulsating arch of blue light. Above the arch Seadacts hovered and squawked. They swooped and dived towards it but were forced back by some invisible force field.

He could feel the force of the Stones tugging at the ring. The carpet turned and moved slowly towards the dome. He held on and the carpet was pulled into the light.

Bathed in light and blinded by its brilliance Izward floated in a world of blue. In an instant he travelled through a thousand dimensions and across an infinite number of universes.

He witnessed the birth of stars and the formation of Galaxies.

He experienced the creation of life and the origins of Universes.

In a blink of an all *Seeing Eye* the Stones transferred their power and were gone.

The bright light vanished and Izward was left alone lying on top of the carpet. The dome had disappeared and Izward caught a glimpse of four columns of light fading quickly under the water.

Suddenly the silence was broken by a flock of Seadacts screeching in the skies above him. He looked up to see hundreds of birds swooping towards him. The sound was deafening. Fearing for his safety he quickly moved the carpet away leaving the confused birds to investigate another strange disappearance.

"Izward?" said a voice, *"I'm back."*

Izward stopped the carpet and looked at the ring. The face of the smiling girl hovered above it. The ring was working again.

"Beth?" said Izward.

The girl in the ring smiled and said nothing.

"The island," said Izward, "I must know what's happening to the island?"

The girl's face vanished and a symbol appeared. He quickly found the symbol and pressed it. He adjusted the ring for maximum view and found himself in an underground tunnel.

Above him hung the roots of trees and below a river of green sludge. Hundreds of green tentacle-like tubes grew out of the river and up the side of the tunnel. An eerie yellow light reflected off the walls and lit up the entire area. All around him clinging to the trees and the walls were millions of worm-like creatures.

He guessed they were the same creatures Hoot had encountered.

He watched as the worms ate.

They crawled up roots and into the trees, up the walls and through the soil. Wherever the worms crawled they ate. Izward could see large holes where the creatures had been and inside the holes a sticky green slime.

Suddenly there was a small explosion and Izward turned to see the green slime in one of the holes had burst into flames. There were more explosions followed by more and more fires.

The green slime secreted by the worms was bursting into flames.

Soon the underground tunnel was ablaze with fire.

Izward watched in horror as the fire began to spread and set light to the underground tunnels.

"Talon" he ordered.

Another symbol appeared and Izward pressed it. Immediately the scene changed and he was in the forest. A yellow smoke swirled up and around the trees and in the distance he could see a red glow.

The fires had reached the surface and were setting fire to the trees.

"This way," said a familiar voice and Izward saw Talon leading hundreds of Terrodacs through the trees. It was the first time he'd seen a Terrodac and was surprised how large they were. They were about three metres high and reminded him of giant bats. He'd seen pictures of bats on his computer and apart from their long pointed beaks they were alike.

"Hoot," yelled Izward and another symbol appeared and he pressed it.

The scene changed.

He was in a different part of the forest. Around him trees were bursting into flames. He enlarged the view and looked for Hoot. Black yellow smoke drifted up from the ground and swirled all around him.

"Sea fogs and serpent's breath," said a familiar voice.

It was Hoot.

Izward hung over the side of the carpet and looked down into the smoke. In reality he was looking into the lake but he knew the ring was showing him an alternative reality.

Through the smoke he saw Hoot struggling with the map. He'd opened it to its full extent and was having difficulty hanging on to it. It kept slipping out of his claw and fluttering to the ground. He kept picking it up and cursing.

"Blast yer! You be as slippery as an eel."

Finally he picked up four stones and placed the map on the ground. He placed the stones at its edges and knelt down. Smoke drifted everywhere forcing him to cough.

"That'll be the place!" he coughed pointing to the X on the map, "over there near the well."

Without warning the map burst into flames and Hoot scrambled clear. It quickly disintegrated and blew away in the wind.

Izward watched as Hoot fought his way through the smoke towards the well. Around him trees smouldered and their branches spat and crackled with the heat.

Hoot reached the well and began to search for the book.

Around him trees were exploding and bursting into flame. Smoke and fire poured out of the well creating a cloud of burning ash. It billowed high into the trees and as the burning embers descended they set fire to the surrounding branches.

Suddenly Hoot's feathers began smouldering and several burst into flames. He quickly fell to the floor and rolled along the ground. The flames went out leaving him face down in the grass.

In the distance Izward could see trees crashing to the ground and exploding in balls of fire. The underground fires had reached the surface and were setting fire to the forest. Suddenly Izward heard a branch snap and looked up to see the top of a tree falling towards him. It fell onto the carpet passing through it and towards Hoot. The owl saw it coming and quickly rolled out of its way. It crashed to the ground missing Hoot by centimetres and burst into flames.

For several seconds Hoot lay still and Izward feared he'd been injured. Then, to his great relief, he saw Hoot stretch out a claw and untangle something from a clump of weeds.

It was a large book. Hoot stood up and examined it.

"Yes!" he shouted, "Hoot me old mate, yer found it!"

Izward watched as the owl tucked the book safely under some feathers and continued his search. Suddenly from out of the forest burst several panic-stricken Tellurians fleeing the fire. They ran into Hoot and sent him sprawling. The book slid across the grass towards the well.

When the last Tellurian had gone Hoot stood up and went over to retrieve the book. Suddenly out of the well came a large snake-like creature. Stones and blazing branches flew everywhere and Hoot was showered with burning debris.

The creature hovered above the carpet its neck swaying from side to side hissing and spitting venom. Izward edged nearer. Around its neck dangled Zardo's Talisman. Its body stretched high into the air and he could see its tail was stuck in the well. It squirmed and wriggled desperately trying to free itself. It lowered its head and its eyes passed through him. He froze and went icy cold.

He knew it was only a projection but the image still sent shivers down his spine.

It opened its jaws and its tongue slithered out of its mouth and down towards Hoot. It wrapped itself around the owl's foot and yanked him off the ground.

"I thought I'd killed you,"protested Hoot.

Hoot came up through the carpet and was held upside down in front of the creature's head. It hissed and began swinging him backwards and forwards.

Izward knew he had to save Hoot. Without help the owl would die, the book would be lost and the Game at an end.

He held both his hand's skyward and cast a spell.

"Thunderbolts and lightning, from where I do not know. Across the fiery island, a lightning bolt I throw," he chanted. "Go fast and find your target, of fiery forest flames. Strike deep and save our hero, so he can save the game."

From the ends of Izward's fingers came rays of light, they arched together to form a spinning yellow ball. Its surface glowed and crackled with energy.

With a flick of his finger the ball flew off into the imaginary forest and on to the real forest many kilometres away. Within seconds it reappeared in the images around him and struck a tree. The trunk exploded and burst into flames. The creature, taken by surprise, let go of Hoot and turned to face the falling tree.

Hoot fell to the ground and scrambled to his feet.

The creature unable to free itself was struck by the tree and set on fire. Both tree and creature fell to the ground in flames. As the creature hit the ground Zardo's Talisman came loose and flew through the air. Hoot followed its path and with a perfectly timed jump intercepted it.

The creature, still in flames, slithered back down the well and disappeared.

With both the book and the Talisman in his possession Hoot left the clearing and disappeared into the smoke filled forest.

Having successfully cast one spell Izward tried to save the forest by casting another.

He ordered the ring to switch itself off and he raised his hands above his head again. Immediately the forest disappeared and the lake returned. He began to chant and his fingers crackled with magical energy.

"In the gathering of a storm is thunder lighting, clouds of rain," he recited, "and in a hundred oceans and in a thousand seas a million tonnes of water my magic shall now claim."

Over the lake storm clouds gathered, they drifted in from every direction gathering speed as they neared the carpet. From the ends of Izward's fingers, bolts of energy shot skyward and rivers of lightning crashed into the cloud. Inside thunder rumbled and it began to rain. The cloud moved taking its rain over the burning forest.

Izward watched as the rain fell and huge columns of black smoke rose above the forest. Soon the forest fires would be out and Izward relaxed knowing he'd saved the lives of many Tellurians.

"What of Vulgor?" asked Izward re-energizing the ring.

The girl appeared and her smile was quickly replaced by a symbol. He pressed the identical symbol on the ring and Vulgor appeared. He adjusted the ring to maximum and saw he was talking to several Gores. They were inside a windmill. He also noticed a large amphibian had joined them. It reminded him of a huge over bloated frog.

Izward sat on the carpet and like an invisible fly on the wall eavesdropped on their council of war.

A Horde of Misfits

"Congratulations my horde of misfits," shouted one of the assembled creatures, "you have done well!"

Izward assumed this was Vulgor by the way the others grovelled when he spoke.

"It is time to strengthen our position and capture the island," urged their leader.

The creatures agreed.

"Gorf?"

"Yes your Darkness!"

The most repulsive amphibian Izward had ever seen stepped forward.

"You'll lead the ground assault," said Vulgor.

"Yes Sire," said Gorf.

"Take Varen and Koor with you."

The twins stepped forward.

Izward noticed they were identical bird-like creatures different from the Gores.

"Find and capture Methuselah," ordered Vulgor, "secure it and wait for me. Understood?"

"Understood Sire!" echoed Varen and Koor.

"Understood," saluted Gorf.

"And you Sire," enquired Gorf, "what will you be doing?"

"The Gores and I will be out there exterminating all opposition."

Gorf nodded and rolls of fat wobbled down his torso.

"With Zardo in the Dark Zone and their precious forest in flames," continued Vulgor, "opposition will be weak."

Zardo's still alive thought Izward, a prisoner in the Dark Zone.

"There will be little resistance and Tellurian will be ours," concluded Vulgor

The room went silent.

"Now go, and may the Forces of Darkness be with you."

Gorf and the twins saluted and left leaving Vulgor and the Gores planning the island's destruction.

The smallest of the Gores flew up to the ceiling and hovered above its comrades.

Izward had the strangest feeling the creature could see him.

"Pheogore?" shouted Vulgor from the ground.

The Gore winked at Izward and turned away.

"Yes Sire?"

"Pay attention!"

"Sorry my Lord thought I saw a Tellurian lurking in the windmill."

Pheogore looked at Izward and winked again.

"But I was mistaken," said Pheogore and returned to the others.

Izward was astounded. In reality he was watching a projected image and therefore should not have been visible.

Had the Gore seen him? He didn't know, but if it had it wasn't telling Vulgor.

Vulgor and the Gores left the windmill and the image changed. Suddenly Izward was flying over Amphibia watching Vulgor struggling against the rain.

Vulgor was angry.

He hated rain and was forced to take shelter in one of the buildings. He cursed his misfortune. The rain would stop the destruction of the forest and make his task harder.

While Vulgor and the Gores sat out the storm Izward eavesdropped on Gorf.

He and the twins had reached the other side of Amphibia and were about to enter the forest. They were wet and covered in mud. They too were struggling against the rain. He watched as they entered the forest and disappeared into the smoke.

Izward turned the ring off. The image of Gorf vanished and he was back over the lake. His plan had worked. Not only had he saved the forest but delayed Vulgor's invasion. He'd gained time to organise the Tellurians and coordinate battle plans.

He pressed the sole of his foot into the carpet and manoeuvred it over the lake towards Amphibia. He had an army to assemble and didn't want to be late.

The City of Amphibia

Dark clouds had gathered over the island and above the abandoned city of Amphibia. Trees smouldered in the distance and black smoke hung over the forest.

Izward came out of the clouds and brought the carpet to a halt. He hovered unsteadily above the city watching the rain run down its deserted streets.

There was no sign of Vulgor.

Most of the city had been destroyed and its buildings lay in ruins. Each building had once been a sphere and together with others had formed circular habitats of about twenty spheres.

Some of the habitats had been constructed with the spheres arranged on top of each other creating large ball shaped buildings of about a hundred spheres. Izward counted about a thousand spheres and estimated the city's population to have been twice that many.

Suddenly three Tellurians came running out of forest and hid inside one of the buildings. Izward could see them through the cracks in the broken roof.

Then from out of the forest flew Koor and Varen who began searching the ruins. Izward knew the three Tellurians would eventually be found and eliminated. He couldn't let this happen, not again, the massacre of the other Tellurians still haunted him. This time he *could* help and ordered the carpet to their rescue.

To The Rescue

"Get ready," shouted Izward, "when I tell you, jump on the carpet."

The carpet descended, carefully manoeuvring itself through a crack in the dome of the building.

Izward found himself inside the ruins of a large banqueting hall. Overturned benches and chairs littered the floor. A long table broken in half arched towards the ceiling its legs broken. Tankards and goblets, plates and cutlery lay in piles at either end of it. Tattered flags and faded banners hung around the walls. Three large circles in the shape of a triangle had been drawn in the centre of each flag and on each banner the silhouette of a strange amphibian like creature. Every flag and banner was the same except the colour of the circles differed on individual flags.

On the banqueting floor the Tellurians were waving frantically. Izward looked over the side and steered the carpet towards them.

"Now!" screamed Izward.

"Behind you," yelled the Tellurians as two dark shadows fell across them. Izward turned to see Koor and Varen flying towards him.

Escape

"Jump!" shouted Izward.

The Tellurians responded instantly and grabbed hold of the carpet. Izward reached out an arm. He felt fingers around his hand and he pulled.

"Thank you," said one of the creatures rolling onto the carpet.

"Hold on," ordered Izward as the shadows of Koor and Varen grew larger. The carpet flew off, with the other two Tellurians hanging on to its edge.

"Don't let go!" pleaded Izward as he steered the carpet up into the room and away from their attackers. Koor and Varen followed, chasing the carpet around the building like predators after an easy meal.

The two terrified Tellurians clambered onto the carpet and clung to each other for fear of being thrown off. Izward flew the carpet across the floor towards the overturned table. Koor and Varen followed. At the very last moment Izward turned the carpet aside and up towards the roof. Unable to execute the same manoeuvre Varen stopped in mid air and Koor flew into her. They collided and fell and skidded along the floor. They crashed into the table bringing it down on top of them. Tankards and goblets, plates and cutlery clattered across the floor leaving the twins buried under benches and chairs.

While Koor and Varen struggled under the wreckage, Izward and the Tellurians were escaping through the roof.

Having safely piloted the carpet outside, Izward turned towards the trees and disappeared into the forest.

When Koor and Varen finally got free, Izward and the Tellurians had gone. Koor scrabbled to his feet and helped his sister remove a large flag that had wrapped itself around her head. She threw it away angrily and something flew off it. Koor scuttled after it.

"It's a ring," shouted Koor picking it up, "I'm having that."

They flew back to Gorf and told him of their failure. He wasn't very pleased and ordered them back into the forest to find them.

Black smoke was everywhere. It drifted through the forest like a thick fog making visibility poor. Izward knew his journey would be difficult. He would have to be extra watchful and alert. He peered through the smog carefully picking out a safe pathway between the trees.

He asked the Tellurians their names and they told him they represented the *Troop* into which they'd been born.

"I'm a *Utan*," said one.

Izward noticed he had longer arms than the others.

"Mines the *Illa*."

"And I'm a *Bonn*," informed the smallest.

Suddenly Izward noticed the ring was missing.

"The ring!"

Izward held up his hand.

"What ring?" asked Illa.

"The one I wear on this finger!"

"Is it important?" enquired Bonn.

"Very! We must find it!"

They began searching the carpet but it wasn't there.

"When did you last see it?" asked Utan.

"When I rescued you," said Izward pointing to Bonn, "remember I reached out my hand and… Oh No!"

"What's wrong?" asked Bonn.

"It must have slipped off my finger when I pulled you onto the carpet."

"I'm sorry," said Bonn, "I didn't mean to."

"I know," said Izward reassuringly, "it wasn't your fault."

"Shall we go back and look for it?" said Illa.

"No!" said Izward reluctantly, "we haven't time."

Izward's future was now in the past and any thoughts of returning to his own time a forgotten memory.

The Game had taken over his life and he was now part of its reality.

He was now a Tellurian with no other memory but that of The Wizard Master, Time Warrior of Tellurian.

The Wizard Master

On board the carpet there was an uneasy silence as they flew through the ruins of the forest. Visibility had improved and most of the smoke had been replaced with a yellow mist.

Izward stared in disbelief unable to recognise the nightmarish landscape around him. Most of the trees had been destroyed and only their stumps remained. Black smouldering shapes with crooked boughs and twisted branches spiked out of the ground in every direction. Trees scattered the undergrowth their trunks still smouldering from the falling rain.

The Tellurians, still not fully recovered from their encounter with Koor and Varen, stared at their beloved forest in disbelief.

Izward quickly explained the reasons for the fire and Vulgor's invasion. He told them about his plan to destroy the invaders and save Tellurian from the Dark Zone. They'd listened intently and after he'd finished they'd volunteered to help.

Ahead of them stood Methuselah. It looked frail and unwell. Its branches had withered and the fire had damaged its trunk. Its bark had turned black and trails of black smoke meandered around its branches.

Izward could see Talon and the Terrodacs. Talon was perched on one of Methuselah's lower branches while the Terrodacs had scattered themselves all over the tree.

On a rough count Izward counted fifty Terrodacs but there could have been more. He spotted Hoot surrounded by a handful of Tellurians. He was standing next to Methuselah's entrance. The Tellurians had formed a semicircle around him and he was showing them Zardo's book. One of them moved away from the group and looked up. It pointed into the sky and turned excitedly towards the others. Soon others had joined him

On the ground Hoot gently forced his way through the Tellurians and looked up at the approaching carpet. He took Zardo's book in both hands and waved it triumphantly above his head.

Izward waved.

The owl handed the book to one of the Tellurians and removed the Talisman from around his neck. He held it up so Izward could see it.

Izwards nodded and waved again.

"Well done," he shouted but the heroic old owl was too far away to hear.

Several Terrodacs escorted the carpet to the ground then returned to the tree. Izward stepped off and was greeted by Talon and Hoot. Together they gave him an enormous hug.

"It's good to see you again my friend," shouted Hoot almost squeezing the magic out of his friend. "We thought you'd been captured."

"No my friend," said Izward throwing his arms around Hoot's waist, "been rescuing Tellurians."

Izward pointed to the three Tellurians stepping off the carpet.

"Welcome home sir," said Talon hugging the pair of them. "Glad to have you back."

They quickly told each other of their adventures and discussed new strategies.

Talon flew back to the Terrodacs and Hoot returned to the Tellurians.

Izward went across to Methuselah to address everyone.

The old tree had suffered severe burning and its bark was black and charred. It looked withered and old. Its lower branches had been burnt away and all that remained were smouldering stumps. Izward stood gazing up at the tree concerned for its survival. Suddenly several Terrodacs burst out of its branches and startled him. For a moment Izward was thrown into confusion and Talon flew down to reassure him.

"All present and correct," saluted Talon enthusiastically, "they await your instructions."

"...Um, thank you Talon," said Izward, "I'll talk to them in a minute."

"Very good sir," shouted Talon responding with yet another salute. He waved the Terrodacs back to the tree and joined them.

"Hoot?" said Izward beckoning the owl towards him.

"Yes Wizard Master?" shouted Hoot saluting.

"A quiet word."

"Yes sir!" shouted the owl.

"What's all this shouting and saluting," asked Izward quietly, "is it really necessary?"

"You be the Wizard Master now, me old mate," said Hoot saluting again.

The owl spun his head in a complete circle then beckoned Izward to one side.

"Don't want the crew to hear," said Hoot looking towards the Tellurians who were busy celebrating the safe return of their lost colleagues.

"What are you talking about?" asked Izward.

"They expect it!"

"Who?"

"The Tellurians and the Terrodacs," whispered Hoot, "they be respectful of authority and honour discipline they do sir."

Across the clearing Talon could be heard marshalling the last few stragglers into their correct positions.

"Zardo be a great leader," continued Hoot whispering into Izward's ear, "respected for his magic and military expertise. You need to follow that tradition. Show them you're as good as he be."

Hoot stepped away from Izward and stood to attention. He winked knowingly and saluted. The Tellurians saluted and Izward saluted back. Hoot then turned towards the Terradacs and saluted again.

"Attention!" order Hoot. The Terrodacs sat upright on their branches.

"At ease!" shouted Izward and stepped forward.

For a moment he panicked and stood there in silence. But this was not the time to show weakness. He had to be strong.

"Wing Commander Talon," shouted Izward confidently putting his fears aside, "has informed you of the sudden disappearance of Wizard Zardo."

Talon stood to attention and smiled to himself. He had never been a Wing Commander before and he liked the sound of it.

"We believe the evil forces of the Dark Zone led by Vulgor, have abducted him," continued Izward.

The Terrodacs looked angry and began whispering to each other.

"An invasion force from the Zone has already appeared and unfortunately we have suffered casualties."

The whisper grew to a hubbub and Izward could see anger on the faces of the Tellurians. Izward waited for the noise to subside.

"We owe it to our fallen colleagues to rid ourselves of this evil pestilence."

There was a sudden cheer of approval.

"Around you are the effects of that pestilence. Your island is being poisoned, infected with evil. Soon it will become as corrupt as the Dark Zone and the yellow poison drifting above will engulf us all."

Without exception they all looked up. The yellow mist had thickened and was slowly drifting closer.

"Vulgor and the Gores are approaching. They have to be stopped," continued Izward. "Wing Commander Talon will take the Terrodacs and engage them in battle."

The branches of Methuselah buzzed with excitement as the Terrodacs discussed their mission.

"Major Hoot will deploy the Tellurians on the ground. They will patrol the forest and protect us from surprise attacks."

The Tellurians nodded their approval.

"There will be other Tellurians still out there, lost and confused and unaware of Vulgor's invasion," said Izward. "These unfortunate creatures will need our help. Major Hoot's patrol will also be responsible for their welfare. He will find them and bring them home. The forest will be our headquarters and Methuselah our fortress. But be aware! Vulgor plans to take Methuselah and use its strength against us."

Izward searched his belt and took out a piece of paper.

"This is a message sent to us from Zardo before he disappeared," he shouted waving it in the air for all to see.

"It gives instructions on how to defeat Vulgor."

"It reads, *the mysteries of the universe are many, open your eyes to understanding. Seek out its darkest secrets and good shall always triumph over evil.*"

Izward turned towards Hoot.

"The book," he asked, "give me the book."

" Aye, aye sir. I have it here,"

The owl handed Izward Zardo's book and he held it above his head.

"Thanks to the bravery of Major Hoot we now have this book," shouted Izward.

The Tellurians clapped and the Terrodacs hooted.

Hoot felt embarrassed and waved them silent.

"It is called *The Mysteries of the Universe*," continued Izward.

"The Talisman?" whispered Izward turning towards Hoot.

"Aye Master," replied Hoot.

The owl removed the charm from around his neck and handed it to Izward. Izward handed the book back to Hoot.

"This is Zardo's Talisman, many of you will recognise it."

There was a buzz of recognition.

"It is also known as the Chard of Creation and has great magical power." Izward took the book from Hoot and held it above his head. He inserted the charm into its image on the book's cover and the metal clasps that kept the book locked suddenly opened.

"Open its eyes to understanding," shouted Izward.

"It is a book of great magic," continued Izward, "written by the great Wizard Zardo himself."

Izward flicked through the pages stopping here and there to read out chapter headings.

"Seek out its darkest secret," quoted Izward.

The Tellurians watched in silence as Izward flicked through the pages. Suddenly Izward stopped at one particular page. He ran his finger along the words and read them silently to himself. He smiled and turned to show the page to Hoot. Hoot took the book and began reading.

"Its all here me old shipmates, it be all here!" announced Hoot triumphantly.

The clearing burst into chatter as each creature demanded to know what was written in the book.

Izward coughed for attention and Hoot handed him back the book

"*Seek out its darkest secrets,*" quoted Izward opening the book at the appropriate page, "and here they are."

The onlookers cheered.

Izward held up his hand for silence and they responded immediately.

"Before I disclose those secrets let me introduce my self. My name is Izward your new leader."

More cheers

"I too am a Wizard Master and Zardo's replacement until he returns."

All the creatures clapped in approval.

"I come from…"

Izward stopped. His mind had gone blank. Where had he come from? He couldn't remember.

All the creatures stared, waiting for him to continue.

"Why it be from the Island of Future," reminded Hoot whispering in his ear.

"Where?" asked Izward unable to recall any such place.

"The Tellurians sir, they be waiting on you?" reminded Hoot who was beginning to worry about him.

"I come from the… The Future," continued Izward unsure as to what that really meant.

Izward began to panic. He could remember nothing before his meeting with Hoot and Talon in Zardo's room. He turned to Hoot for guidance.

"Who am I?"

"You know who you be sir," assured Hoot, "why you be the Wizard Master. It doesn't matter where you be from sir, do it."

"Well not really…but I…"

"Forget the past. It is the future that's important sir. Tellurian needs yer to be strong right now! Me mates over there are all relying on you."

Hoot pointed to the Tellurians who were growing restless wondering why Izward had stopped.

"Me shipmates over there," whispered Hoot, "respect and admire yer. You've proved yourself Zardo's equal and they'll follow you to the ends of the universe. You were sent to destroy the Zone and defeat Vulgor. That's what matters to them. Now talk to them, give them hope, forget yer past and give them a future."

Hoot was right. Izward turned towards the Tellurians and began to talk to them again.

"Major Hoot and I have just discussed Zardo's instructions," he shouted holding out the book, "and this is what we have to do..."

Suddenly a twig snapped and all eyes turned towards the forest.

Without hesitation Talon and two of the Terrodacs flew into the forest to investigate. There was the sound of a scuffle and several heart stopping moments later they reappeared dragging a body. They pulled it into the clearing and dropped the unconscious creature in front of Izward and flew back to the tree.

The creature remained still, face down on the ground.

"A Gore!" shouted Utan, "its a Gore!"

"Quick tie it up," screamed Illa, "before it wakes up and attacks us."

Several Tellurians stepped forward and grabbed hold of the creature's legs while others bound its wings together with thin vines. They tied its legs together and tethered it to a tree stump.

After several minutes of silence the Gore moved and opened its eyes. It struggled to its feet and roared. The Tellurians gasped and took a cautious step backwards.

The creature looked bewildered and tossed its head from side to side. It looked around the clearing looking confused. Izward watched as it tried to get free. It wriggled and twisted in every direct. Suddenly Izward realised he'd seen this Gore before.

The creature looked at him and its eyes pleaded for mercy.

"Its you!" whispered Izward suddenly remembering.

The creature nodded and stopped struggling. It was the Gore that *winked* at him. Izward ordered Hoot to release it. The Tellurians and the Terrodacs gasped in disbelief.

"But sir," pleaded Hoot, "it be our enemy."

"Don't worry Major Hoot," said Izward, "its a friend, trust me! Untie it!"

"At once Master!" said Hoot and ordered Illa and Bonn to assist him. They reluctantly came forward and helped Hoot undo the knots. The rest of the Tellurians watched nervously, unsure as to why Izward had ordered their enemy to be released.

"I believe this Gore to be a friend," shouted Izward trying to reassure them, "I have encountered this creature before and he has proved to be a friend."

The Terrodacs stopped arguing and demanded an explanation.

"Izward is right," said the Gore suddenly breaking the silence.

Surprised by the creature's outburst Bonn and Illa quickly let go of the vines and scrambled back to their colleagues. Hoot continued to untie the Gore.

"Thank you," said the Gore as Hoot untied the final vine.

"I wish you no harm," said the Gore. "I've been sent here by...*a friend* to assist you. I have information that will help you defeat Vulgor."

"How do we know we can trust you?" asked one of the Tellurians. Others also voiced their doubts.

"You can call me Pheogore," said the creature, "but that is not my true name. I am not what I appear to be."

"How do we know it's telling us the truth," questioned Talon, "he could have been sent by Vulgor to spy on us."

Others agreed.

"I'm returning this," said Pheogore handing Izward his ring, "I stole it back from a creature named Koor. I know it to be of great importance to you."

Izward took the ring and put it on his finger.

"You said you had information that will help us," demanded Bonn who was still unsure of the Gore's true intentions. "Prove it!"

Pheogore nodded and sat down. He waited until there was silence and then began.

"Zardo is a great wizard, whose knowledge of the Dark Zone has helped keep you safe from its evil. I too have that responsibility. A great book exists called *The Mysteries of the Universe* within its pages are many secrets. One of those secrets is the proof of my loyalty."

The book was produced and handed to Izward.

"Find the chapter on the Dark Zone and look up the names of the Gores." Izward turned to the chapter and began scanning through its pages.

He stopped and looked up at Pheogore.

"Out loud," demanded Pheogore, "so all can hear."

"Beware the Ogres of Evil," shouted Izward, "these are the wicked ones. Remember their names, disguised falsehoods hide their true nature. Seek out hope and follow his guidance."

"And their names?" said Pheogore.

"Their names are Vengorey, Stulgore, Degoreger, Aerogeth, Predigore and Pheogore," shouted Izward.

Talon looked puzzled.

"But this proves you an enemy," insisted Talon, "It names you as one of Vulgor's Gores."

The Tellurians too were confused. The Terrodacs shuffled nervously on the branches unsure as to what this Gore was trying to prove.

"I don't understand," repeated Talon, "where's the proof?"

Izward and Hoot looked at Pheogore as if seeking guidance.

"What is a Gore?" asked Pheogore.

"I don't know," said Talon. "You?"

"A Gore is an ogre of evil," said Pheogore repeating part of Zardo's message.

"Beware the ogres of evil," quoted Izward reading from the book.

"Correct! So look at the words Gore and ogre carefully," said Pheogore, "can you see the connection?"

For a moment there was silence while Hoot, Talon and Izward looked at the book. The Tellurians too remained silent, wondering what their comrades would discover.

"They have the same letters," shouted Izward, "rearrange the word Gore and you have ogre!"

"Well done!" said Pheogore, "now do the same with the Gore's names."

The forest suddenly burst into noise as every creature in the clearing rose to the challenge.

"Vengorey!" shouted a Tellurian, " is *ENVY!*"

"Stulgore is *LUST!*" shouted another.

"Both unspeakable evils best kept hidden away in the Dark Zone for ever," said Pheogore,

"Degoreger!" informed Hoot, "is *GREED*."

"Good!" said Pheogore, "what about Aerogeth?"

There were several incorrect guesses until Izward gave the correct answer.

"*HATE!*" announced Izward.

"The most vile of all evils," said Pheogore, "the carrier of death and destruction."

"Predigore is *PRIDE*," said Illa.

"Correct!" said Pheogore, "well done."

"And my name," asked Pheogore, "what about my name?"

"That's easy," said Talon, "*HOPE*."

"Seek out Hope," quoted Pheogore, "and follow his guidance!"

Talon looked at Pheogore and smiled.

"Convinced?" enquired Pheogore.

"Convinced!" said Talon.

The Tellurians cheered and the Terrodacs hooted their approval. They had found a friend and ally.

It was time to consult the book again and discover even more of its secrets.

Zardo Speaks

"In the beginning was the circle of life," read Izward out loud.

Every creature went silent not daring to interrupt.

"The planet rotated and the cycle began," continued Izward.

Pheogore moved closer to Izward and stood next to Hoot and Talon. The four of them stood in a line like generals facing their troops before the eve of a battle.

"For every day there was a night and for every sunrise an evening moon. The stars had the night and sun the

day," read Izward. *"Spring followed Winter and the seasons lived and died."*

A gust of wind whistled through the trees and across the clearing making the creatures shiver with an unexpected chill.

"Such was the balance of nature and Tellurian evolved," recited Izward.

Suddenly there was a loud *crack* from behind one of the trees and a hundred pairs of eyes turned towards the sound. Izward stopped reading and looked at Hoot. Talon looked at Hoot and they all shook their heads.

The forest froze. Nothing moved. Everyone feared the worse.

"I'll go!" said Hoot volunteering himself for the task. He told the others not to move and went into the forest and disappeared in the trees. He reappeared holding two pieces of twig.

"It's just an old twig cooling down," said Hoot reassuringly, "nothing to worry about me old shipmates. There's no one there."

He threw the broken pieces onto the ground. Everyone relaxed and Izward began to read again.

"...But an oversight in the planet's construction had created evil abnormalities forcing the Creator to construct the Dark Zone."

There was another loud snapping noise but this time everyone ignored it. Izward paused and looked up.

"What's the matter?" asked Talon.

"I thought I heard something," answered Izward, "over there."

He pointed towards a burnt out tree stump.

"Its your imagination," suggested Hoot, "there's nothing there, I've checked."

Pheogore strode across to the stump and looked behind it.

"Nothing!" shouted the Gore.

Izward returned to the book and started to read.

"With the evils of creation banished life could freely evolve".

A gust of wind swirled a yellow mist down through the trees. Izward paused. Reading out loud was tiring. He felt a little dizzy and needed time to clear his head. He took a deep breath and filled his lungs with air. The air tasted strange and sour, forcing him to cough. He noticed others too had begun to cough. The mist was getting closer.

He returned to the book and turned over to the next page. To his surprise it was blank. The page was empty apart from a tiny black and white sketch of Zardo in the centre of the page. Izward stared at the picture then flicked to the next page. This too was empty. He went to the next and then flicked forward through the rest of the book. All the pages were empty.

Izward returned to the page where Zardo's image had been etched and looked across at his colleagues.

"What's the matter?" asked Hoot seeing the puzzled expression on Izward's face.

"The rest of the book's a blank," explained Izward.

"What?"

"It can't be!" uttered Talon who was hovering over Izward's shoulder. Izward showed him the blank pages.

"He's right!" uttered Talon, "there's a picture of Zardo and that's all. The rest of the book's empty."

"Let me see?" said Hoot taking the book from Izward.

"Barnacle bottoms and naked starfish," swore Hoot as he turned each page carefully.

"What are we going to do," asked Talon landing next to Pheogore seeking his advice.

"Don't worry," insisted Pheogore, "Zardo's a wizard trust him."

Suddenly Zardo's image on the page winked at Hoot.

"What the..." blasted Hoot dropping the book in surprise.

The book fell open at the sketch of Zardo. He looked down at the picture wondering if he'd been mistaken. Zardo smiled at him.

"By all the myths of Creation," muttered Hoot, "it's true!"

Izward who'd been busy explaining the missing sections of the book to the Tellurians suddenly heard Hoot cursing. Talon looked at Pheogore and the Gore smiled at him.

"Always trust a Wizard," said Pheogore, "to make an impressive entrance."

Suddenly the image in the book started to get bigger. It grew and grew until it filled the entire page.

I Am Zardo

"Well I'll be a sea monster's mate," exclaimed Hoot as Zardo stepped out of the book. The image continued to grow until it was three times Hoot's height. Everyone including Izward watched open mouthed as Zardo walked across to the centre of the clearing and stopped.

Towering in front of Methuselah like a giant statue Zardo began to speak.

"I am Zardo, Wizard Master of Tellurian," said the image. *"Together we face a great danger. Once again the evil forces of the Dark Zone have invaded our lands."*

Izward and all the Tellurians stared at the image astounded by its size. It now stood twenty metres tall and filled the entire clearing. It hovered in front of Methuselah slowly turning around.

"I have failed you! My weakness, old age and stupidity."

The image turned as if rotating on an invisible wheel.

"Creatures of Tellurian! Please forgive me."

For a moment the image stopped and looked about the clearing moving its giant head from side to side.

"I fear I may have unleashed a terrible evil upon you."

The image began to turn again.

"My only hope is that you can forgive me and I can atone for my error."

All the Tellurians turned to each other and nodded. Zardo had been a great inspiration and they weren't about to abandon him now.

"I can only hope for a miracle and my successor has found my book and deciphered my clues.

Izward and Hoot looked at each other, nodded and smiled. The image of Zardo turned towards Izward and stopped rotating. It paused for a moment looking down at him.

"To the new Wizard Master I offer hope. Throw the book into the Eye of Genesis and the Dark Zone will cease to exist."

Suddenly the image shrank and went back inside the book. The book slammed shut and Izward picked it up. He began flicking through the pages but to his utter amazement every page was blank. Every word Zardo had ever written had gone.

Suddenely the forest errupted with noise as all the Tellurians started talking at the same time. They demanded to know what had happened to Zardo.

Izward asked for quiet and eventually regained order.

"The ring," suggested Phoegore, "show them the ring."

Izward nodded and activated the ring.

"I must ask you all to remain calm," insisted Izward, "what you're about to see is but an illusion."

Suddenly the world around them exploded into fire. The sky turned red and particles of ash drifted through the air. Thunder rumbled in the heavens and lightning lit up the sky. Silhouetted against the crimson horizon stood jagged edged mountains pouring out molten lava into rivers of fire.

They stood in the centre of what appeared to be a castle courtyard surrounded by black lava walls. A dense yellow mist swirled across the courtyard spiralling towards Zardo who was suspended between two black towers. Above him hung a large stone. A yellow staircase led out of the stone and down to the ground. Zardo had been suspended a hundred metres above a large altar spewing out yellow smoke. Curled around the bottom step of the staircase was a huge creature with enormous claws. It snored loudly unaware of the chaos around it. Suddenly a giant fireball raced out of the sky and headed towards them. They panicked and dived to the ground expecting to be incinerated.

"You'll not be harmed!" shouted Izward above the roar of the approaching fireball. The Terrodacs, fearing they too would be incinerated, panicked and flew off into the forest. Suddenly there was a mighty roar and several Tellurians looked up and saw a fireball heading towards them. They froze in horror as it passed through them and on into the fiery sky. Another exploded overhead, sending a hail of smaller fireballs into the courtyard. One struck the sleeping creature on its head and it woke up. It lifted its three heads and roared loudly.

"That's Tyrann!" informed Pheogore, "Vulgor's pet dragon."

The Tellurians watched as Tyrann moved towards the stairway. It stopped and looked up. It roared angrily and green slime dribbled out of the corners of its mouths. It placed a foot on the first step and cautiously lifted the other on to the next. It stood for a moment balancing between the two.

"What's it doing?" enquired Hoot.

"Waiting for Zardo's *Life Force* to expire," answered Pheogore.

"Then what?"

"Tyrann's a carnivore," said Pheogore, "fresh meat is scarce!"

For a moment there was silence. Hoot looked at Talon and together they stared at Pheogore.

"You mean?"

"Yes, it's going to eat him," concluded Pheogore.

Suddenly a distant volcano erupted and the castle began shaking. Walls crumbled and large pieces of lava toppled into the courtyard. Tyrann unable to keep his balance fell off the stairway and onto the ground.

"Once Zardo's *spirit* expires," said Pheogore, "Tyrann will devour him."

They turned and looked at Zardo. They could see a thin column of yellow gas venting from his chest and spiralling up into the stone.

"Soon Zardo will die and Vulgor will get his revenge," continued Pheogore, "Tyrann will get his meat and Tellurian will be lost to the Dark Zone."

"Never!" shouted Izward. The others agreed.

The earthquake stopped and the images around them ceased shaking. They watched as Tyrann crawled up the staircase. On reaching the step opposite Zardo it raised its three heads towards the Stone and howled loudly. It swung a head over to Zardo's body and began nudging and sniffing it. Zardo groaned and Tyrann grunted disappointingly.

"Zardo's still alive," shouted Hoot.

Tyrann withdrew its head and flopped down on the step to wait.

For a moment all eyes focused on Zardo. If they were going to rescue him they'd better do it quickly.

"What's that?" shouted Bonn.

A large yellow dust storm was coming through the forest towards them. At first they thought it part of the fantasy but as it came closer they could see it was no illusion. They could see the Terrodacs flying ahead of it trying to get out of its path.

"Quick," shouted Izward turning off the ring, "hide in Methuselah!"

Zardo and the Dark Zone disappeared as a cloud of yellow dust engulfed the clearing. Blinded by the thick yellow fog the Tellurians panicked and lost all sense of direction. The Terrodacs, their eyes protected by transparent eyelids, were able to see through the dust and guide Izward and the rest of the Tellurians into Methuselah. Once they were all safely inside Izward closed the door.

Having found Methuselah the dust storm blew away leaving Koor and Varen standing at its entrance. They'd been searching the forest for hours using the dust storm to conceal their approach. Now that they'd found it they entered and began the opening phase of Vulgor's plan to capture the tree.

Tellurian Forever

The room was in chaos. It was noisy and overcrowded. The Terrodacs flew about the room looking for somewhere to land whilst the Tellurians stood in a circle around the wall. Sections of the floor had collapsed and a large hole in the centre of the floor had appeared. Wisps of yellow smoke filtered through cracks in the remainder of the floor making the air unpleasant and smelly. Izward entered the room and was overwhelmed by the noise. He put his hands over his ears and turned to close the door.

"Silence!" he screamed and slammed the door shut.

The Terrodacs scattered and found perches where they could. Izward coughed and the room went silent.

"Look about you!" ordered Izward, "the evils of the Dark Zone have decended upon us."

A cloud of yellow smoke belched up out of the hole in the floor filling the room with an evil odour. Suddenly a tremor deep underground shook the tree. The room shuddered violently and several Tellurians were thrown off their feet. Illa, unable to prevent himself from staggering forward, toppled into the hole and was engulfed in yellow smoke. There was a gasp of horror when a ten-metre ball of flame shot up out of the hole. The tree stopped shaking and the column of fire collapsed back into the hole. The Tellurians rushed to the edge of the fissure. To their surprise Illa was still alive. He was balancing on a branch clutching the sides of the hole. With two Tellurians holding his legs Utan was lowered into the hole. He grabbed his friend's outstretched hand and pulled him to safety.

Pheogore, who was standing next to the door, was convinced he could hear breathing in the corridor.

"Izward!" shouted Pheogore, "can you hear...?"

But the Gore's question went unheard drowned by the noise of the Tellurians as they congratulated Illa on his safe return.

"Talon," shouted Izward. The room went silent.

"Yes Master."

"We haven't a moment to lose," urged Izward, "take the Terrodacs, find Vulgor and destroy him."

"At once sir," said Talon saluting.

"Be careful! He'll be heavily guarded," said Izward, "you'll have to fight the Gores to reach him."

"I know! Trust me your Wizardship, we'll not fail you."

The Terrodacs squawked in agreement.

Pheogore pressed his head against the door and listened. He could definitely hear breathing on the other side.

"Izward," insisted Pheogore, *"something's* in the passage."

But again his voice went unheard lost by the squawking of the Terrodacs.

"Hoot?"

"Yes Sir?" said the owl.

"Take the rest of the Tellurians and guard the forest."

"Yes sir."

"Set up regular patrols and keep a watchful eye. Vulgor is very cunning expect the unexpected. He'll try to trick us and I don't want us unprepared."

"I can assure you sir," said Hoot, "we'll be vigilant."

"Remember he intends to capture Methuselah," said Izward, "make sure he doesn't."

"Trust me sir," said Hoot saluting, "Methuselah is safe in our hands."

Pheogore had decided to investigate the passage on his own and was about to open the door when Hoot suddenly stepped forward and began speaking.

"Comrades!" saluted Hoot, "TELLURIAN!"

The Tellurians stood to attention and raised both their arms in the air and together began to sing the Tellurian Anthem.

Tellurian Forever,
For Ever May It Stand
Tellurian's My Homeland
A Free And Cherished Land

May Its Goodness Last Forever
And Spread Far Across Our Land
We pray to our Creator
Forever May It Stand

"Caught you," shouted Pheogore finally pulling the door open. Two identical creatures fell into the room.

The singing stopped and all eyes looked at two bird-like creatures struggling on the floor on top of each other.

"Koor and Varen!" yelled Pheogore.

"Traitor!" yelled Koor directing his anger at Pheogore. "Wait till Vulgor hears of this!"

Koor scrambled to his feet accidentally standing on his sister's face.

"Ouch! You brainless peacock!" scolded Varen.

"Dodo!" retaliated Koor.

"Dactyl brain!" insulted Varen.

"Enough of this nonsense," said Koor, "we've a mission to complete. Give me the Sphere."

Varen produced a round ball from under her feathers and tossed it to Koor. Koor caught it and began rolling it around in his claws. It started humming.

"Quick," shouted Varen, "now!"

"Stop them," ordered Pheogore.

He went to grab Koor but was far too slow.

Koor took off and flew to the centre of the room. Varen snatched a Tellurian and joined her brother. She dangled the unfortunate creature over the hole threatening to drop him.

With a squawk of satisfaction Koor released the orb. It floated over the hole emitting a deafening high-pitched wail. The noise was overpowering and the Tellurians were forced to shield their ears from the sound.

The orb began to spin and four razor sharp blades appeared around its centre. Slowly it descended into the hole its blades slashing the air like a sickle cutting corn. Koor and Varen smiled to each other as the orb disappeared into the floor. Their plan to capture Methuselah had begun well.

By the time the Tellurians had recovered Koor and Varen were heading back down the corridor and the open door to freedom. Their hostage lay in a heap against the wall. It was injured but still alive.

There was a chaotic scramble as the Tellurians chased down the corridor after them.

"Stop them!" cried Illa.

"Its too late they've escaped" cried Bonn.

"Warlocks!" cursed Hoot.

They all watched as Koor and Varen disappeared into the misty forest. Talon ordered the Terrodacs to follow but Izward stopped them.

"Let them go!" insisted Izward, "its too late."

Izward ordered them back into the tree and they reluctantly returned to the room.

Izward asked Hoot to bring him Zardo's Book. He took the book from Hoot and ordered the magic carpet to come to him. It appeared from behind the bookcase, unrolled itself and came to a stop in front of him. He hid the book in the bookcase.

"I'll find Zardo and bring him home," said Izward stepping onto the carpet. "Hoot?"

"Yes sir?" saluted Hoot.

"You know what you must do?"

Hoot dropped his salute and turned towards the Tellurians.

"Tellurians! Attention!" yelled Hoot.

There was a unified sound like a twig snapping and every Tellurian stood upright.

"Single file, every Tellurian to his post," yelled Hoot, "quick march!"

Like ants across a forest floor the Tellurians, led by Hoot, marched out of the room, through the corridor and into the forest.

"May the Creator protect you all," shouted Izward saluting the last Tellurian as it left the room.

"Talon?"

"Yes Sire?"

All the Terrodacs sat to attention.

"Vulgor and the Gores must be stopped!" pleaded Izward, "before any more innocent creatures die."

"Consider it done your Wizardship," said Talon.

"May the Creator give you victory"

"I'm sure he will," replied Talon."Terrodacs! Prepare for flight."

Like swarming bees the Terrodacs took to the air and hovered in the room waiting for orders.

"Follow me!"

Talon flew through the open door, down the corridor and into the mist. The rest of the Terrodacs followed leaving Pheogore and Izward alone in the room.

"Pheogore my friend," said Izward, "search the underworld and find that orb. Destroy it before it can do more harm."

Pheogore nodded.

By the time Izward had manoeuvred the carpet over the hole Pheogore had gone. As Izward stared down the fissure he began to wonder who this mysterious Gore really was and why was he helping them?

Only time would unravel that mystery.

He took the carpet across the room, down the corridor and flew into the forest. He stopped and looked back at Methuselah. The tree looked frail and fragile, sad and unhappy. He looked around at a forest he no longer recognised. It was eerie and frightening and bathed in a yellowish haze. Thick clouds of yellow dust drifted everywhere and tree stump shadows loomed out of the mist. The forest had an evil supernatural look and he shivered with fear knowing the Dark Zone was all around him.

Following the yellow mist Izward set off to find the Dark Zone.

Visibility in the forest was poor and he was having difficulty breathing. The mist had a strange odour and it made him feel dizzy. Around him it swirled into strange and terrifying shapes. He left the forest and followed its trail high into the sky. The higher he climbed the more transparent it became. Finally through the mist he could see a large dark cloud. The closer he came to the cloud the stronger the resistance from the mist and he had to increase the carpet's speed to overcome its force.

He entered the cloud and headed towards its centre. Immediately the carpet was engulfed in a dark yellowy fog and he lost all sense of direction. For several minutes he meandered aimlesly unable to get his bearings. Finally the fog lifted and he could see the Gateway.

At its centre was a black hole and spiralling around it a dark red cloud. Bolts of energy forked across it like veins in a blood-shot eye. Weeping out of the hole was the yellow mist that had led him here.

Suddenly the force that was slowing him down was gone and he found himself hurtling towards the Gateway. He clung on as the carpet raced towards the hole. The carpet suddenly shuddered to a halt and he was thrown forward into the Dark Zone.

An Exchange Of Minds

Izward was falling, bouncing uncontrollably down a stairway of steps. Around him a yellow fog blurred his vision and he could hear the hiss of escaping steam.

Suddenly he came to an unexpected halt.

Something large and smelling of rotting meat stopped his descent. At first he felt relieved, falling headlong down a flight of stairs had been painful and he was grateful it was over. However when the object began to move and make loud growling noises he feared the worse.

It was Tyrann.

He quickly scrambled to his feet and ran back up the stairway.

Having retreated to what he thought would be a safe distance he stopped hoping he hadn't disturbed Vulgor's pet.

He hadn't. He could still hear loud snoring noises drifting up from several steps below him.

For the moment he was safe.

He crouched down and looked around. What he saw horrified him. The Dark Zone was indeed a most terrifying place.

He was at the top of a stairway that came up from the ground and ended at a large oval stone above his head. The stone hung between two black towers with no visible means of support. He remembered falling out of it just before he hit the steps.

From the top of the stairway he could see right across the Dark Zone.

He'd seen all this before, in the ring!

This was Vulgor's castle and the figure suspended between the two towers was Zardo. He looked across at the wizard. He was still and lifeless. Suddenly something hot and wet splashed down the back of his neck.

"Ugh!"

His hand went to his neck and he froze. He heard a loud snort and a blast of air struck the back of his hand. A shiver of fear ran down his body, Tyrann was awake and had crept behind him. Another snort lifted his hair making it stick up like the quills on a *Porcudact's* back. He could hear the creature breathing and feel its hot breath on the nape of his neck. It sent goose pimples running down his spine. Again Tyrann snorted spraying his neck with more sticky liquid. Izward remained still; he didn't want to panic the animal into attacking him. Suddenly its three heads began examining his body and it made his skin crawl.

Izward slowly turned and faced his assailant. It stood four steps above him its three heads posed to strike. Suddenly, it swung a head in his direction and he dropped to his knees. Tyrann's jaws snapped shut missing his head by a whisker. It roared angrily and lifted itself up on its hind legs. It attacked again but Izward kicked hard at its under-belly and the creature toppled backwards. Its legs slipped off the step and it fell on its back. It lay there, its heads dangling over the edge.

Izward looked for an escape. His only option was down but that meant leaving Zardo. Suddenly another violent explosion rocked the ground and the staircase started shaking. He stumbled and fell, landing on his back. To his horror he saw Tyrann sliding down the steps towards him. With only seconds to spare Izward got up, jumped onto the creature's stomach and began running along its body. All three of its heads attacked but he managed to dodge their snapping jaws and jump to safety. Tyrann continued its descent down the steps and came to a bedraggled heap at the bottom of the staircase.

The aftershock abated and the stairway stopped shaking.

Izward looked across at Zardo and thought him dead. The mist had gone and he could see the wizard's body. His face was white and his bones protruded from under his skin. Suddenly Zardo moved and Izward knew the wizard was still alive. He quickly consulted the ring and the girl appeared. She smiled at him.

"I've found Zardo," said Izward, "but how do I release him?"

But before she could answer a fireball exploded over his head and he was showered with hundreds of molten lumps of lava.

"Quick," shouted the girl coming to Izward's rescue, *"use your cloak, fire cannot harm it."*

He quickly removed his cloak and wrapped it around himself. He crouched down and waited for the firestorm to stop.

It was dark under the cloak and the girl's face shone in the darkness like a full moon on a dark night. He felt strangely attracted to her and reached out a hand to touch her cheek. He hesitated and withdrew it knowing she wasn't real.

How he wished she were.

"You have Zardo's power," said the girl bringing him out of his trance, *"use it!"*

Izward was confused.

"You are protecting Zardo's magic, it is time to return it!"

Suddenly she faded back into the ring and everything went dark.

Below, in the castle's courtyard, the altar opened and released an unseen entity. It spiralled up towards Izward intent on killing him.

From under the darkness of the cloak Izward heard a strange howling sound. Suddenly it was all around him screeching and shrieking like a flock of angry birds. His cloak was ripped away from his head and his body was lifted in the air. He clung to the step with both hands his legs flapping like a rag on the end of a stick. Using what strength he had left he let go of the step with one hand and increased his grip with the other. He pointed a finger at the altar and cast a spell. An energy bolt arched from the end of his finger down into the hole. On contact it exploded destroying the altar and its contents. The howling stopped and Izward fell onto the step with a thud. He stood up, retrieved his cloak and put it on.

Overhead the fireballs continued their assault turning the sky a bloodier red. He turned to Zardo and raised both hands in his direction. He felt a strange tingling sensation, it starting at his toes and steadly crept up his body. He could feel Zardo's magic all over him and he began to shiver. It swirled around him meandering over his skin like liquid gold. It gathered at his fingertips and arched across to Zardo. There it swirled around the wizard's body before entering his mouth.

For several minutes the pair were linked, joined together in magic. Izward felt weak and tired. His head ached and his eyes hurt. He closed his eyes hoping the darkness would make the pain go away. It didn't and the throbbing inside his head continued. As the magical exchange continued the pain increased and Izward felt his thoughts spinning out of control. He tried to open his eyes but couldn't and felt his mind drifting off into the blackness. Then Izward's mind joined with Zardo's and they shared the same thoughts and experiences. In that brief exchange of minds they sensed another's presence.

"You are Time Warriors! Heroes of Tellurian," said the Creator, *"together the greatest force in the universe."*

Then it was gone!

Both sensed its departure but on waking, it was a forgotten memory lost in the unexplored regions of the mind.

Izward opened his eyes and looked across at Zardo. The skeletal shape had gone. In its place was the restored figure of Zardo.

"Zardo," shouted Izward from the staircase, "it's Izward, I've come to rescue you."

But before the wizard had time to open his eyes he was gone, falling through the air towards the ground.

Izward watched in horror as Tyrann, now fully recovered from its fall, stood opened mouthed, ready to catch the unsuspecting Zardo.

Back Home

Zardo fell, his beard flapping around him like a sail in a storm. Below, the jaws of a three-headed creature snapped and snarled waiting to devour him. Izward panicked and started down the steps two at a time.

Suddenly, through the Gateway, flew the carpet and went to Zardo's rescue. As Tyrann was about to catch Zardo it swooped under him and swept him clear of its mouth. Tyrann's jaw snapped shut missing Zardo by centimetres. Its teeth tore into the edge of the carpet bringing it to a temporary standstill. There was a loud ripping sound and the carpet tore free. Skilfully the carpet dodged the snapping heads and escaped, carrying the liberated Zardo to safety.

Tyrann roared angrily irritated by the piece of carpet lodged in its teeth. It tried to shake it free but failed. It twisted and twirled, snapped and snorted. It coughed and spluttered, sneezed and spat but the carpet wouldn't budge. The more it tried the more enraged it became. Suddenly it flew into an uncontrollable rage and started snapping at its own head with the other two.

Izward watched with growing amusement as the crazed creature tried to dislodge the carpet from out of its own mouth. Suddenly he was struck from behind and toppled backwards onto something soft.

It was Zardo and the carpet!

"Welcome aboard!" said a voice, "hang on, this could be a little bumpy!"

But before Izward had time to answer the carpet swerved to the right almost tipping him over its edge.

Izward gripped the carpet even tighter and hung on.

The removal of the torn piece of carpet proved impossible and Tyrann finally gave up leaving it lodged in his teeth. It had ripped and shredded itself into several strands and hung out of his mouth like seaweed over a rock. The tattered fibres were wet and soggy and covered with saliva. Tyrann roared angrily and began searching the castle for the intruders.

In the fiery skies above the castle Izward, Zardo and the carpet were heading towards the Gateway.

"Almost there!" shouted Zardo, "hang on a few more seconds and we'll be safe!"

A fireball exploded just above them showering the carpet with red-hot embers. Most fell harmlessly to the ground but one very large cinder landed on the carpet. It fell next to Izward's feet and began to smoulder. Quickly he kicked it over the edge before it could set fire to the carpet.

"Well done Izward," said Zardo, "the Creator chose well!"

Suddenly the carpet lunged backwards and they almost fell off. They turned to see one of Tyrann's heads biting into the back of the carpet. The creature had climbed up the stairway and was balancing on the top step stretching out its heads towards them. Immediately Izward and Zardo began rolling around the carpet hoping to confuse the attacking heads. For several death-defying moments Izward and the wizard dodged the snapping jaws, slithering across the carpet like hunted fish in a river of crocodiles.

Finally, confused and extremely dizzy, Tyrann's three heads slumped lethargically onto the carpet to rest. Quickly Izward kicked out at one of them catching it hard on the snout. The creature roared with pain.

"Take that!" shouted Izward.

"And that!" added Zardo zapping the creature's other heads with two well-aimed bolts of energy. One struck the creature on the forehead while the other exploded between its eyes. Both heads were knocked sideways and tumbled off the carpet. Tyrann tottered momentarily at the top of the staircase and then fell.

Izward and Zardo watched as the creature plummeted towards the ground. As it fell it wriggled and thrashed in the air like an eel out of water. With a mighty thud Tyrann smashed onto the ruins of the altar. Instantly it exploded in a ball of fire engulfing Tyrann in flames. When the flames died, Tyrann had gone and where the altar once stood was a very large hole.

Suddenly a down draft of air hit the carpet and it dropped sharply. Izward's and Zardo's hearts rushed towards their mouths. The carpet tipped crazily to one side almost tipping them off.

"Look!" shouted Zardo, "something's coming through the Gateway."

The yellow mist that had engulfed the forest was returning. It was rushing back through the Gateway and disappearing down the hole created by Tyrann.

They watched as the yellow mist was sucked back into the ground.

"Without my power it grows weak and ineffective," explained Zardo, "the yellow mist can no longer exist in our world and must return to its own dimension."

"We have to hurry," urged Zardo, "soon the Gateway will close and if we don't escape we'll be trapped in this nightmare forever."

Now that the Gateway was open the carpet slowly moved forward. It headed towards the centre of the stone and the yellow mist.

Izward could see nothing, the yellow mist blotted out everything. Forced by the incoming mist into yet another standstill the carpet hovered between the two dimensions waiting for the pressure to ease. The sound was deafening and they both covered their ears for fear of damaging their eardrums. Suddenly, the carpet shot forward into a bright blue sky. The yellow mist disappeared and there was silence.

They were back in Tellurian.

For a moment Izward and Zardo stood on the carpet listening to the silence. "Out of my way," squawked a voice.

Suddenly a Gore flew out from behind a cloud and struck Izward on the head.

"See you in Hell!"

It flew off and disappeared back in the cloud.

Having been stunned by the blow Izward toppled backwards and fell off the carpet.

A Welcome Home Party

Izward was tumbling through the bright blue sky like a bird without wings. Above him he could see Zardo and the carpet getting smaller and below him the ground getting closer and closer. He was plummeting towards the ground at an impossible speed and knew he would hit the ground well before any rescue attempt by Zardo could reach him.

He was falling towards a smouldering tree stump. Its trunk had split in half during the fire leaving two spiked shafts of wood protruding from its centre. Every second fetched him closer to the stump and death on those deadly spikes.

He closed his eyes not wishing to witness his own death.

As he fell strange visions rushed through his head. There were boxes filled with bright lights and strange flashing words.

PATIENT flashed one box
EMERGING blinked another
FROM COMA said another.

Around him floated masked faces with large bulging eyes and he swore he saw the girl in the ring smiling at him.

ELIZABETH she kept saying BUT YOU CAN CALL ME BETH

Suddenly there was an almighty thump and his waist exploded with pain.

The vision vanished and he was surrounded by blackness. He had reached the ground and knew he was DEAD. He imagined himself impaled on the tree stump.

However it didn't feel like he was dead and he could feel wind rushing across his face.

"That was a close one," said a familiar voice, "another second and we'd have lost you."

Shocked at being able to hear voices Izward opened his eyes. To his great relief he saw Talon flying above him. The eagle had snatched him from certain death and was carrying him away to safety.

Izward winced, his waist hurt. The pain was due to the bird's talons digging into his waist.

"Sorry, " said Talon apologetically, "but we mustn't let you fall must we?"

Izward agreed. The pain was a small sacrifice to make considering the alternative.

Talon headed towards the carpet and when above it carefully dropped Izward next to Zardo. The pair watched as Talon flew around the carpet several times. Having satisfied himself there were no more Gores lurking in the skies Talon joined his colleagues on the carpet.

"Welcome home your Wizardship," said Talon.

Zardo nodded in acknowledgement.

"That was very brave of you," said Zardo.

"Thank you," said Talon looking anxiously around.

"What's the matter?"

"We've got to go, its not safe your Wizardship, there are Gores everywhere."

Suddenly one swooped out of the cloud and dived towards them. It flew past and Izward tried to shoot it. Nothing happened. The creature turned and headed back. Izward tried again but there was nothing, he no longer had the power. Suddenly a bolt of energy flashed over his head. The creature came to a sudden halt clutching its chest. It fell out of the air and corkscrewed down to the ground. It landed in a pool of mud face down. It lay there for several seconds then slowly got up and limped away into the forest.

Izward looked across the carpet at Zardo. Zardo smiled at him and held up a finger. It sparked with energy and Izward knew the old wizard had got his magic back. Izward returned the smile although he was feeling a little sad. He'd enjoyed being a wizard but he knew that was now over.

"We have to go," urged Talon. "Now!"

Without asking for an explanation Zardo turned the carpet towards the forest and headed for Methuselah.

"Vulgor has the Terrodacs," informed Talon.

There was an angry silence. Izward looked at Talon and waited for an explanation but Talon looked too upset to answer.

"What happened?" asked Izward.

"I'll explain later," replied Talon.

"But the Zone? We have to destroy it!" urged Izward.

"I know, but Vulgor will kill the Terrodacs first."

Izward and Talon looked at Zardo hoping his wisdom could solve their dilemma.

After some discussion it was agreed to rescue the Terrodacs.

They were unsure as to what would happen to Vulgor once his dimension had gone. Destroying the Zone first would be too big a risk.

They would return to Methuselah, find Hoot and rescue the Terrodacs. While this was happening Izward would fly to the Gateway and wait until the Terrodacs were safe. Once they'd been rescued he would enter the Gateway and destroy the Zone.

"But how will you know when to destroy the Zone?" asked Talon,

"I'll use the ring," answered Izward.

To demonstrate Izward switched on the ring. The face of the girl appeared and flickered unsteadily. Her image faded in and out and although she spoke, her words could scarcely be heard. She smiled but Izward knew the ring's power was diminishing. He quickly turned it off to save what little energy it had left. He hoped it would be enough when the time came.

"What's wrong with it," enquired Talon.

"Nothing," lied Izward, "its fine!"

"But what if we fail," said Talon, "and we don't rescue the Terrodacs."

"Then I'll destroy it anyway, what have we to lose?"

The carpet sped on meandering its way through the trees at great speed. On board were three Tellurian heroes about to experience a rather unusual welcome home party.

Talon's Story

"What happened to the Terrodacs?" asked Izward looking down onto a landscape of burnt trees, pools of water and waterlogged swamps.

"We were ambushed," answered Talon, "we flew straight into a trap!"

As Talon told his story Izward leaned over the side of the carpet and looked at the forest. Scattered amongst the artificial lakes were unburnt trees and patches of green. These areas had escaped the fire and he thanked Zardo's magic for helping him send the rain that had saved the forest from total destruction.

"We left Methuselah and headed towards Vulgor's last known position," continued Talon. "We flew in three clusters, each group flying a V-shaped formation. We looked magnificent."

Talon stopped for a moment and turned towards Zardo.

"You would have been proud of us Sire."

"I already am," said Zardo. "The whole of Tellurian will know of your bravery."

"We were strong and resolute," continued Talon, "determined to destroy the evil that was invading our land."

"I'm sure you were," interrupted Zardo trying to reassure Talon.

Zardo had sensed an uneasiness in Talon's voice and knew the bird was blaming himself for the missons failure.

"So what happened?" asked Izward, "what went wrong?"

"It was my fault," said Talon sadly, "I should have realised it was a trap."

"Don't blame yourself," comforted Zardo, "leaders have to make decisions."

"They knew we were coming," continued Talon, "we didn't stand a chance."

There was a moment's silence. Talon was angry with himself and shook his head dejectedly. Clearly the eagle was upset and his emotions were showing.

"They'd heard everything," continued Talon.

Izward closed his eyes and pictured Vulgor's two spies flying off through the trees and disappearing into the yellow mist.

"I should have gone after them," said Izward, "tried to stop them. I never thought they'd make it back and tell Vulgor."

"Stop blaming yourselves," interrupted Zardo, "what's done is done!"

More silence.

"It was sitting next to a large fire," said Talon breaking the silence.

"What was?"

"Vulgor," answered Talon.

Silence.

"The Gores were building shelters and that odious amphibian creature was on guard," narrated Talon. "They didn't even know I was there, well, I thought they didn't."

Izward and Zardo looked across at Talon. Talon was struggling with his emotions.

"I'm sorry," apologised Talon, "I'm getting ahead of myself, all this must sound a little confusing."

"No, not at all."

Zardo looked up just in time to steer the carpet through a flock of Seadacs. They squawked loudly as the carpet scattered them apart.

"Do go on."

"My plan was simple," said Talon continuing with his story, "while I searched for Vulgor, the Terrodacs would hide in the forest and wait for my return. Once I'd discovered Vulgor's location I would return for them and lead them into battle."

"A good plan," said Zardo.

"It meant only I was put at risk," said Talon proudly, "and not our entire army."

"An excellent idea," said Izward thoughtfully, "so how come the Terrodacs got captured?"

The expression on Talon's faced changed.

"I'm coming to that!" said Talon.

"The day had almost come to an end when I spotted a column of smoke rising out of the forest," continued Talon. "Using the darkness as camouflage I flew cautiously towards the rising smoke. I was able to land unnoticed on an overhanging branch just above the smoke. It was then I spotted Vulgor sitting on the ground, next to a fire, six metres below me. His very presence sent a chill down my feathers and I almost toppled off the tree from fear."

"Clearly you didn't," said Izward.

"Didn't what?"

"Fall off the tree!"

Ignoring Izward's sarcasm Talon continued.

"I assumed they were staying the night because the Gores had constructed shelters. They had used three large black triangular sheets of cloth and a single wooden pole. One corner of each sheet had been tied to the top of the pole allowing the three triangular pieces of cloth to hang down like a giant triangular pyramid. The two remaining corners had been fixed to the ground with large wooden pegs. An opening, large enough for a single Gore to enter, was left in the cloth facing the fire."

Talon paused.

"What's wrong?" enquired Izward.

"Nothing," replied Talon, "just gathering my thoughts together."

"Look! We're nearly there," informed Zardo pointing towards the horizon.

They all turned. In the distance, silhouetted high above the forest line, stood Methuselah.

"Home," whispered Zardo.

Realising he was running out of time Talon quickened the pace of his story.

"I realised Vulgor had made a tactical error," said Talon.

"How?"

"His campsite!" continued Talon, "offered no protection. The surrounding trees would give an approaching enemy cover."

"Enough to mount a surprise attack!" enquired Izward.

"More than enough," replied Talon.

The carpet banked to the right slightly as Zardo changed course and headed directly towards Methuselah.

"I decided to attack them while they slept," continued Talon, "so I flew back to the Terrodacs and told them of my discovery. We made large nets out of tree vines and creepers, large enough to carry a Gore. The idea was simple. If we took them by surprise they would panic and scatter in different directions. If we attacked in pairs, from four different directions, using the nets as giant scoops, we could either capture them on the ground or net them as they took off. Once inside the net they would be helplessly trapped."

"What about Vulgor," asked Izward, "how were you going to capture him?"

"We constructed a special leather-lined net that would cover his eyes and stop him from using his energy bolts."

"Did the nets work?" asked Zardo.

"Yes, perfectly," replied Talon, "we practiced them on the Terrodacs before we set off."

"Clever!" praised Izward.

"But not clever enough," replied Talon.

"So what did go wrong?" asked Zardo.

"As I said," continued Talon, "it was a trap. Vulgor had deliberately picked that site knowing he could ambush US just as easy as WE could trap him. Whoever sprung the trap first would be the victor."

"So you flew into a trap!"

"Like a fly into a spider's web," said Talon.

"Because of the information given by those spies of his?" said Zardo.

"Yes. They knew we were coming. They were all sitting around the fire laughing and squawking. The amphibian was pretending to be asleep and Vulgor was sitting alone away from the rest of the Gores. Unknown to us, he had constructed giant nets hidden in the trees all around the campsite. As we flew past the first set of trees he released them and they sprung up behind us trapping our retreat. From between the trees in front of us more nets shot up blocking our way forward. Our only escape was upwards but that too had been carefully planned. The Gores, who'd been watching our capture from the centre of the clearing, suddenly disappeared from view. They re-appeared seconds later carrying a giant net which they quickly unrolled and dropped across the gap between the two rows of trees. Our escape from above had been blocked and we were trapped like birds in a cage."

"But how did you escape?" asked Izward unclear as to how Talon had escaped such a well-executed trap.

"If you remember," explained Talon, "I was to capture Vulgor so I carried that special net. I was ahead of the main attack when they ambushed us. Fortunately the net I carried got caught in theirs and when the net shot up it took me with it and catapulted me away from the compound. The darkness hid me and I escaped."

The carpet came to a stop and hovered above the forest. Ahead of them stood Methuselah. They could see Hoot standing by the doorway. The door was open and he was waving at them. The trio waved back and Zardo ordered the carpet to land.

An Underground Hideaway

Hidden underground, in an old abandoned *Rabtor* burrow next to Methuselah, cowered Mrs Clutter. She was cold and frightened and very confused. She couldn't remember how long she'd been there.

It felt like a lifetime.

The hole smelt of fusty leaves and sour soil and she could taste an unpleasantness on the back of her tongue. She swallowed hoping the metallic taste would go away, it didn't.

She trembled in the semi-darkness staring up at a circle of daylight fearing the world above her.

The events of the last few hours had terrified her and she remembered having to crawl into the burrow to escape a raging fire that had swept through the forest.

Then had come the water.

It had rushed down the hole and into the burrow almost drowning her. She had struggled against its force clinging on to roots and small plants growing on the walls of the hole. Finally the rain had stopped and the water in the burrow had subsided. She had released her grip and had fallen exhausted on the wet soggy earth. She had fallen into a deep sleep and had drifted into a nightmarish dream of sea monsters and river serpents. In her dream dark creatures from her bedtime story days came out of the shadows to get her and take her away. One such vision had caused her to cry out in her sleep and she had awakened shivering from fear.

All that had seemed a long time ago and as she shivered in the burrow wondering what was to happen to her she heard the familiar voice of someone she knew.

"It's me!"

It was a voice she recognised.

"I've returned!"

It was a voice she trusted.

"Hoot my old friend, glad to see you're well!"

It was Wizard Zardo.

Suddenly the terrors of the last few hours dissolved like hailstones in a hot spring. She relaxed knowing everything was back to normal. If Zardo had returned then Tellurian was safe again and whatever danger had threatened the island was gone.

Eagerly she wriggled her way up the burrow and emerged out of the hole. She scrambled to her feet ready to greet Zardo and apologise for being late.

At first she couldn't see him but as she turned towards Methuselah she could see him surrounded by creatures from her nightmare. To her horror they had tied his hands and feet and were flying around him snapping and pecking at him.

Watching over them was the creature that had frightened her when she was cleaning the step, the one Zardo had said was a Seadac. It stood behind a large owl squawking out orders.

She recognised the owl. It was Hoot, a trusted friend of Zardo. He too had been bound.

Suddenly two more flying creatures appeared holding a humanoid figure she didn't recoginse. They held him by the ankles and flew over a spike. They dangled him over it threatening to drop him. This amused them and they squawked and howled with pleasure.

Her instincts told her to run, go back down the hole and hide, but she resisted the temptation and remained hidden.

Suddenly a large amphibian appeared in the doorway. It was the fattest creature she had ever seen. It stood for a moment watching, then went back inside the tree. The others followed dragging their captives with them. Two then waited until everyone was inside then slammed the door shut. The sound of the door closing echoed around the forest like distant thunder.

Mrs Clutter came out of hiding and stood for a moment looking at Methuselah.

She shivered with fear. Her childhood nightmares had come back to haunt her but this time it wasn't a dream.

The monstrosities inside were real.

Suddenly two claw-like talons grabbed her from above and took her off into the morning sky.

Her nightmare was beginning all over again.

Slime and Fire

Izward was hanging upside down over a bubbling mixture of slime and fire. His feet had been tied together with a long rope attached to a horizontal pole. To his left hung Hoot and on his right dangled Zardo. They too had been tied to the pole but Hoot hung several metres lower and Zardo a few metres higher.

All three had been bound with rope wrapped tightly around their bodies. They each hung, dangling on the end of a single cord staring down into a pulsating pit of evil.

The pole on which they'd been tied was supported at either end by three long pieces of timber tied together to form a pyramid. At each end of the pole a large wooden wheel had been assembled out of branches lashed together with creeper vines. On the hub of the left hand wheel a thin belt of twine circled itself around the wheel and down onto a smaller one at the base of the pyramid. The smaller wheel formed part of an intricate mechanism of cogs and levers attached to three cylindrical drums. Wrapped around the drums were three taught ropes that went up through the pyramid and beyond his view. He assumed these were the same ropes that held him and his colleagues captive.

Izward swung his body over to his right and saw a similar mechanism had been constructed in the other tower. However this combination of cogs and levers controlled a different array of vines. He counted about twenty ropes shooting out of the machinery and up into the roof of the tree beyond his vision. The function of these cogs and levers remained a mystery.

Swaying slightly from side to side, Izward stared down into the pit of slime watching the bubbles pop and explode into little flames of fire. Blood was rushing to his head making him feel sick and dizzy. His head throbbed and it felt like it would burst. He wriggled like a worm hoping to loosen the knots around his ankles but the more he squirmed the tighter they became. Finally he gave up and just hung there, resigned to his fate.

As he dangled over the slime he tried to recall the events that had led up to their capture.

They'd seen Hoot standing in the open doorway of Methuselah waving to them. They had eagerly waved back pleased to see him safe and uninjured. Zardo had shouted down to him but Hoot had remained silent. He had continued to wave at them pointing to a spot on the ground where they could land. They'd suspected nothing and followed his directions landing the carpet in a copse next to several burnt out trees.

They had stepped off the carpet and were immediately attacked by Gores. They'd been hiding inside the trees that surrounded the carpet.

It had been the perfect trap and Hoot had led them straight into it. They'd been taken prisoners, bungled inside Methuselah and strung up like carcasses of meat.

A sour rancid taste insulted his mouth and Izward spat. A globule of green liquid fell from his mouth and landed with a hiss in the slime. His head spun and he could feel himself becoming sleepy. The gas from the bubbling slime was affecting him. He wondered what the slime was and why he and his friends had been suspended over it.

He strained his head trying to get a better view of his surroundings. Below him was Zardo's room, or what was left of it. It had changed from the last time he'd been here. The pit of slime had replaced the hole in the floor and the inside of the tree had been covered in a black tar like substance. It covered the walls like solidified wax down the outside of a candle.

Suddenly from the centre of the pit a bright spinning ball shot up out of the slime and hovered over the bubbling mass. It howled and crackled with energy shooting lines of fire around its surface. Izward recognised it immediately, it was the orb he'd sent Pheogore to destroy.

On the edge of the pit was Vulgor and next to him stood Gorf. They were ordering the Gores onto the machines. Koor and Varen were sitting against the wall reading Zardo's book. He cursed himself for not hiding the book more carefully.

Three Gores had flown inside the tower to his right and were perched on levers inside the machine. They looked across at Vulgor awaiting his orders.

"Now?" asked one of them eagerly.

"No!" squawked Vulgor angrily," I want to play with them awhile."

A look of disapproval spread across the Gore's face.

"But your Darkness…"

Suddenly it was hit in the chest by a bolt of energy and knocked off the lever.

Vulgor's eyes faded from an angry red to a sedate pink.

"I won't tolerate insubordination," scolded Vulgor, "the next time I'll blow your unworthy head off!"

"Sorry your Darkship, it won't happen again," said the Gore untangling itself from out of the machine.

Vulgor turned angrily towards Gorf and stared deep into the creature's over bloated eyes. Gorf felt Vulgor's power violating his mind, searching for signs of weakness.

"Shall we proceed?" questioned Vulgor menacingly.

Gorf nodded, more out of fear than of approval.

"Good! I promise you, you won't be disappointed."

Vulgor's eyes went red and he turned towards his prisoners. A bolt of energy shot across the room and glanced off Izward's foot. It ricocheted into the wall and exploded. A hail of red-hot embers lit up the tree disclosing twenty pairs of eyes hidden in the shadows above him. The embers dimmed and the eyes disappeared back into the darkness.

The impact sent Izward into a spin knocking him unconscious.

Vulgor looked at Gorf and smiled.

"Fun isn't it," beamed Vulgor.

Gorf nodded.

"Now let's see if I can hit the other two."

Voices From The Past

"Izward!" shouted a voice inside his head, *"wake up!"*

Izward ignored it.

A bright light shone all around him.

"Look into the light."

In the brightness floated several human figures. He could only see the upper half of their bodies. They wore long white gowns that sparkled and glittered like veins in a silvermine. Red masks covered the lower half of their faces and they each held strange metal objects in gossamer gloved hands. He thought he recognised them but his mind couldn't recall where or when.

"*Wake up!*" said one of the faces, "*it's over.*"

"*You're at the Institute,*" said another, "*the operation is over and it's a success.*"

Unable to respond Izward looked up at the faces and remained silent.

"*It's the anaesthetic doctor,*" said a female voice, "*we had to keep him under a long time.*"

Suddenly a familiar face appeared above him.

"*Izward my darling,*" said the girl in the ring," *I love you. Please wake up.*"

Beth! reminded his memory, the girl in the ring was Beth.

But who was Beth and why were these faces so familiar? He was sure he knew these people but from where? But before he could unmask their identities Vulgor appeared riding a huge winged serpent. Emitting a terrifying ray from its nostrils the serpent blasted the masked strangers with a river of fire. They burst into flames and became fiery skulls. Gradually the flames died and the skulls faded into the light. Vulgor and the serpent rode into the brightness and he drifted into blackness.

Izward awoke to the sound of creaking timber and the throb of moving machinery. It clattered and rumbled like wooden wheels on cobbled stones. He panicked his mind a jumble of confusion.

Where was he? What was happening?

To his right he could hear the whirling of spindles and the grinding of cogs. Fearing for his sanity he twisted his body towards the noise. Several winged creatures were pulling and pushing levers on a large wooden contraption. At first he didn't recognise them then suddenly his memory cleared and he remembered where he was.

Inside The Hollow Tree

Mrs Clutter was terrified.

She'd been snatched up like a fish from a pond and carried into the air by an unknown abductor. At first she'd struggled to get free but as her captor gained height she'd stopped, fearing the creature would drop her.

"Are you all right?" said a voice above her head.

She said nothing.

"Don't be afraid, I'm here to help you."

Mrs Clutter didn't move.

Talon flew towards the trees where he'd earlier been ambushed and flew down inside one of the stumps. He gently placed Mrs Clutter on the ground and released her. She remained still and lifeless.

The inside of the tree was dank and dark and smelt of rotting vegetables. Above him a disc of blue sky outined the top of the tree.

"Excuse me," said Talon politely, "you can get up now, we'll be safe in here."

Suddenly a twig cracked and he felt a stabbing pain in his left leg just above the claw. Mrs Clutter had bitten him. He howled with pain and tried to dislodge her but she only sank her teeth deeper into his skin.

"I'm a friend," said Talon, "I'm here to help you. Please let go you're hurting me!"

Mrs Clutter was unconvinced and kept her teeth firmly embedded in Talon's leg.

"Look!" said Talon a little more sternly, "I'm not your enemy and if you'll stop biting me I'll prove it!"

"How?" she snapped unwittingly releasing the grip on Talon's leg.

Talon jerked his leg free and limped out of reach.

"I have the *Birth Mark*."

There was silence.

"I was born beyond the great forest," continued Talon lifting up a wing, "look!"

She noticed several feathers were a different colour and made a pattern she recognised.

♌

This creature was indeed born a Tellurian. All creatures born on the island carried that mark.

"What species are you?" she asked.

"I am an eagle," he said proudly, "we are newly evolved and form part of the island's future."

Indeed Mrs Clutter had witnessed great changes in her lifetime. The island had been the *Birth Mother* of a thousand different species. Tellurians were the life force of the planet and the future of the universe.

"Forgive me for doubting your loyalty," said Mrs Clutter, "but something terrible is happening to the island and I don't know who to trust."

"There's nothing to forgive," said Talon. "We need to talk."

They quickly exchanged adventures and formulated a plan. Then Talon grabbed hold of Mrs Clutter and gently lifted her off the ground. Together they flew out of the hollow tree and headed towards Methuselah.

Tellurian Mutants

Izward pretended to be unconscious.

Above he could hear creatures breathing and below the sound of Gores clambering over the machinery.

Hovering above the pit of slime was the orb.

"Lower the Tellurians," said a voice he recognised.

The Gores responded and began pushing and pulling levers. The machine rumbled into action and Izward heard the scraping of rope across timber. He felt movement and heard objects being lowered from above.

Suddenly a Tellurian dropped into view quickly followed by others. They were all bound and gagged and appeared lifeless. They continued their descent dangling on the end of ropes, heading towards the slime.

"Stop!" squawked Vulgor.

The machine came to a grinding halt and the Tellurians came to an abrupt stop a few metres above the bubbling slime.

Izward half opened his eyes. Vulgor was staring into the orb. Suddenly a bolt of energy came out of his eyes and into the ball.

"Prepare Zardo and the other two," ordered Vulgor.

Izward watched as the orb spun towards him. It stopped and began to emit a loud wailing sound. His ears exploded with pain.

"Lower Zardo," ordered Vulgor.

"At once!" came the reply.

Degoreger pushed a lever and the machine burst into movement. Stulgore pulled at another and a single rope unwrapped itself from around a cylinder and fed itself through the machine.

The ache inside Izward's eardrums was unbearable but he resisted the urge to cry out. Suddenly Zardo came into view. He looked still and lifeless.

"Stop!" shouted Vulgor.

The machine came to a halt leaving Zardo dangling next to Hoot.

"Now the other."

The machine started up again and Izward felt himself being lowered.

"Stop!"

He came to a stop hanging beside his colleagues. The wailing stopped and the orb spun out of sight. Izward looked across at his comrades, they were awake but their eyes stared wildly.

"Hoot," whispered Izward, "its me Izward."

But the owl said nothing, his eyes fixed on the bubbling slime below him. Izward turned to Zardo. He also stared into the slime unaware of Izward's presence.

"Now?" asked Gorf, scratching a rather irritating boil on his neck. The boil burst and yellow liquid oozed down his neck.

Vulgor looked up at his captives and smiled. They were about to become *Darklings*, creatures of the Zone. He smiled at the thought, trying to visualise a Tellurian Empire under his rule.

"Yes," answered Vulgor, "but transform the Tellurian creatures first, they make excellent *Mutants*."

Izward watched as the first of the Tellurians approached the pit. Slime leaped out of the pit and attached itself to the creature's head. It slithered up and around the body creating a shell of burning slime. It solidified cocooning the unfortunate creature inside. For a brief moment it hovered over the pit like a giant chrysalis, then dropped and disappeared under the slime.

Others followed and the pit was engulfed in flames.

"Now!" shouted Vulgor after several minutes of submersion. Vengorey pulled a lever and the machine clattered into reverse. Slowly the Tellurians rose out of the slime.

Izward stared in disbelief. He no longer recognised them as Tellurians. Suspended over the slime were several very large egg shaped objects dripping with yellow sludge.

"Move them to the incubation chamber," ordered Vulgor.

The machine clattered into action.

The eggs swung gently across the pit as the machine moved them to the outside of the room. They were lowered to the floor besides an opening Izward had never seen before. Suddenly three creatures came out of the opening and stood beside the eggs. At first Izward didn't recognise them They weren't Gores or any offspring to Vulgor or Gorf. They were humanoid in appearance and walked on two legs. Thin orange hair covered their entire bodies and they waddled as they moved. They had translucent flesh and their skeletal shape was clearly visible through the skin. An uneven row of misshapen humps grew along their spine forcing them to stoop as they moved. They had long spindly arms and claw like hands. When they moved their long pointed nails scraped along the ground making an irritating screeching sound.

"Move them to the incubation chamber," ordered Vulgor.

The creatures obeyed and shuffled forward. They each took hold of an egg and started sliding it along the floor into the opening.

Suddenly it all became clear and the reality of what was happening horrified him, the creatures were Tellurians. Vulgor was harvesting the

Tellurians and making them slaves. Suddenly more Tellurians were lowered into the slime. They re-emerged as eggs and were taken into the incubation chamber by their mutant colleagues.

"Prepare Zardo and the others for mutation," ordered Vulgor.

"Yes your Lordship," answered Degoreger.

Degoreger threw a lever and Zardo moved towards the pit. Izward could see the slime gathering on its surface. Unless he thought of a way to escape, it would engulf them all and turn them into zombies.

To The Rescue

Mrs Clutter looked at her beloved forest and felt sad. The trees she had known from childhood had gone. All that was left were their stumps smouldering in the evening twilight. Smoke drifted everywhere and the smell of burning wood filled the air.

Visibility was poor and Talon was having difficulty finding his way across the clearing. Having Mrs Clutter between his claws only added to his problems. If he flew too low she might be injured and to go too high would leave him lost in the smog.

His dilemma came to an end when, avoiding two shadowy figures lurking in the mist, he crashed into the limbs of a very large tree.

"What was that?" came a voice through the fog.

"What was what?" came the reply.

Mrs Clutter and Talon were a little dazed but unhurt. They had landed safely between the branches of a very large tree and were able to move freely from one to the other.

"Up in the tree. I'm sure I heard a noise."

Talon looked at Mrs Clutter and told her to remain silent. She nodded and they both moved to the edge of the branch. They carefully leaned over and looked down. Immediately below them, less than twenty metres away, were Koor and Varen. They were standing next to a large wooden door.

"You're mistaken," insisted Varen, "there's nothing up there."

"Well I could have sworn I heard a noise."

Mrs. Clutter looked up at Talon and smiled.

"I know where we are," she said and let out a squeal of excitement. "We've landed on Methuselah."

"There it is again!" shouted Koor, "you must have heard that?"

Varen didn't answer.

"You must have done!" said Koor getting annoyed, "up there, in the fork of the tree."

Talon and Mrs Clutter moved out of sight. For several seconds Koor and Varen stood in silence staring up at the tree.

"Well I can't see anything," said Varen.

"I'm telling you, there's *something* up there."

Suddenly Talon couldn't see Mrs Clutter anymore. For a moment he panicked fearing she'd fallen to the ground.

"Over here!" she whispered.

She was standing next to a large branch covered with leaves.

"I use this when I forget my key," she said.

She pulled back the leaves and disappeared through them. Talon didn't move.

"Well what are you waiting for?" she insisted suddenly poking her head back through the foliage. "Follow me!"

Talon made his way across the tree and pulled back the branch. Mrs Clutter had gone. Several tree roots had twisted together to form a tunnel into the tree. Down the passage he could hear Mrs Clutter scuttling along in the darkness. He bent down and put his head into the hole. He pulled it back immediately. The entrance was narrow, barely wide enough for his head.

"Ok! I'll prove it, I'll go and have a look."

Koor flew off leaving Varen to guard the door.

Talon tried again. He crawled in as far as his shoulders and stopped. The sides of the tunnel were pressing hard against his wings. If he carried on he might get stuck. The thought of being wedged in a hole horrified him so he carefully retraced his steps and crawled back out.

"Well," shouted Varen.

Koor had almost reached the fork in the tree.

"Anyone there?" she asked sarcastically.

Talon spun around. The voice had startled him and he could hear wings beating the air.

"Well?" questioned a voice at the foot of the tree.

Fearing he'd be seen Talon dived head first into the tunnel and came to an abrupt stop. As he had feared he had become wedged against the sides of the tunnel and was stuck. The sound of flapping wings grew louder and Talon knew he would be discovered. Suddenly two scrawny hands gripped his throat and began tugging at his neck

"Wriggle," ordered Mrs Clutter, "while I pull."

Talon obeyed and as Mrs Clutter pulled, Talon twisted and turned his body until he'd squeezed himself through the hole and into the safety of the tunnel.

"Thank you," wheezed Talon nursing his throat.

"You're welcome," replied Mrs. Clutter politely. "Now follow me, I've something to show you."

Together they crawled through the tunnel into the tree. It was dark and damp and smelt of rotting vegetation. The passageway led up, twisting and turning its way up the tree towards its branches.

"Not far now," encouraged Mrs Clutter, "its around the next bend."

She reached the corner and turned into the final section of the tunnel. Some fifty metres ahead of them was a large opening.

"Do you see them?" asked Mrs Clutter.

"See who? "asked Talon.

She crawled the last few metres on her hands and knees and stood up. Talon followed some several metres behind her. On reaching the opening he stood up beside her.

"See for yourself," said Mrs. Clutter.

What he saw terrified him.

The Challenge

Slime slithered under the surface of the pit like an unseen assassin. It surfaced as a pulsating mass of goo growing steadily larger with every throb. Izward watched as Zardo neared the pit. There was nothing he could do to save the wizard. He himself was trapped and would inevitably suffer the same fate. He grew angry and frustrated.

The slime reacted to the wizard's presence and spat tentacle-like arms towards him.

"Monsters!" yelled Izward.

There was no longer any point in him pretending to be unconscious. Vulgor and the rest of his legion suddenly looked up.

"Coward," accused Izward suddenly realising he'd caught Vulgor unprepared.

"Stop the machine!" bellowed Vulgor.

The machine came to a shuddering halt and Zardo came to a stop two metres above the slime. Izward could see the slimy tentacles trying to attach themselves to his body, but he was out of their reach.

Izward saw the look of surprise on Vulgor's face and decided to take advantage of this unexpected opportuntity.

Gorf was astounded.

"Impossible!" muttered the amphibian.

Vulgor stared up at Izward in disbelief.

"Coward," taunted Izward trying to anger Vulgor further.

"I thought you said the orb took away all resistance?" questioned Gorf.

Gorf looked at Vulgor then at the orb. The orb was hovering beside Hoot preparing him for the slime.

"Well I was wrong," said Vulgor angrily, "it appears *that* creature's immune."

Gorf stepped back sensing anger in Vulgor's voice.

"You're a coward Vulgor!" shouted Izward, "and to prove it I challenge you. Just *you* and *me*."

Gorf and the Gores watched Vulgor's reactions wondering how long their lord and master would take such insults.

Vulgor remained silent.

"Thought so!" continued Izward, "*you* are a coward."

Vulgor didn't reply.

"I hope you rot in hell," continued Izward.

Vulgor remained silent then suddenly smiled and answered.

"I'm already *there*," he said smugly, "and if I'm not mistaken, you and your meddlesome friends will soon be joining me!"

Vulgor turned to Gorf and grinned. Then he started to laugh. The Gores, who felt obliged to laugh, joined in and soon the room echoed with false laughter.

"I'm already there," repeated Vulgor staring menacingly into Gorf's eyes. "Get it?"

Gorf nodded and started to laugh.

"You're scared," shouted Izward, "you laugh out of fear. You're afraid of me."

The room went silent.

"Am I?" stormed Vulgor, "then this should amuse you!"

A bolt of fire shot out of Vulgor's eyes and thundered towards Izward. Izward jerked his body aside and the projectile missed. It struck the wall behind him and disintegrated. Izward started to swing backwards and forwards across the room.

"You don't frighten me!" called out Izward as he swung wildly around the room, "catch me if you can!"

Izward's swinging began to affect Zardo and Hoot's ropes and they too started to swing. Vulgor watched as all three of his captives swung backwards and forwards over the slime pit. He looked up at the remaining Tellurians hanging above them and noticed they too had started to sway. The timber towers on either side of the pit of slime were creaking under the strain and he feared for the machine's stability. Izward was beginning to annoy him.

Vulgor frantically followed Izward's path around the room trying to blast him with energy bolts, but every time he fired he failed. After several aborted attempts Vulgor's energy weakened and he was forced to stop.

"Curse you!" said Vulgor weakly.

Suddenly one of the beams supporting the tower snapped and fell into the slime. The slime swam towards it and devoured it. The constant swinging of Izward and the others was weakening the tower's foundation and they begun to creak under the strain.

"Lower Zardo into the pit," ordered Vulgor in a panic. "Now!"

The machine clattered irratically into action. Zardo suddenly dropped and hit the surface with a splat. Slime splashed everywhere.

Izward, still swinging across the room, watched as the slime regrouped itself and gathered around Zardo's submerging body.

Suddenly Zardo flew up out of the slime and disappeared from view.

Talon To The Rescue

Talon hovered above the room and looked across at Mrs Clutter. She was standing in a tunnel about a hundred metres below him. Gripped between his claws was a rope and attached to the end of the rope was Zardo.

When Zardo had plunged into the slime Talon had grabbed his rope and had pulled him out of the pit.

Zardo was heavy and Talon's claws ached under the strain. He carefully manoeuvred Zardo towards the passage. Suddenly there was a loud snapping sound and a piece of wood flew off one of the towers. It narrowly missed him and tumbled to the floor. It landed in the slime and burst into flames. There followed more snapping sounds and several more pieces broke away. They too landed in the slime and were quickly devoured by flames. He noticed the Gores had abandoned the machine and were frantically running around the room looking to escape.

Fearing he'd be hit by more falling timber, he quickly guided Zardo to the tunnel's entrance. Mrs Clutter reached out a hand and grabbed him. She guided him through the entrance, laid him down and untied the rope. The rope slithered out of the passage and Talon released it. He watched it fall, snaking itself through the air towards the pit. It struck the surface with a splat and was immediately sucked under. As he watched the rope sink under the surface he noticed the slime was rising. It was slithering out of the pit and pouring into the room. He could see something rising through the slime and coming to the surface.

Suddenly a huge black bubble burst through the slime and into the room.

A River of Slime

At first it had gone unnoticed, a distant rumble barely audible against the sound of falling timber and clanking machinery. Vulgor had been too busy yelling at the Gores to notice the room was vibrating.

The Gores, mindful of being struck by falling beams and bits of machinery, were ignoring his orders and scrambling off the machine towards the safety of the corridor. As they huddled in the doorway they too failed to hear the rumblings beneath their feet.

The Tellurians oblivious to anything other than the hypnotic effect of the slime remained ignorant of the chaos around them. They swung precariously on their ropes swinging madly from side to side.

The three mutants, unaware of its futility, stood waiting for an egg that would never come.

A rising river of slime swept around the room threating all in its path. It splashed angrily around the walls setting fire to the falling timbers. Vulgor flew out of its path landing unsteadily inside one of the towers. It rocked unsteadily and parts of the machine began to disintegrate. Levers and cogs, ropes and pulleys began to fly off in every direction and Vulgor was forced to duck and hop around avoiding them.

The Tellurians, still attached to their ropes, were swinging madly around in every direction. The poles to which they were tied were buckling and bending under the strain.

Izward, who had instigated all of this, watched with growing satisfaction. Vulgor and the Gores were in disarray and the destruction of the machine looked certain. Suddenly he felt a sharp tug on his rope and was surprised to see Hoot above him. The owl's rope had swung around his and the two ropes were twisting together. The added weight of Hoot brought Izward's rope to a standstill and he stopped swinging.

Gorf, desperately trying to out run the oncoming river of slime, slipped at the entrance to the incubation chamber and was swept inside. He came to a stop inside the hatchery lying on his back. He struggled to stand but his immense weight pinned him down. He could feel the slime slowly rising over his body and eating into his skin. Boils burst and sores exploded.

Hanging above him were the cocooned mutants awaiting birth. He could see them moving about inside their shells. Several shells had already cracked and were about to hatch. Suddenly the whole of the chamber shook and several eggs fell to the floor. He felt the slime rising over his body and beginning to solidify. He couldn't move. It rose to his head and began to flow between the folds in his neck. The last thing he saw were the newly hatched mutants standing over him before his head was covered in slime and he fell into unconsciousness.

Encounters

Talon had been the first to see the bubble looming up from the depths of the slime. He'd been rescuing Zardo when he noticed slime coming out of the pit and into the room. The tree had shaken violently and Talon had flown Zardo to safety.

Izward, who'd been wrapped around Hoot, was the first to encounter the bubble. It burst through the slime and struck him hard on the side of the head. For a moment he was temporarily dazed and speckles of bright light danced around his eyes. When the stars had gone he'd found himself lying on something hard with the unconscious Hoot on top of him. The owl blocked his view and Izward tried to push him aside but he was too heavy. As he struggled with Hoot's huge frame he noticed that vacant stare had gone. Hoot was waking up. Suddenly there was a tremendous crash and objects started falling on them.

Vulgor watched with horror as the bubble rose out of the pit and spun towards him. It was twenty metres in circumference and covered in green slime. Unable to get out of of its way he'd flown onto it. But its surface had been slippery and he'd lost his footing. He'd spun off knocking over the Mutants. He'd scrambled to his feet but had slipped on the slimy floor. He'd heard wood snapping as the bubble grew and crashed into the machine. He'd fallen again, tripping over broken machinery parts. He'd kept trying to get to his feet but kept slipping on slime or fallen debris. Finally he crawled along the floor and headed towards the door and the safety of the passageway.

The Gores had managed to avoid the slime by hiding down the passage. They'd tried to escape but had found the outside door locked. They'd pleaded with Varen and Koor to open it but they'd refused. Vulgor had told them *nothing came in or went out* and they were standing by those orders. They'd returned to the room and were just in time to save Vulgor from being crushed by a Tellurian. Vengorey had spotted Vulgor crawling along the floor and had grabbed him. He managed to pull him into the doorway before the room was overrun with falling Tellurians.

Tellurians fell from everywhere.

After saving Zardo, Talon had flown around the machine releasing Tellurians. Without the hypnotic effect of the orb some of them were waking up. He'd released these first. He'd managed to release seven before the bubble destroyed the towers and the whole of the machine had come crashing down. He'd given these seven a plan and once they were on the ground they were to release the other Tellurians and attack Vulgor and the Gores. With the collapse of the towers there had been nothing to keep the Tellurians aloft. They had fallen onto the bubble and had dropped to the floor.

Talon had watched as the Tellurians bounced and rolled down the sides of the bubble. Then he had flown back to the passage to be reunited with Zardo.

Inside the tunnel they had hugged each other and Zardo had thanked them both for rescuing him. Talon had quickly explained how he'd escaped Vulgor's trap and how he'd found Mrs Clutter. He'd hidden inside a tree stump and had found Mrs. Clutter wandering around outside Methuselah.

Zardo had listened intently to the rest of Talon's story and after he'd finished insisted it was now up to *them* to rescue the Terrodacs.

Talon had wanted to go back and rescue Izward and Hoot but Zardo had assured him they would be safe.

"The Creator was looking over them," he'd said.

Reluctantly Talon agreed and Mrs Clutter led them all back down the passageway and out of the tree.

Caught on the top of the bubble were ropes and pieces of wood. These had tangled together to form a makeshift net. Trapped inside the net were Hoot and Izward. Both creatures struggled to free themselves unaware the bubble was about to open.

The Ogre Of Hope

The room stopped shaking and the bubble stopped spinning. It dropped to the floor and rolled to a stop on top of the pit.

Inside the sphere the Ogre of Hope prepared for departure. Disguise was no longer necessary and Pheogore became the Overseer once again. His mission was almost over. Finally after an eternity of guilt he would be forgiven. He'd blamed himself for the Dark Zones creation. Earth's late arrival had unbalanced nature and the Creator had been forced to create the Zone to restore order. When Vulgor escaped for a second time he'd been asked to disguise himself as a Gore. He'd spied on Vulgor and under the Creator's guidance had gone over to the Tellurians. He'd followed the orb down the hole and watched as it created the slime. He'd been faced with a dilemma. Let Methuselah die or violate the *Prime Directive*. Faced with no alternative but to disobey the *non-interference rule*, he'd quickly created the *Sphere of Hope* and went to the Tellurians rescue.

A Heavenly Guardian

Quickly the freed Tellurians scurried around the room untying their comrades. All but three had survived the fall and as they gathered around the bottom of the sphere they heard a familiar cry. They turned and saw Hoot sliding down the sphere. He quickly took control and positioned them in a circle around the base of the sphere.

Suddenly several mutants shuffled out of the incubation chamber carrying an enormous egg. They dropped the egg on the floor and stood against the wall. The egg cracked and Vulgor could see it contained the mutated shape of Gorf. The brainless dimwit of an amphibian had gone and got covered in slime, well good riddance to it thought Vulgor.

With the appearance of the mutants the mood of the Tellurians changed. They stared in horror at their lost colleagues but before their sorrow had turned into anger Vulgor launched his assault.

The Gores flew out of the passage and attacked the Tellurians. Several were knocked to the ground with blows to the head and left lying unconscious on the floor. Some panicked and tried to escape up the sphere but came sliding back down. Those left standing lashed out with their hands hoping to grab a Gores' leg and snatch it out of the air.

Degoreger, having dived too low was captured and dragged to the floor. The Tellurians swarmed all over him but he managed to escape by dragging himself along the floor pulling several Tellurians along with him. Finally one by one they let go and he flew back to the passage to regain his strength. Vulgor looked at him angrily and the Gore reluctantly returned to the battle.

Hoot attacked Vengorey and sent him crashing into the sphere. The Gore was knocked unconscious and slid lifelessly on to the floor. He came to a stop sprawled out over Gorf's egg.

Vulgor ordered the mutants into the battle but only one responded. It blundered forward leaving the rest motionless. With its knees bent and its arms swinging wildly across its body it waddled across the room in the wrong direction. Vulgor swore, cursing the creature's lack of understanding. Finally it walked into Vengorey and tripped over Gorf's egg. The egg went spinning across the floor. The mutant hopelessly out of control tried to climb up the sphere.

Vulgor watched, knowing the battle wasn't going well. The Tellurians had kept retreating to the sphere and were successfully fending off his Gores. The mutants, still refused to move and something was blocking his thoughts and preventing him from firing his energy bolts.

Inside the incubation chamber more mutants were being hatched. They waddled out into the room and stood motionless beside their colleagues.

Vengorey, still weak from his first encounter, was once again snatched out of the air and dragged towards the sphere.

Suddenly the sphere started to glow.

Vulgor sensed defeat and magically produced a large green egg. He began to chant and roll it around in his claws. It crackled and bolts of energy ran around its surface. It too began to glow and reflect the fiery-red eyes of its Master.

Suddenly everyone in the room stopped and turned to face the sphere. Something unexpected was happening. It pulsed so bright the room was blinded by its brilliance and hovering above it was a figure floating inside a transparent globe.

To the watchers the creature inside the light took on different forms.

Hoot saw the mermaid who had rescued him from drowning whilst the Tellurians saw their heavenly protector. Vulgor, still nursing the egg, saw the traitor Pheogore and the Gores, a small grey spidery creature with a large head and black oval eyes. Even the mutants saw a silvery angel floating about in the brightness.

Suddenly the sphere imploded and the room exploded with brilliance never before experienced. When the eyes of the onlookers had adjusted to the glare they found the sphere gone.

In its place floated several large transparent bubbles.

The Gatherers

Izward was inside a bubble bobbing in a sea of light. Above him was the girl in the ring. She too drifted on the same sea encased in a similar bubble. She looked at him and smiled. He felt calm and relaxed, reassured by her presence. Transfixed by her beauty he stared lovingly into those hypnotic eyes wishing she were real.

Earlier he'd been trapped on top of the sphere with Hoot. The owl had managed to wriggle himself free and slide down the sphere. Izward had tried but had failed. He'd been trapped on top of the sphere when it had imploded. To his great surprise he'd awoken inside a transparent globe with the girl floating above him.

He looked again for the girl but she'd gone and her bubble was empty.

More bubbles floated into view and began drifting around him. They floated through the air colliding with each other. Izward moved to the edge of the bubble and looked out. It rolled as he walked keeping him upright. His feet sank into its surface forcing him to bend his knees as he moved. The curvature of the bubble distorted the view making everything look bloated and misshapen. Below the Gores had resumed their attack on the Tellurians.

From the bubble Izward could see the remains of Vulgor's mutant-making machine scattered over the floor. The hole in the floor had gone, replaced by a small hill. Standing on the hill were the Tellurians. They'd formed a circle and were fending off the Gores. They'd taken timber from the collapsed towers and were using them as spears. As the Gores flew over they stabbed at them with the ends of the broken poles. Other Tellurians were throwing lumps of wood and bits of shattered machinery.

Izward watched as Hoot ran towards a Gore knocked out of the air by a well-aimed piece of wood. The creature lay in a heap on the floor, but before Hoot could reach it two of its comrades dragged it to safety. Hoot pursued them, waving a makeshift spear at them. Suddenly Hoot was taken by surprise by a Gore he thought dead. The creature had been slumped against the wall pretending to be killed. It now attacked and Izward watched with growing concern as the owl received blow after blow from the resurrected Gore. Finally Hoot fell and lay motionless. The triumphant Gore, overjoyed by its victory, put a claw on Hoot's chest and roared loudly.

Izward thumped the bubble with his fist, angry at not being able to help his comrades. The bubble responded and moved several metres forward. From his new position Izward could see Vulgor. He was standing by the door holding what looked like an egg. Izward could see Vulgor's eyes turning red. The Lord of the Dark Zone was gathering his forces for a final showdown. Suddenly the mutants stepped forward and stood beside the Gores. The Tellurians, anticipating another attack, huddled closer together.

Suddenly two Tellurians, carrying homemade spears, rushed off the hill to try to rescue Hoot. Izward watched as they repeatedly attacked the Gore, poking at it with the end of their poles. They would have succeeded if not for Vulgor's intervention. With the bubble gone Vulgor's strength had partly returned and he blasted them. They slid along the floor smoking and smouldering.

Izward felt angry, he wanted to be down there with his comrades, fighting. He kicked the bubble and it lurched forward. He toppled backwards and landed on his back. As he hit the bubble he bounced back over and landed on his stomach. He lay there staring through its outer skin at the battle beneath him.

The Gores were attacking once again and the Tellurians were fending them off with makeshift weapons. Poles and spikes stabbed the air and the Gores flew off unable to break through their defence. The mutants who were advancing on foot were being bombarded by large pieces of wood. They too were having difficulty. Several had already been struck by flying debris and lay motionless on the ground

Suddenly Izward had an idea. *The bubble had rolled forward when he'd kicked it*! He struggled to his feet and began to experiment with his idea.

It worked.

He could move the bubble by *walking it* in any direction. To go up and down you stayed in one place and jumped.

Simple.

Delighted with his discovery Izward prepared to join his comrades but before he could carry out the manoeuvre something quite extraordinary happened.

Around him the empty bubbles had been drifting around the room occasionally colliding with each other. They'd appeared harmless so he'd ignored them. Suddenly one of them deliberately came towards him and rammed his bubble. His bubble shot forward whilst the other rebounded towards the ground. It bounced off the inside of the tree and onto the floor. It gathered speed and headed towards the Gore on top of Hoot. It rolled over the astonished creature trapping it inside. It then bounced passed Hoot and headed towards the other Gores who panicked and scrambled out of its way. It struck the wall behind them and bounced over their heads. It flew through the air and hovered over the Tellurians. They looked at it with utter amazement. Inside they could see the terrified Gore kicking and thumping the sides of the bubble trying to escape.

Suddenly all the Tellurians started to run off the mound. At first Izward was puzzled but as more of the hill became visible he saw the reason for their panic. The mound was collapsing and a large circular hole was appearing.

With a *whoosh* the bubble suddenly fell towards the mound. The Tellurians, who'd gathered around the hill's perimeter, let out a mighty *gasp*, as the bubble shot past them and disappeared down the hole. For a moment there was silence, then suddenly the sounds of cheering. The Tellurians began jumping up and down and hugging each other.

"I have sent you the *Gatherers*," said a girl's voice from inside Izward's bubble, "they await your guidance."

It was a voice he recognised.

Whoever had created the bubble had created the Gatherers. It had given him a weapon to defeat the Gores.

Now he knew why he was in the bubble. His mission was to guide the *Gatherers* to their targets.

Quickly calculating the trajectory of his next target he carefully walked his bubble into position and braced himself for the impact.

The Last Of The Gores

Degoreger watched as another bubble bounced into the room. He panicked as it bounced over the Tellurians and headed towards him. He turned and ran for the door.

The bubble bounced after him.

He slammed into the door, but it wouldn't move, something was preventing him from opening it. He slowly turned to face the bubble. It hovered a few centimetres off the floor directly in front of him.

The other three Gores had also abandoned the battle and were being chased by three other bubbles. Unable to escape the room the Gores were desperately trying to avoid capture.

Two Tellurians dragged Hoot to safety whilst the rest cheered the bubbles to their targets.

The leaderless mutants remained motionless waiting for orders that never came.

Finally, utterly exhausted, the Gores gave up.

Degoreger watched with horror as Stulgore, unable to stay ahead of his pursuer, was snatched and taken inside the bubble. He saw the look of fear on his comrade's face as the bubble disappeared into the hole.

Suddenly, above him, hovered another bubble. Inside was the terrified Predigore. It sped off and disappeared behind the cheering Tellurians. Aerogeth tried to hide behind Gorf's egg but couldn't hold on to it. Slime dribbled out of the cracks and his claws kept slipping off its surface. Eventually he lost control and the egg rolled out of reach and struck the wall. It cracked open and the mutant Gorf flopped out. The exhausted Gore was snatched and taken inside the bubble to the centre of the room. The last Degoreger saw of Aerogeth was his terrified expression as the bubble disappeared down the hole.

More bubbles flew into the room and headed towards the mutants. The mutants offered no resistance and were quickly taken.

Gorf had been too large for a single bubble to carry and two bubbles had to combine to create one large one.

Degoreger watched as the huge bubble bounced along the floor and onto the unconscious Gorf. The bubble had struggled to gain height, but eventually succeeded and carried the mutant

Gorf to the mound. Inside Degoreger could see Gorf's grotesque shape thrashing about. The hole had been too small and the giant bubble had been forced to squeeze itself down the opening. The mutant Gorf had been squashed and as the bubble finally disappeared Gorf had been squashed into a greenish pulp.

More Gatherers appeared and bounced into the incubation chamber. They returned several seconds later with the un-hatched eggs. They headed towards the mound and vanished down the hole.

Suddenly the room drifted into an uneasy silence and Degoreger knew the time for extinction had arrived.

He was the last of the Gores.

The bubble drifted closer. He tried to get away, but the Tellurians had moved either side of him and blocked his escape. In desperation he turned to the door and began hammering on it again but it remained closed.

Escape was impossible. He turned to face his adversaries knowing his fate. Suddenly he was spinning through the air heading towards the mound. It was hot inside the bubble and his skin started to tingle. It felt as if he were melting. Then suddenly he pludged into darkness and his reality ended.

Children of the Dark

One by one the Gatherers carrying the mutants dropped to the floor and rolled to a standstill behind the unsuspecting Tellurians.

The Tellurians had been too busy celebrating to notice their arrival and while they sang and chanted victory anthems the mutants were changing. Inside each bubble time appeared to be travelling backwards and the mutants were changing back into Tellurians. Soon every bubble had dissolved replaced by a resurrected Tellurian.

Their discovery started a Tellurian celebration that would have lasted forever but for the sudden appearance of Vulgor. Without warning, he came from his hiding place behind the door and burst into the room. He was still holding the egg. He quickly chanted a few unrecognisable spells and the egg flew off and hovered over the mound.

Vulgor's sudden appearance had taken the Tellurians by surprise and they stood open-mouthed watching the egg getting bigger. Suddenly it cracked open and two more eggs popped out. These continued to grow until they were twice Vulgor's size. There was a loud crack, and out of the eggs hatched two terrifying apparitions.

The Tellurians froze with fear. Never in their wildest nightmares could such monstrosities be imagined.

Vulgor smiled at his creations. They were his last hope of victory. They were creatures of the Dark born from the primeval slime of the Dark Zone. They were kindred beings of evil, children of the Zone. They would be its future and mankind's destruction.

Vulgor watched anticipating their every gesture. They hissed and swayed, growled and roared. They spat and dribbled, oozed and leaked. Slimy green liquid poured out of their mouths and yellow pungent goo bubbled and gurgled out of thick fatty folds in their skin. Large open sores seeped yellow gunge that quickly congealed into patches of crusted gore. Yellow syrupy slime slithered down their bodies and along their tails. Large transparent hump-like growths grew out of their skin each containing beetle like creatures.

Vulgor could see the creatures scurrying around inside the humps. Occasionally one would break through the surface and scurry off to bury itself somewhere else on the creature's body.

Hoot, who had recovered from his ordeal with the Gore, was the first to react. He scrambled to his feet and carefully ventured forward. Several Tellurians followed keeping a safe distance behind him. The rest cowered against the wall.

What he saw sickened him. They were the most diabolical creatures he had ever seen. Each had a snake-like face with skin that stretched tight over a bird-like head. Their skulls jutted through the flesh and Hoot could see the creature's veins. They were yellowish in colour and appeared to be pumping a blood-green liquid across the beast's heads. The veins fed several tentacle-like creatures that appeared to be living on top of the animals' heads. They reminded Hoot of giant worms but much longer. They were black in colour and intertwined across the creatures' heads. At the end of every tentacle a cone shaped cavity opened and closed. It rippled as it moved creating concentric rings of moving flesh. From out of these holes came a loud recurring hiss as if the creatures were breathing through these pulsating slits. From out of the creatures' mouths snaked long black tongues. They swayed in the air, hovering in front of the creatures like eels swimming against the tide. At the ends of the tongues were two grotesque heads that snapped and snarled, growled and spat. They reminded Hoot of Vulgors' hideous features but much smaller. Each of the heads appeared to be leaking. He could see rivlets of slime spurting out of cuts sliced into the forehead. The holes bled a greenish liquid that oozed down the side of the face and into the eyes. Most of the liquid ran off and splashed to the floor but a little found its way along the tongue and back into the creatures' mouths.

Hoot remained calm. He had to be! The Tellurians would be waiting for his reaction. He was their Commander and they trusted his judgement and he in return respected their loyalty. He stood his ground and looked up at the creatures.

They hovered above the hole in the centre of the room flapping giant crooked wings. On the ends of the wings were giant claw-like talons that dripped slime. He shivered at the thought of being attacked by such fearsome weapons. Where the bird-like skulls ended several layers of leathery skin formed the neck. It wrapped itself under the head creating a collar of fatty tissue that resembled coiled up snakes. The neck wobbled when the creature moved squirting a yellow gunge onto the skin. The liquid became trapped in the coils and squelched when the creature moved its neck. This layered coil-like structure continued down the rest of the body, widening at the centre then tapering into a point at the tail. It reminded Hoot of the body of a giant bloated slug about to burst.

Their entire bodies were covered with boils and sores, lumps and humps, that oozed and dribbled, trickled and bled. Dried yellow and green crustaceans clung to the skin like fungus on trees.

Hoot noticed their skins appeared to ripple and he ventured closer. Movement around the lower abdomen confirmed his fears. Insect-like beings *were* living on their bodies. He saw several scurrying across the skin and burrow into the flesh.

Hoot turned to look at Vulgor. The Lord of the Dark Zone smiled and flew across the room and positioned himself between his creations.

"Now my Children of the Dark," he squawked, "I have *tasks* for you to perform."

The creatures snaked closer, hissing and swaying from side to side. Vulgor turned to the larger of the two monstrosities.

"I want you to kill the Terrodacs."

The creature suddenly grew several metres taller and spat venom across the room.

"They *were* to be *mutated* but that's no longer possible," he growled.

He looked across at the Tellurians and glared angrily at them.

"Instead I shall exterminate their species forever," he continued, "make an example to others who dare challenge my superiority."

Hoot and the Tellurians stepped forward angrily but the creature spat at them and they reluctantly shuffled back.

"I have them prisoners in the forest, find and kill them."

The creature took to the air and flew towards the passage.

"Go my *Reaper* of destruction, bring me back their skulls."

It disappeared down the corridor smashing its way along the corridor and through the outer door. Once in the forest it stopped only to pick up the Terrodac's scent, before vanishing through the trees in pursuit of its prey.

"These are yours," said Vulgor turning towards Hoot and the Tellurians. "Dispose of them."

The other creature flew to the passage and hovered in the doorway leaving Hoot and the Tellurians trapped inside the room. It moved towards them and they were forced to hide inside the Incubation Chamber. As the Tellurians crowded into the room several lost their footing and slipped on the slimy floor.

Suddenly the creature appeared at the entrance and unable to enter the room because of its size, started spitting venom through the entrance. Poison splattered everywhere. The Tellurians panicked and rushed about the chamber slipping and bumping into each other. Finally Hoot calmed them down and ordered them to the rear of the chamber.

Vulgor flew across the room and stood beside his offspring.

"What *are* you waiting for?" questioned Vulgor, "kill them… *Now!*"

The creature didn't move it just grew bigger and shot more venom into the chamber. Vulgor grew more and more angry.

"Why you overgrown bag of slime," squawked Vulgor, "I gave you an order!"

The creature reluctantly moved forward and squeezed its head into the chamber. Vulgor could see the Tellurians huddling at the far end of the chamber.

"Kill them," ordered Vulgor impatiently. "What *are* you waiting for?"

The creature couldn't move. It struggled to free itself but its head was stuck. Hoot and the Tellurians saw an opportunity to escape and charged the entrance. They ran past the creature and into the room. It responded and managed to pull its head clear. The chamber entrance collapsed trapping several Tellurians inside. Hoot ran to the door but was shot in the wing and knocked to the floor by one of Vulgor's energy bolts. The Tellurians, being no match for the creature, were swept aside with a single blow from its tail and sent crashing into the wall. They were knocked unconscious and lay where they fell. Hoot tried to stand but couldn't. The energy-blast had left him dizzy and he remained on the floor clutching his wing. It hurt and there was a small hole in the skin where the bolt had hit.

Suddenly the creature let out a deafening roar and a slit across its head opened. Hundreds of long black snakes sprang out of the gash and began coiling around each other. They remained at the hole slithering around its rim like worms over a carcass. Each snake–like tentacle secreted a sticky yellow substance that glistened and smelled of rotting meat. As they moved they made unpleasant squelching sounds and spat out jets of yellow slime. Around the slit several slivers of bone appeared. They quickly increased in size until they formed a row of razor sharp teeth around the opening.

What happened next surprised them all.

The Ring

The sound of an approaching wind echoed around the tree and Vulgor looked up. What he saw terrified him. A tornado of light was spiralling around the room and coming towards him. In its centre hovered a ball of light so bright he had to look away for fear of being blinded. As the tornado touched the floor it divided into several versions of itself and began searching the room. As it searched it made strange whistling sounds.

Hoot watched as the whirlpools of light explored the room. One spun up to Vulgor and wrapped itself around his legs while others spun around the creature's body. He could see Vulgor struggling against the unknown force unable to move his legs. The creature too was acting strange.

It was shaking, vibrating to the sound within the light. It too appeared unable to move.

It was the opportunity Hoot had been waiting for and he dragged himself over to the unconscious Tellurians. His wing hurt and blood had started to flow from the wound. He tried to stop the bleeding with a piece of rag he found on the floor. He tied it above the cut and pulled it hard using his teeth. It worked and the wound stopped bleeding.

The Tellurians looked dead. They lay beside each other face down on the floor. Neither moved and Hoot feared the worst. He gently shook one of them and it moaned, thankfully this *one* was alive. He shuffled to another, but before he could assess its condition, a bright yellow flash obliterated his sight.

When his sight returned there was a bright object directly above him. He looked up but couldn't see it clearly. It was too bright and the glare hurt his eyes. Eventually the brightness faded and he could see it was a bubble similar to the ones that had taken the Gores. It was slowly coming towards him and rapidly dissolving into the whirlpools of light that held Vulgor and his creature captive.

The more it dissolved the more saucer–shape it became. It was coming directly towards him. He closed his eyes and flipped his wings over his head and waited for the impact. It never came.

When Hoot finally opened his eyes the bubble had gone and Izward was standing next to him smiling.

"Hoot my old friend," said Izward dropping to his knees, "quick, we haven't much time."

Izward helped Hoot to his feet and hugged him.

"Izward me old shipmate is it really you?" muttered Hoot.

"Delighted to see you're alive," beamed Izward releasing Hoot from the hug. "You've done well."

Hoot staggered forward and Izward caught him.

"Steady me old friend," said Izward, "here, sit down and get your strength back!"

"But what about them?"

"Don't worry about Vulgor and the creature," answered Izward leaning Hoot against the wall. "Not yet, any rate."

Hoot slid to a sitting position.

"The light will hold them," said Izward, "but its power is limited."

"Get rid of them now, while we can!" squawked Hoot struggling to get up.

"We can't," said Izward, "they're inside the light-force."

Hoot fell back into a sitting position.

"You mean those whirligig things are protecting them?" said Hoot angrily.

Izward nodded.

"But at the same time stopping *them* from attacking *us*!" added Izward.

Hoot frowned.

"It's a standoff!" said Izward.

"A what?"

"A standoff," repeated Izward, "neither side has the advantage."

Hoot thought for a moment.

"Well if that be true captain, we'd better set sail and get the Hell out of here while we can. We need to regroup and devise new strategies."

Izward agreed.

"If we stay here we'll be fish food," concluded Hoot.

Hoot looked across at the creature. The whirpools of light had lost their brightness.

"There's another one of those things," informed Hoot pointing at the creature. "It's out there somewhere."

"I know," said Izward, "I saw it from the bubble."

Hoot looked puzzled.

"Never mind," said Izward, "I'll explain later."

"We've got to find it,"urged Hoot, "kill it before it destroys the Terrodacs."

"All taken care of," said Izward confidently.

"How?"

"Trust me I'm a Time Warrior."

"Zardo and Talon?" enquired Hoot.

"I haven't seen them,"said Izward, "but both are strong and resourceful. I'm sure they're safe."

One of the Tellurians on the floor moaned and Izward knelt down to comfort him. It smiled and Izward smiled back.

"You'll be fine," said Izward, "a little sore perhaps but you'll live. We'll get help to you soon."

The Tellurian nodded weakly and closed its eyes. Izward shuffled sideways and examined its colleague. It had a large open wound in its stomach and blood trickled over its chest onto the floor. He could see the creature was seriously injured.

"Hold on comrade," said Izward reassuringly, "help's on the way."

"I didn't betray you," said Hoot grabbing hold of Izward's arm. "They made me do it."

"I know," said Izward sympathetically, "don't worry."

"They said they would torture the Tellurians. Kill them if I didn't help them."

"Your loyalty was never under question," reassured Izward.

"Please forgive me!"

"There's nothing to forgive," said Izward, "you saved their lives and that took courage."

Hoot smiled. Several Tellurians had woken and were helping their colleagues to their feet. Izward thought he heard scraping sounds coming from inside the collapsed chamber and went over to investigate.

There it was again. He began removing the collapsed timbers.

"Over here," shouted Izward.

Those Tellurians who could went over to assist. Soon they'd cleared the entrance and four Tellurians scrambled out.

Hoot was beginning to feel a little better. The cut in his wing had stopped throbbing and the fuzzy feeling in his head had gone. He stood up and began to help other Tellurians to their feet. Illa and Bonn made a makeshift stretcher out of two poles and a plank of wood and carefully lowered the injured Tellurian onto it. Suddenly the whirlpool of light around Vulgor started to dim and he opened his eyes. The Tellurians gasped and started to panic.

"Stay calm!" hollered Izward, "we've a few minutes yet."

The creature moved its head and several snake-like tentacles hissed angrily.

"Quickly," said Izward, "into the forest."

The Tellurians scrambled towards the door and began running down the passage. Suddenly the creature was slithering towards the door in pursuit. But it was far too slow and by the time it reached the passage all but one of the Tellurians had escaped. It lashed out at the one remaining Tellurian viciously slicing the air with its claws. Nimbly the Tellurian dodged the blow and ran down the corridor to safety. The creature roared furiously and turned towards Izward and Hoot.

Suddenly the ring on Izward's finger began to glow. A blue light lit up his hand and above the ring the familiar smile of the girl. The smile faded and Zardo's symbol appeared. Izward pressed the corresponding sign on the ring and the most amazing thing happened. The ring exploded in a ball of blue light. When the glare had faded an angel-like creature hovered above them.

It was humanoid in appearance and had long thin arms and legs. It had a large head with oval black eyes and grey skin.

Suddenly Izward realised Vulgor wasn't in the room and cursed his lack of forethought. He'd let him escape taking Zardo's book with him. He had to find him before Vulgor disposed of the book. Without the book all would be lost and the Dark Zone would exist forever. Leaving Hoot and the being from the ring to deal with the creature he left in pursuit of Vulgor.

An Appointment With Destiny

It was daylight and it was raining heavily. Izward stood outside Methuselah wondering where the Tellurians had gone. A blanket of smoke drifted through the trees obscuring the sky. The forest still smouldered from the fire and Izward knew it would take days for the trees to cool down. The rain would help and as he watched the raindrops cascading down the branches he knew the island would recover.

Time was against him and he couldn't delay any longer. The whereabouts of the Tellurians would have to wait. He summoned the magic carpet and it unrolled itself from out of a tree and flew towards him. He'd fortunately got the carpet to hide itself in the forest when the Gores attacked. It came to a halt in front of him and he stepped on.

A twig snapped and he turned to investigate. He could see nothing but smoke swirling around the charred trunks of the trees.

"Crack!"

Another! This time it was behind him. He turned but could see nothing. He kept staring at the trees trying to see beyond the smoke, but there was no one there.

"Its me!" shouted a voice immediately behind him.

Izward turned to face the voice. It was Utan. Rain was running down his face and dripping into a pool of water under his feet.

"They told me to wait for you," said the Tellurian shuffling the water about with his feet.

"You scared the dying nightmares out of me!" blasted Izward.

"Sorry!"

"Where are the others? I thought I told you to wait here for Hoot and myself."

"We would have," insisted Utan, "but we all decided to rescue the Terrodacs. They left me behind to explain where they'd gone."

"Utan, my friend?"

"Yes, Wizard Master?" replied Utan

"Have you seen Vulgor?"

"Yes!" said Utan, "he flew off in that direction."

Utan pointed towards a clump of burnt out trees covered in smoke.

"He flew right over me carrying a large book."

Izward could see a faint yellowy trail of mist going up through the trees.

"Sorry Utan my friend, but I have to leave you," apologised Izward, "I've an appointment with destiny to keep."

Utan stopped splashing the water and stood to attention. He saluted and looked straight into Izward's eyes.

"Permission to come with you Sire," said Utan.

"Sorry, Utan," said Izward, "you must remain here."

Utan looked disappointed and dropped the salute.

"I must do this alone," said Izward, "my future is uncertain and I know not what the fates have planned for me."

Utan frowned and looked puzzled.

"I go to the Dark Zone."

Utan nodded.

"This is my destiny and the outcome of this encounter will shape the future of the universe. You must stay here."

"But Master?"

"Trust me I'm a Wizard Master," interrupted Izward, "Hoot will soon be joining you, tell him where I've gone."

Before Utan could utter another word Izward was heading towards the yellowy trail of mist.

"Thanks again," shouted Izward and disappeared into the trees.

A Council of War

Zardo stood hidden behind a tree looking across the clearing at two creatures sat beside a fire. It was raining and the fire hissed in protest. It had almost gone out and smoke drifted slowly upwards mingling with the smoke coming from the surrounding trees.

Zardo turned to the tree next to him and put a finger to his lips.

"Sh!" he whisperd.

Talon and Mrs Clutter nodded. Over at the fire one of the creatures picked up a stick and poked the sodden embers. Smoke bellowed out and they started to cough.

"I should never have listened to you," said Varen.

Koor looked at his sister and smiled at her.

"I tell you Koor, when Vulgor finds out we left Methuselah to look for these mysterious creatures of yours, he'll roast us alive."

"Not if it turns out to be Wizard Zardo he won't."

"Warlocks!"

Koor looked angrily at his sister then pointed towards the trees.

"Trust me my dear he's out there. I saw him escape with two of his comrades."

He turned to the fire and began poking it again with his stick.

"He'll try and rescue the Terrodacs, I'm sure of it. When he does I've got him!"

"Well I hope you're right, for both our sakes."

"Damn!" muttered Koor, "the blasted thing has gone out."

Koor kicked the fire and logs scattered across the clearing.

"And as for locking the door on the Gores," continued Varen, "well that was utter stupidity."

"What?"

"Back at the tree," reminded Varen, "you stopped the Gores leaving."

"Only following instructions my dear," said Koor, "only following Vulgor's orders."

Back at the tree Zardo waited for the rain to stop. Rain interfered with his magic and made it very unreliable. If he tried to use it now the chances were it wouldn't work and they'd be discovered. He would have wait.

He sat down against a tree and recalled the events of the last few hours. They had followed Mrs Clutter down the tunnel and had crawled out onto a branch several metres above the ground. It had been raining and the bark of the tree had been wet and slippery. He'd slipped and had been saved from falling onto Vulgor's guards by Talon. The eagle had quickly taken to the air and had snatched him to safety.

With Mrs Clutter hanging onto Talon's neck and himself dangling under the bird's belly, they'd set off in search of the Terrodacs. Talon had known the way but the smoky atmosphere had made the journey difficult. Finally they'd arrived at the clearing to find the two guards from the tree already there.

Without a fire the stick was useless and Koor threw it back into the forest. It went flying through the air and hit the tree Zardo was hiding behind. It bounced off the trunk and hit Talon on the head.

"Ouch!"

"Did you hear that?" squawked Koor looking in the direction of the stick. "It's them!"

"Oh warlocks!" swore Varen, "here we go again."

Talon and Mrs Clutter ducked out of sight.

Varen wished she hadn't come. Koor had convinced her he'd seen Zardo and that they should follow him. He'd reasoned the old wizard was trying to find the Terrodacs and it was their duty to stop him. He'd known a short cut through the forest and she had reluctantly gone with him. With no sign of Zardo, she feared the worse.

Suddenly, another sound, far deep in the forest attracted their attention.

"You see," squawked Koor, "its him, I told you Zardo would come."

Varen stood up and looked in the direction of the noise. She could see smoke swirling between the trees and hear branches snapping. Something very big was coming through the forest towards them.

"That's not Zardo," said Varen, "its too big."

Zardo looked across at his colleagues and indicated for them to follow him. Silently they sneaked across the clearing, passed the two guards and headed towards the Terrodac compound.

The Terrodacs could smell them coming and flew across the stockade to meet them. Unable to get any further than the netting that held them captive they gathered in front of Zardo noisily pecking through the holes in the mesh.

Zardo quickly calmed them down and Mrs Clutter asked them to be patient while they found a way of setting them free.

Talon was sent to inspect the outside of the netting for possible signs of weakness. He returned several minutes later shaking his head the mesh appeared to be impregnable and impossible to break. A sudden hissing sound distracted them. It was coming from the clearing where Zardo and his comrades had been hiding. It was impossible to see clearly but Zardo swore he saw a large snake-like shadow moving about in the mist. It was huge almost as tall as the lower branches of the trees. Fearing it had come to destroy the

Terrodacs, Zardo quickly convened a council of war.

Meanwhile a strange creature had slithered through the smoke and into the clearing. Varen and Koor gasped in horror. It was twice their size and was hissing at them angrily. It glistened as the rain trickled off its body.

"Told you it wasn't Zardo," sneered Varen.

Suddenly snakes uncoiled out of the creature's head and spat venom at them.

"Told you he'd find out!"

"O! Shut up!" scolded Koor, "no one knows we're here."

"Exactly!" said Varen.

"And what's that surpose to mean?" asked Koor.

"You'll see!" scolded Varen.

The tentacles on the creature's head suddenly stood on end and started swaying like seaweed on the ocean bed. They emitted a strange howling sound and pulsed in and out as if sniffing the air.

"It's looking for something." said Koor.

"Us!" replied Varen.

"It's not come for us," said Koor a little uncertain, "its come for... them!"

He pointed across the clearing to the Terrodac enclosure. Ignoring his sister's warning Koor approached the creature. It hissed at him and suddenly grew much larger. It stretched out its wings to reveal large claw-like hands. Each claw had razor sharp talons that dripped rain.

"Um...you want to be over there," muttered Koor, "the Terrodacs are over there."

Suddenly an assortment of spider-like insects covered in hair and legs appeared all over the creature's body. They crawled and scurried, scuttled and scampered across its skin until they came together to form one large moving mass.

"I don't think it understands you," said Varen trying to pull her brother away from the creature. Koor resisted and stood his ground.

Suddenly they were covered with hundreds and hundreds of hairy spiders. Within seconds the spiders had devoured them both.

Having satisfied their hunger, they returned to their homes on the creature's skin. The creature moved on, its ravenous appetite for flesh unfulfilled. Only its master, Lord Vulgor was immune from its lust, all other creatures offered a constant source of sustenance.

Instinct told it there was more food beyond the trees and it slithered through the clearing towards its next meal.

Arachnoids

"Over here!" shouted Utan.

Hoot ran out of Methuselah and looked across at Utan.

"Hide," shouted Hoot without stopping. He ran across the clearing towards the Tellurian looking anxiously behind him.

"They're coming," yelled Hoot.

Utan ducked behind a tree stump and pulled Hoot beside him as he ran past. Hoot was panting and it took several seconds for the owl to get his breath back.

"What's happening?" asked Utan.

Hoot took a deep breath and slowly raised his head over the stump. Utan did the same.

"What are we looking for?" asked Utan.

"Arachnoids," replied Hoot.

Utan looked puzzled.

"Arachnoids, what's an arachnoid?"

Hoot, realising Utan knew nothing of the events inside the tree, quickly explained what had happened in Zardo's room. He described how the ring had changed into a grey humanoid figure and how it had attacked Vulgor's creature by spitting poisonous quills out of its mouth.

Utan sat engrossed trying to visualise the encounter. The *Being* from the ring had psychic power and was able to communicate by implanting images in Hoots mind. The poison had attacked the tentacles on the creature's head, which according to the telepathic images Hoot had received enabled the creature to breathe. The creature had fought back but eventually the poison had taken effect and one by one its tentacles had dropped off.

Hoot paused and looked back over the stump at the tree.

"So what happened?" asked Utan eager to know the outcome.

"It toppled over and died."

"So the creature's dead?"

"Well…yes and no," stuttered Hoot.

Utan looked confused.

"The creature from the Dark Zone's dead… but the *Arachnoids* aren't."

"What the warlocks is an Aracnoid?" swore Utan.

"There were hundreds of em… came scurrying out of the dead creature's body, "narrated Hoot ignoring Utan's question. "Big black hairy things they were with lots of legs."

Utan's face suddenly froze and he looked at Hoot horrified.

"You mean an Aracnoid is a… spider?"

"Well kind of, yes," answered Hoot, "but with carnivorous appetites."

"I hate spiders," screamed Utan unable to stop himself from shaking.

"I ran and left them eating the creature," said Hoot. "They'll have probably finished it by now."

"And there's hundreds of them inside that tree?"

Hoot nodded.

Had they listened they would have heard a strange scuttling noise coming from the direction of the tree. Had they looked over the stump they would have seen two large black spider-like insects scurrying out of the passage. Instead they'd sat against the tree stump talking and failed to see two of Utan's greatest fears scampering towards them.

Aracnoidphobia

The rain had stopped and most of the smoke had vanished into a pale blue sky and for the first time in several days the island witnessed the re-birth of the sun. It looked pale and watery and gave little heat. Its light was weak and feeble and barely visible above the silhouette of scorched and broken branches. Clouds filtered its brightness and it struggled to be seen.

Utan was the first to sense their presence. He suddenly went cold and felt a familiar tingle at the back of his neck. He put his hand on his neck and gripped Hoot's wing with the other. His neck felt clammy and instinct told him they were in danger. All Tellurians hated spiders and Utan's primitive intuition had told him they were close by.

"Don't move!" he insisted.

Hoot responded immediately and remained still. Utan slowly turned his head and looked upwards. Two giant spider-shaped creatures were perched on the stump above him.

"There on the tree!" whispered Utan turning quickly away.

"How many?"

"Two!" responded Utan.

"One for each of us," joked Hoot.

Utan shivered, his worst nightmare was coming true. Hoot ventured a look. "What shall we do?" asked Utan.

"Run!" whispered Hoot unable to think of another solution.

"On three then," responded Utan.

"On three," agreed Hoot.

"One!" said Utan.

"Two!"

"Three!" concluded Utan.

Together they stood up and ran. Immediately the spiders responded and sprang after them. But they'd been far too slow for the agile spiders and were quickly overtaken. Like hungry predators at the end of a chase the spiders jumped onto Hoot and Utan's back sinking their fangs deep into the flesh. Both Hoot and Utan screamed with pain and fell to the floor. Hoot couldn't move. The bite had paralysed his legs and he could feel its poison creeping through the rest of his body. Utan, about to face a nightmare that had haunted him all his life, panicked and screamed.

The spiders, having caught two tasty meals, were about to satisfy their hunger, when something quite unexpected stopped them.

The sun having spent several days in hibernation suddenly awoke and burst through the cloud cover. Its beams struck the trees in spectacular rays of brightness showering the forest with sunlight.

Having come from a dimension of darkness, sunlight had been an unknown enemy. Unaware of what sunlight could do to them, they ignored the approaching beams of light and carried on with their attack. Hoot's spider had been the first to experience its affect. It had scuttled up his body and into a shaft of light that had fallen across the owl's face. On entering the beam the spider immediatley burst into flames and disintegrated. Its partner, on seeing this, abandoned Utan and scuttled off to find the darkness. But that had proved difficult to find. Eventually it too was struck by sunlight and exploded.

Whilst Hoot and Utan recovered from the spider-bites the rest of the spiders scurried out of the tree and into the clearing. The first two, once out of the shadow of Methuselah burst into flames. The others tried to stop but their colleagues in the rear knocked them forward into the sun. They too burst into flames. Those remaining turned back towards the tree but were suddenly confronted by the ring being. It was standing inside a huge transparent sphere that blocked the entrance to the tree.

In the sky above Methuselah the sun had reached its zenith. A time, say *Tellurian Legends*, when the planet stops and for that brief moment in time, shadows don't exist and the terrors of the dark are driven from the island. Methuselah cast no shadow and the spiders, unable to escape the sunlight, burst into flames.

Utan stood up and helped Hoot to his feet. The effects of the poison had worn off and they could move feeely again. They both heard a twig snap and turned towards the sound. Smoke and ash drifted through the hazy sunlight and they could hear voices.

"What's that?" shouted Hoot.

Coming out of the smoke were three black shadows.

One Last Miracle

The Overseer could do no more. It had already broken more Universal Laws than it cared to remember and would no doubt face the wrath of the Creator for having done so. However its conscience was clear and it could rejoin the Cosmos a forgiven immortal. It was now up to the mortals to save Tellurian.

Inside Methuselah the Overseer had one last miracle to perform.

He would save Methuselah and make it whole again. He stood inside his transparent bubble and ordered it to spin. Soon it became a whirling orb of energy and he floated in its centre like an angel in a halo of light. Then it drifted to the top of the tree and disappeared.

Instantly the room changed and all of Zardo's belongings returned. They floated back into place leaving the room exactly as it had been on Mrs Clutter's first visit. Outside an even greater miracle was taking place. Methuselah was growing new leaves and repairing its wounds.

In space and time above the clouds The Overseer stopped for a moment to consult the Creator. Having agreed the universe was almost back to normal the Creator thanked the Overseer for his assistance and wished him a pleasant journey through the Cosmos.

The Final Conflict

Before Hoot and Utan could identity the figures in the smoke, a loud scream above their heads frightened them. The scream increased until the whole of the sky was a crescendo of screeching and squawking, hooting and squealing. Hoot looked up and to his great relief saw they were Terrodacs.

Over on the other side of the clearing Zardo emerged through the smoke. Behind him came Talon and Mrs Clutter his housekeeper. Illa and Bonn were the next to come through the smoke closly followed by the Tellurians.

More Tellurians crowded into the clearing and the noise became deafening. Every creature was talking and squawking all at the same time and Hoot wondered how each of them could possibly hear the other above all the commotion. Utan shook hands with Illa and Bonn and together went over to the other Tellurians and joined in the general hullabaloo. Suddenly Talon spotted Hoot and flew across the clearing towards him.

"Hoot my old friend," wrapping his wings around him, "It's over. The Dark Zone's been defeated."

Hoot nodded more out of friendship than of conviction.

"I'm not so sure," queried Hoot. "What about Vulgor?"

Talon didn't answer.

"Zardo wants to talk to you," said Talon, "there's a lot to tell you."

Talon flew back to Zardo leaving Hoot to walk across the clearing alone. As he made his way towards Zardo, the Tellurians took it in turns to congratulate him. What should have taken him a minute took him ten. Eventually he reached Zardo and they hugged each other.

"Well done Hoot," said Zardo, "Tellurian has a hero."

"Only doing my duty Sire," replied Hoot, "those are your real heroes."

Hoot pointed to the Terrodacs and Tellurians milling around in the clearing. Zardo agreed.

"I have much to tell you," said Zardo.

"And so have I," answered Hoot.

"But first let me speak to the Tellurians."

"Very well your Wizardship."

"Fellow Tellurians," shouted Zardo, "brave Terrodacs, your attention please."

The clearing fell silent. Suddenly there was movement to Zardo's left and all eyes turned towards Methuselah. Something quite extraordinary was happening to Tellurian's oldest resident. It was restoring itself, repairing damaged branches and growing back new foliage. Zardo stared, unable to believe his own eyes. This had nothing to do with him. Some greater force was responsible for this miracle.

The Terrodacs took to the air and circled around Methuselah squawking and hooting with excitement. They watched as new bark grew along the trunk and millions of new leaves burst out along newly formed branches. Soon a luscious blanket of green covered the upper canopy of the tree its leaves sparkling in the afternoon sun.

It took less than a minute for the tree to restore itself. So amazed had been the onlookers, they fell silent and watched in awe as the tree suddenly grew taller and several metres wider. Finally it stopped and all eyes turned to Zardo.

Only Hoot saw the ring-being darting through the skies in a bubble of light. It came out of the tree and disappeared in a cloud. Then it was gone and the vision was over. He would say nothing of this to the others, this was for his eyes only.

"We may have won a battle."

Zardo's words echoed inside Hoot's head and his mind returned to the clearing.

"But the war is far from over!"

"Look around you Sire," insisted a Tellurian voice, "the island recovers, the evils of the Zone have departed."

"Methuselah is re-born."

"Please try to understand, while Vulgor lives our existence is threatened," pleaded Zardo, "Vulgor seeks revenge and won't rest until he carries out his threat."

"Zardo's right," shouted Utan.

He stepped forward out of the crowd.

"You all know me."

The Tellurians nodded and mumbled in agreement.

"We Orangs have lived on this island for centuries," he continued.

"Too long!" joked one of the Tellurians.

Everyone started laughing.

"Our fathers and their fathers before them fought to keep this island safe and secure for the generations that followed," continued Utan. "Our generation!"

The Tellurians agreed.

"Take Bonn," said Utan turning to his friend.

"I wish I could," shouted a good-looking female Tellurian, "but he won't have me."

The clearing burst into laughter again and Bonn blushed with embarrassment.

"His great great grandfather Gibb helped the Amphibians build the twin cities of Amphia and Hibia."

The Tellurians started clapping.

"But today those cities stand in ruins," said Utan, "and the Amphibians gone!"

Utan paused for effect.

"Why?"

"Vulgor!" shouted most of the Tellurians.

"Vulgor!" repeated Utan. "While he lives we live in fear of suffering the same fate as the Amphibians."

"Zardo's right," added Illa. "Grandfather Gor once told me nightmares do come true. Vulgor is that nightmare and unless we rid our land of such dreams our children's children will be haunted by them for all eternity."

The Tellurians went silent.

"Well said!" responded Zardo, "spoken like a true Tellurian."

Zardo started to clap and the rest of the Tellurians took up his gesture. Soon every Tellurian was clapping. Bonn looked uncomfortable as if all this praise was too much to handle. He smiled and waved awkwardly.

"So what do we do?" asked a voice from the crowd.

"Nothing," replied Zardo. "We wait."

The Tellurians began mumbling to each other and the Terrodacs unsure as to what Zardo meant, shuffled uncomfortably on their perches.

"Look, let us all go into Methuselah," said Zardo trying to calm everyone down, "and I'll explain everything."

Zardo turned and walked towards Methuselah. Mrs Clutter ran ahead and was the first to see the new front door. Hoot and Talon followed leaving the Tellurians to drift across the clearing at their leisure.

"Ooh! Look at the door," beamed Mrs Clutter rubbing her bony fingers over the polished oak.

It had been completely restored.

"It'll be a pleasure polishing that your wizardship," she said opening the door to allow Zardo to walk into the corridor. He entered the passage and walked down the corridor. He opened the door at the end of passage and went into his room. Mrs Clutter, Hoot and Talon followed behind.

On entering the room Zardo paused for a moment. Everything was back to normal. The books were in the bookcase and a fire blazed in the fireplace. His clock had been fully restored and ticked noisily on the mantelpiece. Even his mirror had been restored. Zardo smiled contentedly and sat down in his favourite chair. It felt warm and homely.

Mrs. Clutter entered the room and looked about her.

"Bigger, much bigger," she muttered, "more for me to clean."

She was right. The room was bigger, about twice the size of the old one.

"I'll raise your wages," joked Zardo.

Mrs Clutter laughed and went over to the clock.

"See you do!" she teased. The clock looked brand new.

Hoot and Talon entered the room. Hoot noticed the door had been repaired and hung sturdily on shiny new hinges. The room looked enormous far too big for one wizard to live in. Talon flew off and examined the upper sections of the room. The blackness had gone from around the wall and new roots had started to grow across the ceiling. The secret passage was overgrown with vines and its entrance barely visible. The hole in the floor had gone and nothing of Vulgor's machine remained. Suddenly the room was filled with noise and Talon looked down to see the Terrodacs and the Tellurians crowding into the room. They surged through the door and gathered excitedly round Zardo's chair. Soon Zardo disappeared under a sea of Tellurians. Hoot and Mrs Clutter went to Zardo's aide but they too vanished inside the crowd. The Terrodacs unable to get near Zardo took to the air and perched on whatever they could find.

Talon could see his colleagues needed help and went to their assistance. Suddenly, Zardo came floating out of the crowd and hovered above them. The Tellurians stood back in amazement and while Mrs Clutter assembled them around the fire Talon explained to Hoot how they'd freed the Terrodacs.

They'd found them trapped inside a copse of trees covered by a large net. The net had proved impossible to break. They'd pulled it, pushed it, tugged it and even tried gnawing through it, but it had been unbreakable. They'd even tried to dig under it but the net had run all the way under the ground.

It had been raining and Zardo had been unable to use his magic. It appeared rainwater created a *dampening effect* on his spells. So they had decided to wait until the rain stopped then try again. Suddenly a snake-like monstrosity had come through the trees and had attacked them. Talon described it and Hoot realised it had been Vulgor's second creature.

The creature had spat and clawed at them and they'd been unable to destroy it. It had slithered towards the Terrodac enclosure where it had released hundreds of spider-like creatures from inside its body. They'd squeezed through the holes in the net and had attacked the Terrodacs.

Talon explained how the spiders had rolled into tight little balls and pushed themselves through the netting. Once inside, the spiders had returned to normal size and had begun attacking the Terrodacs. At first, the Terrodacs had fought well and the spiders had found them difficult to catch. They'd flown up to the top of the net and had attacked the spiders from above. Unable to pursue them into the air the spiders had been forced to scuttle along the ground or crawl along the net in order to defend themselves.

There had been an endless supply of spiders and as the *mother-creature* released wave upon wave of reinforcements the Tellurians had become outnumbered. With no way of escape and the enclosure overrun with spiders the Terrodacs had tired. Eventually they'd become too weak to fight and were hunted down and caught.

Talon paused.

Mrs Clutter had almost finished and Zardo's chair was beginning to descend. Eager to know more, Hoot urged Talon to finish his story.

Just when Talon thought the Terrodacs had been overpowered the rain stopped and a giant rainbow had arched across the enclosure. A shaft of sunlight had come through a cloud and struck one of the spiders. To everyone's surprise the spider burst into flames. The spiders had panicked and had looked for shade, but could only find their own shadows. They'd massed at one end of the cage hiding in each other's shadow. The only shade had been trees on the other side of the enclosure. Realising the spiders were now vulnerable the Terrodacs come down off the nets and blocked their escape. Forced by approaching sunlight the spiders had scuttled across the compound but by the time they'd reached the Terrodacs less than fifty remained alive.

Talon stopped again and pointed to Zardo.
"Look, I think he's ready," said Talon.
Mrs. Clutter sat the last Tellurian on the edge of the circle and asked for silence.
"But what about the spiders?" enquired Hoot.
"Sh!" demanded Talon, "Zardo's about to speak."
Hoot felt a little annoyed, he out-ranked the eagle and didn't like being *shushed!*
"So how did the Terrodacs escape?" insisted Hoot sternly.
"Later," uttered Talon, "I'll tell you later after Zardo has spoken."
"But…"
"Sh! Zardo's about to speak."
"I must ask you all to be patient," said Zardo. His chair floated gently to the floor and he stepped off.
"I need a little time to prepare the mirror." He walked over to the fireplace and began polishing the mirror.
"Well?" asked Hoot. "What happened next?"
While Zardo polished the mirror Talon finished his story.

The remaining Arachnoids had hidden in the shadows of the Terrodacs but the birds had flown aside. Immediately the spiders had burst into flames and had ran around the compound on fire.

Zardo, now able to use his magic, had conjured up a spell and had directed it at the creature. Lightning had spiralled around its body and bolts of energy had raced across its skin. Its skin had scorched and burst into flames. Tentacles on top of its head withered and it had staggered around the clearing gasping for breath. Finally it had crashed into the Terrodac's enclosure and became trapped in the netting. The more it had struggled the more entangled it became. The Terrodacs had then attacked it, pecking at its skin through the netting, causing a yellow slime to ooze from the wounds. The slime had dribbled down the creature's body and dripped onto the net. To their surprise the strands in the mesh had started to dissolve. They'd continued their attack inflicting more wounds thus increasing the flow of slime. The more the creature bled the bigger the hole became. Eventually the hole had been large enough for the Terrodacs to squeeze through and they escaped.

They had left the clearing and had returned to Methuselah leaving the creature to be devoured by its own blood.

"Tellurians," shouted Zardo turning away from the mirror, "Tellurian stands at a crossroads, its future uncertain."

Talon stopped his narrative and looked at Zardo. Hoot and Mrs Clutter did the same as did every Tellurian and Terrodac in the room.

The room went silent.

"Our fight against evil is not yet over," said Zardo, "Vulgor lives and hastens to the Dark Zone."

Suddenly inside the mirror Vulgor appeared. There was a gasp of alarm as the Tellurians saw him flying towards them.

"Don't be afraid," reassured Zardo, "Vulgor cannot harm you, this is only his image. He is in fact many kilometres away approaching his own dimension."

In the mirror Vulgor was flying towards a whirlpool of cloud.

"If Vulgor were to survive," said Zardo, "then Tellurian would face an uncertain future. He has been seduced by evil and therefore beyond redemption. He poses a threat to mankind's future and must be destroyed."

The room went quiet only the ticking of the clock could be heard over the silence.

"The Dark Zone has outlived its usefulness," continued Zardo, "and it too must come to an end. We no longer need it. We must put our prejudices aside and learn to accept all the Creator's creatures."

Vulgor was about to enter the vortex and all eyes turned to the mirror. Suddenly another figure flew into view and approached Vulgor from behind.

"It's Izward!" shouted Hoot recognising his comrade.

In the mirror Izward manoeuvred the carpet towards Vulgor.

"Look," directed Zardo, "Izward battles for our future."

All eyes focused on the events inside the mirror. They watched as Izward flew towards the vortex and the unsuspecting Vulgor. Gripped between Vulgor's claws was Zardo's copy of 'The Mysteries of the Universe.'

"Izward needs the book," shouted Zardo.

Every Tellurian willed Izward towards the book.

"He'll not be able to destroy the Zone without it," informed Zardo.

All eyes focused on the mirror.

Vulgor disappeared into the vortex and the Tellurians groaned with disappointment. The Gateway was closing and they feared their hero had left it too late. But Izward had timed his approach to perfection and as the vortex closed he disappeared through the Eye. Every Tellurian cheered. There was a bright flash and the mirror went blank.

"Now we wait," said Zardo, "the final conflict has begun and we must pray for Izward's success."

Into The Dark Zone

On entering the portal Izward had been surrounded by a dense cloud. It had wrapped itself around the carpet creating an impenetrable wall of whiteness. He remembered he'd encountered this before and recalled how the carpet had come to a sudden stop and he'd been catapulted forward into the Dark Zone.

He'd waited, anticipating the sudden thrust forward, but it had never come. Eventually he'd realised he'd been tricked. The swirling cloud around the carpet had created an illusion of movement and he'd been fooled into thinking the carpet was moving, when in fact it had been cleverly brought to a halt.

Izward stepped forward and stood on the edge of the carpet staring into the void. He cursed himself for not realising the deception sooner. The Eye had given Vulgor vital minutes in which to prepare for their encounter and he wondered what tricks Vulgor and The Zone were preparing for him.

A sudden flash of light heralded the first. A bolt of lightning forked out of the cloud and headed towards him. He stepped aside and it ripped through the carpet setting it on fire.

"So it begins," thought Izward.

Another quickly followed and Izward scrambled out of its path. It too ripped through the carpet creating a second fire. Realising the danger Izward tried to smother the flames. He tried stamping on them but that failed. The fire spread rapidly and Izward was forced to take refuge at the back of the carpet. Suddenly the carpet pitched sideways fanning the flames towards him and he felt the heat burn his face. It was now or never. Wrapping the cloak around his body he ran through the flames and across the carpet. He closed his eyes and jumped hoping the Gateway was just ahead of him. For a brief second he hung in the air waiting for gravity to take control. Then he started to fall. Over and over he tumbled gaining speed as he plummeted downward. He felt a redhot wind scorching his face and he dared to open his eyes. He was back in the Dark Zone.

Suddenly a staircase interrupted his descent. He struck the step nearest to the top with both his feet and stumbled forward onto his stomach. He continued his descent sliding down the steps on his belly. Suddenly an energy-bolt struck the staircase below him destroying several steps. He slid to a halt gripping the last step firmly with both hands. His momentum flipped his legs over the edge and he quickly adjusted his grip and held on. There he dangled some twenty metres above a bubbling pit of molten lava.

A yellow dust mixed with ash and smoke filled the air and the smell of sulphur was everywhere.

Whoosh!

Another energy-bolt narrowly missed his head and exploded harmlessly against one of the pillars either side of the Eye. He was too easy a target and knew he had to move. Using all his strength he hauled himself up onto his elbows and crawled forward onto his knees.

Whoosh!

Another bolt thundered past.

He quickly clambered up the stairway and crouched down on the top step.

From his position at the top of the staircase Izward could see the whole of the Zone. It was exactly as he had remembered it. Vulgor's castle looked the same and its high outer ramparts still offered protection against the volcanic mountains that surrounded it. Fireballs raced across the sky and the ground still shook from re-occurring earthquakes. However on the horizon Izward noticed something sinister was happening. A menacing black cloud was forming above the distant volcanoes. Izward strained to see why the cloud moved in such a strange way and to his horror saw it contained hundreds of creatures swirling around inside it.

He looked at the volcanoes. They erupted a strange slime-like substance that snaked up into the cloud. He could see creatures moving and sliding about inside the slime and knew the volcanoes were the source of the cloud's monstrosities. As more of the creatures entered the cloud the larger it grew.

Inside the cloud the creatures were dissolving, melting together to form new and more terrifying monsters. Legs grew out of heads, claws from inside jaws. Grotesque shapes with differing heads snapped and snarled, hissed and howled. Izward could see all sorts of hideous beings writhing and slithering around inside it.

Suddenly the volcanoes stopped erupting and the cloud, now almost a kilometre long, began to move towards him. He looked down the staircase. He was trapped on its upper level with little chance of escape. Several steps were missing and there was a gap of twenty metres before the staircase began again. It was crucial he found a way down. He couldn't jump, it was too far to fall and he couldn't risk getting injured.

Suddenly he had an idea. He walked back up the staircase and sat down. He removed the belt from around his waist and took off his cloak. He began ripping it into strips and tying them together. Soon he had a makeshift rope long enough to reach the bottom half of the stairway. He buckled his belt around a step and tied the rope to it. He tugged to test its strength and climbed down it.

With less than a metre to climb another earthquake hit the Zone and the stairway collapsed. Izward fell and was buried under piles of rubble. For a moment he lay half buried under a pile of broken steps. Slowly he pushed aside the debris and sat up. His back hurt and he felt sick. His head ached and unscheduled stars sparkled in front of his eyes. He coughed and yellow particles of dust flew out of his mouth. But to his great relief he appeared to be uninjured.

Suddenly two large claws gripped his shoulders and pinned him back down onto the rubble. He struggled and wriggled but the claws held him tight. They were too strong to shake off and he was far too weak from his fall.

He lay there, unable to escape, waiting for the owner of the claws to show itself. He waited and waited but nothing happened. The grip suddenly slackened and Izward was able to grab the claws and pull them off his shoulders. They fell lifelessly either side of his out-stretched body. He quickly scrambled onto his knees and began removing the rubble from around the claws. Whoever had grabbed him was buried somewhere under the rubble. He dug down tossing the remains of the staircase over his shoulder.

In the distance the cloud with its cargo of atrocities slithered nearer.

Suddenly Izward could see the tip of a nose, a glimpse of a tooth and finally an eye. Immediately he recognised the eye. It was Vulgor. He let out a yell of delight and punched the air.

"Found you!" he shouted.

For a split moment in time everything went black and Izward found himself floating in a sea of darkness. An elderly face, he thought he should have recognised, floated towards him.

"Found you!" said the stranger's face as it dissolved back into the blackness. Then, like a dream at daybreak, it went unremembered and Izward returned to the past.

The creature that lay beneath him was Vulgor, the fiend he'd come to destroy. It appeared dead and lifeless. Its own chaotic dimension had crushed it to death under a pile of rubble.

Justice thought Izward.

But his mission was far from over, he still had the Zone to destroy and that meant finding Zardo's book. He continued to dig hoping to find

Zardo's masterpiece somewhere on the dead creature's body.

"It's got to be here," uttered Izward picking up a large slab of step and throwing it aside.

"It has to be!"

The more he searched the more frustrated he became. Suddenly he spotted something sticking out from under Vulgor's left wing.

"What's this?" he shouted and dug it out.

It was an oval piece of lava about the size of his fist. It had three triangular shaped blocks poking out of it. It was rough and uneven and covered with hundreds of tiny holes. He picked it up but could see nothing of interest.

"Oh Warlocks!" he swore and hurled it away.

The object bounced down the rubble and rolled onto the ground. It wobbled towards the lava pit and was saved from certain destruction by a large tooth. There were several of them scattered around the rim of the pit and the object rolled up against the largest of them and came to a stop.

Izward continued to dig around Vulgor's body convinced the book was there. Suddenly the ground started shaking and Izward was forced to stop searching. He scrambled off the rubble fearing he would be buried again.

He looked up and realised The Dark Zone was changing. It looked darker and more malevolent. Vulgor's castle was beginning to collapse. Its ramparts were crumbling and huge fireballs were destroying its wall. The two towers either side of the Eye were swaying unsteadily and Izward feared they would collapse at any moment. Around him the ground split open and huge fissures appeared. Inside one of the fissures Izward could see Vulgor's underground lair. A labyrinth of tunnels and chambers lay beneath the castle's surface. As

Izward stared into Vulgor's secret underground world he suddenly realised where Zardo's book had gone.

"Its down there," thought Izward, "Vulgor has the book hidden somewhere under his castle."

Izward silently stood by the fissure gathering his thoughts. Around him the Dark Zone continued to change.

"Of course! It's a key!" shouted Izward suddenly realising the lump of lava he'd found on Vulgor's body. He remembered throwing it towards the lava pit. He moved towards it but the heat was overpowering and he held back for fear of being burnt. Suddenly he spotted something glistening near the edge of the pit. Through the heat-haze he could see a silver sphere about the size of his hand. It stood in a pool of molton lava next to what looked like a large green tooth. The heat from the pit had melted the lava exposing Vulgor's key hidden inside.

Trying to retrieve it would be his next problem.

The heat from the pit was too intense, any closer and he would be incinerated in seconds. He would need a long pole or something similar. He looked but could find nothing. He'd have to risk a quick dash forward and hope for a miracle. It was foolish but there was nothing else he could do.

He prepared himself and started to count to three. He'd reach two when a sudden earthquake shook the castle and he was thrown to the floor. The ground beneath him started to shake and he was tossed around like a boat on a stormy sea. Suddenly something silver rolled past him. It was the key. He shot out a hand and grabbed it before it rolled away and back towards the pit. He felt a stabbing pain in the palm of his hand and smelled the odour of burning flesh. The sphere was red hot and burnt his hand. He held on suffering the pain for fear of losing the only chance he had of obtaining the key.

Finally the earthquake stopped and the ground ceased shaking. Izward stood up still clutching the sphere. The pain had subsided to a dull ache and Izward opened his hand. He removed the ball and inspected his palm. A strange symbol had been burnt into his skin.

Dragomir

The Dark Zone was changing, shifting and sliding itself into a new era. It was preparing itself for a new Master.

The horizon faded replaced by a shimmering image of movement. Contours collapsed and changed into giant peaks of solid rock. Volcanoes erupted and exploded out of existence to suddenly return more violent and twice as large. The earth cracked open, throwing a thousand pieces of lava into the air. From out of the ground came monstrous mountains of liquid rock bubbling and spitting fire, that quickly solidified into high peaks of solid rock. The sky, a rainbow of changing colour, spun itself into a spiralling vortex creating a wormhole of dimensional change. At the centre of the vortex, rivers of energy formed and streaked out across the Zone giving power to the emerging landscape.

Inside the cloud Vulgor's replacement was being created. Absorbing the evils and draining the energy from the monstrosities around it, *Dragomir* was growing in strength and increasing in size.

Like a ravenous animal desperate for food it gorged on the entities in the cloud, inheriting their sins and taking their likeness. Finally the cloud was replaced by a single mass of repulsion that hovered in the air breathing and pulsating evil.

Dragomir had no shape of its own, taking up the forms of the creatures that inhabited it. They would appear and disappear at random, their grotesque shapes bulging out of a thin membrane of skin that surrounded it.

The new Lord of the Dark Zone looked out upon its domain with great satisfaction. It was pleased with its creation. The Dark Zone would live again and the creatures it protected would once again bring chaos to the universe.

Dragomir sensed the approval of the *Collective* and its body rippled with contentment. But outside its body Dragomir sensed an alien intruder planning its destruction.

It had to be found and eliminated.

Dragomir belched loudly and a grotesque head with three oval eyes and insect-like jaws spewed out of its body. It grew in length snaking out of its host like an uninvited guest. Long tentacles with pincer-like claws sprang out of its head and wrapped themselves around the creature's elongated tail.

Still attached to Dragomir and growing continually in length it spiralled down towards the unsuspecting Izward.

Undisturbed by the catastrophic events around him Izward examined the key. He ripped a thin strip of material off the bottom of his tunic and threaded it through the key. Then he hung the key around his neck and turned towards the fissure. The steps that led into Vulgor's lair were to his right. He turned and walked towards them. Suddenly he felt a stabbing pain in the palm of his hand. The symbol on his hand had started to hurt.

He rubbed it and walked down the steps to the bottom of the stairwell.

Another quake suddenly shook the Zone and Izward rocked unsteadily at the foot of the steps. An array of tunnels lay ahead of him, each more twisted than the other. Like vines around a tree they spiralled under the castle and disappeared from view.

But which tunnel to choose, they all looked the same.

He quickly looked down each passage hoping to find a clue but it was impossible to know which of the tunnels led to the book. Strange shadows flickered around them creating an illusion of movement. Like flowing rivers of darkness the shadows rushed down the tunnels and disappeared into the blackness. He stared at them his mind creating all sorts of unspeakable terrors. Then he saw a familiar symbol etched above one of them. He looked at the mark on his palm and again at the symbol above the passage, they were identical. He stepped into the tunnel with the symbol above its entrance and was suddenly surrounded by shadowy shapes. He paused but a moment before they swept him off his feet and carried him down the passage.

The tunnels wound themselves together like tree roots and Izward felt himself twisting and turning around in circles as the shadows carried him deep under the castle. Suddenly the shadows were gone and he fell to the floor. He skidded along in the darkness and came to a stop in front of solid wall of lava. The shadows that had carried him faded back into the passage and slithered back the way they had come.

Izward stood up and in the half-light examined the wall at the end of the tunnel. It felt sticky and warm to the touch and rivers of lava dribbled across its surface. A small keyhole appeared and he inserted Vulgor's key into it. Immediately the key melted into the wall and the hole started to grow bigger.

Suddenly he heard a howling noise in the tunnel behind him. He turned in horror to see a grotesque head with three eyes racing towards him.

A Secret Chamber

Izward stood with his back to the wall facing the creature. It had dark green eyes and its worm-like body stretched the entire length of the passage. Wrapped around it were long tentacle-like limbs that grew out of its head. These were slowly unwinding themselves and hovering around its face. He could hear strange clicking sounds and discovered the noise was coming from pincer-like claws on the end of each tentacle. A more sinister grating sound overshadowed the clicking and through the approaching darkness Izward could see two giant mandibles snapping together. The creature shuffled forward and Izward moved away from the wall into the shadows. A beam of green light fell across the creature's face and Izward caught a glimse of its insect-like jaws. Green ooze dribbled out of its mouth and splashed to the floor.

Izward had a plan. He would hide in the darkness and wait for the hole to get big enough to climb through. The creature was far too large to come after him and hopefully he would escape.

The creature's huge size prevented it from moving freely through the passage and it was forced to use its tentacles to search for Izward. Izward could hear it clicking and snapping its way around the tunnel and caught glimses of its body as it passed into the shaft of light coming from the hole.

Suddenly the passage was bathed in a bright yellow light.

Unable to find its prey the creature had released a fluorescent yellow liquid into its skin. Its body had glowed and the passage had been bathed in an eerie yellow light.

It spotted Izward hiding near the hole and shuffled towards him. Izward felt a tentacle wrap itself around his waist and another around his legs. Soon he was covered with hundreds of them slithering and sliding all over his body. The creature's head snaked nearer and its giant mandibles snapped hungrily at his face. They opened and closed creating that terryfying clicking noise he'd grown to fear. He grabbed them and tried to prevent them sliding around his throat. The creature resisted and it took all his strength to prevent them from snapping shut. Suddenly an earthquake shook the tunnel and the creature coiled backwards. Izward let go of its claws and fell to the floor clutching his throat. Suddenly a huge rock broke through the floor and tore into the creature's body. It crashed through the ceiling taking its head with it.

Izward got to his feet and saw the hole was now large enough to climb through. He clambered through it leaving the headless creature thrashing about on the other side of the wall. Suddenly he heard clicking sounds and turned to see two long tentacles growing out of the creature's severed neck. They slithered along the floor and through the hole towards him. He stepped back but the tentacles followed. Then to Izward's utter delight the hole closed cutting the tentacles off the creature. They fell to the floor and flayed about for several seconds before shrivelling up. He kicked them away fearing they would come back to life. They didn't.

He was standing in a small chamber at the foot of a spiralling staircase no wider than himself. Light came from green flames flickering inside a translucent wall that encircled the chamber. Izward felt he was standing inside a giant icicle of green fire. The stairway spiralled up at a very steep angle and disappeared into the flames beyond. Carved into the wall was a hole shaped like Vulgor's key.

Suddenly Izward felt that cold fear of failure. Was Vulgor's key meant to be inserted here and not in the wall? He panicked knowing he no longer had the key.

"Damn you Vulgor!" he cursed and struck the hole angrily with the palm of his hand. "Now what do I do?"

Suddenly a panel in the wall opened exposing a secret compartment hidden inside. Inside the chamber was Zardo's book.

"Well I'll be a Warlock's Wart!" exclaimed Izward realising the symbol on his palm had acted as the key.

Izward leant inside the chamber to take the book. Immediately the panel snapped shut. Only his quick reactions saved him. He quickly grabbed the book and pulled it to safety. The panel thundered back into place and vanished back into the wall.

Having rescued the book he held it tight against his chest and headed for the stairs. He suddenly stopped and stepped backwards.

Standing at the top of the stairway was...*Vulgor*.

Vulgor's Return

"You're dead," blurted Izward unsure as to what stood on the staircase.

It certainly looked like Vulgor. It had the same head and facial features.

Even its body looked the same. But its skin had become transparent and Izward could see Vulgor's skeleton moving around inside it.

Vulgor stepped forward and flopped down onto the next step.

Out of its mouth snaked claw-like tentacals similar to the ones Izward had seen on the other creature. Realising the two creatures must be linked in some way he took a closer look at the reincarnated Vulgor. His suspicions were confirmed. A long tube-like membrane ran out of the creature's back and up the stairs. The tube was translucent and Izward could see strange shapes wriggling along inside it. He recalled the gathering monstrosities in the cloud and knew Vulgor was but one monstrosity amongst a collective of many.

The creature moved forward and Izward stepped back. Suddenly Izward felt something slither across his shoulders and wrap itself around his neck.

It was a tentacle.

He felt it tighten around his throat and found himself being dragged towards Vulgor. Suddenly Zardo's book flew out of his hands and hovered in front of Vulgor. It opened and began flapping and flicking through its pages at great speed. It stopped abruptly. There was a blinding green flash and out of the book came...*Zardo*.

Changes

Dragomir wrapped itself around the top of one of the castle's twin towers and looked down upon its domain.

The Dark Zone was changing, adjusting to his demands.

It had become an inferno of green fire.

A firestorm of flames raged across the skies and giant monoliths of rock came crashing up through the earth. Columns of fire rushed out of the ground and volcanoes erupted a fiery green sludge into the air. Rocks melted into eerie green shapes and rivers of sludge slithered into giant lakes of burning liquid.

Below, Dragomir could see the walls and ramparts of Vulgor's old castle. It too had gone about change and now lay in ruins. Only the Eye and the two towers remained intact.

A new fortress would eventually rise from these ruins but first the Tellurian interloper had to be destroyed.

Dragomir had found the Tellurian in one of the underground passages and had sent out an agent to dispose of it. But the Tellurian had escaped and the agent had returned minus its head.

But this time it wouldn't escape

He'd got it trapped at the bottom of one of the towers and had sent an old advisory of the Tellurians to dispose of it...*Vulgor.*

Deception

Zardo stepped out of the book and faced Vulgor. The book slammed shut and returned to Izward. At first Izward thought it was the real Zardo, but on closer examination could see it was a copy. Viewed from the side Zardo lacked dimension and appeared flat.

"Go," said the paper image, "find the Eye and destroy it."

Izward stepped forward and looked at Zardo for direction.

"At the top of the tower," shouted Zardo.

Escape up the tower looked impossible, the duplicate Vulgor blocked the stairway. Izward again looked at Zardo for guidance.

Dragomir looked at Zardo through Vulgor's eyes and attacked. It stepped off the staircase and snapped its jaws over Zardo's head. At the same time it coiled its tentacles around the wizard's body and squeezed. But there was no head to crack or a body to squash. Zardo crumpled like a piece of paper crushed in a fist and fell to the floor. By the time Dragomir had realised the deception Izward had escaped and was running up the staircase towards the Eye.

Wizard Master-Time Warrior of Tellurian

Izward spiralled his way up the tower taking two steps at a time. Trailing along the stairway beside him was Vulgor's umbilical tube. It was moving and he could see creatures inside it following him up the steps.

Around him green flames flickered off the walls and he could hear the umbilical tube sliding up the steps behind him.

Vulgor was pursuing him up the tower.

Suddenly a section of the tube stretched upwards and a huge claw tried to grab him. It missed and it dissolved back into the tube. As he ran he could see the heads and faces of other creatures looking at him from inside the translucent duct.

Izward ran on trying to ignore the creatures inside the tube.

He was nearing the top of the tower. The walls had begun to narrow and the steps were getting steeper. As he rounded the next bend the steps suddenly disappeared and he nearly fell into empty space. He tottered dangerously on the edge of the staircase rocking backwards and forwards before grabbing the wall and steadying himself.

The top section of the tower was missing and he was staring out into the Dark Zone. It had changed and a green eerie fire now raged over the whole of the landscape.

Above him was the Eye of Genesis. Across on the other tower clung the creature he'd earlier seen evolving. Attached to the creature was the umbilical tube that had created Vulgor. It stretched out across the gap between the two towers and down the steps he'd just ascended. Suddenly it began to move and Izward could see creatures thrashing about inside it. They were coming out of the monstrosity on the tower, down the tube towards him.

He looked up at the Eye. It was too far away and he daren't risk throwing the book from this position. If he missed, his mission would be over and he would have failed. He had to get nearer but before he had time to devise a plan Vulgor emerged from out the stairway and attacked him from behind.

Tearing away from the tube Vulgor sank his teeth into one of Izward's legs and held him captive. Izward felt a stabbing pain in his left leg and shouted out in agony. He tried to shake Vulgor loose but the more he struggled the more painful his leg.

Immediately an assortment of monstrosities poured out of the severed tube and joined in the attack.

One slug-like creature with dragon-like claws grabbed Izward's other leg and together they tossed him high into the sky. Izward spun hopelessly out of control, twisting and turning over and over in the air. He spiralled within throwing distance of the Eye but he'd begun to fall before he'd realised it. He cursed himself for not realisng it sooner.

More creatures poured out of the tube and joined the others.

Izward hit the floor with a thud and almost let go of the book. Around him were the most hideous and indescribable atrocities he'd ever encountered. They snapped and snarled, hissed and spat at each other as they fought to get at him. Eventually a gigantic jaw came through the chaos and bit into his shoulder. Izward screamed with pain and felt blood trickling down his arm. Suddenly the creature flicked its enormous head and tossed him high into the air again.

Izward smiled, as he approached the Eye.

He'd been given a second chance and this time he would not fail.

He was a Wizard Master, a Time Warrior of Tellurian and he would be worthy of the title. As he tumbled past the Eye he hurled Zardo's book into its centre. There was an almighty explosion and everything went black.

He felt himself falling through the air. For a second he was the hero of a fantasy game flying from danger. But this wasn't a game and he knew he couldn't fly. He thought he heard the thud of his own body strike the ground but he couldn't be sure. All he could remember was a stabbing pain in his back then nothing but blackness.

Location   *The Planet Earth*

Time Zone   *The Present*

End Game

"Izward!" whispered a voice, "I'm here!"

Izward didn't understand. He opened his eyes and stared into the brightness.

"Help's on its way!" echoed the voice, "you're going to be fine!"

The brightness faded a little and a wrinkled old face came into focus.

"Don't move," continued the image, "leave everything to me!"

Izward was confused. Where was he? He certainly wasn't in the Institute the chill on his face told him that. He tried to move but a sharp pain in his back told him to remain still.

"Can you move?" asked a familiar voice.

"Yes, I think so, but my back hurts," said Izward. "Where am I?"

"You've had an accident," said Zeeman, "you've fallen off a cliff."

Suddenly Izward heard the crashing of waves and tasted salt on his lips and everything came flooding back.

The Lighthouse! The Fog!

"I'm sorry," pleaded Zeeman interrupting Izward's recollections, "I shouldn't have left you."

"Not your fault," said Izward, "I should have listened to you."

With the help of Zeeman Izward sat up. His back ached but nothing was broken. He was sat on the sand facing the river. The storm was over and the fog had gone. The sky was cloudless and a bright yellow sun gave warmth to the air. A slight breeze brought the taste of salt back to his lips.

"I'm fine," said Izward, "my back's a bit painful but other than that I'm Ok!"

"Thank God for that," said Zeeman.

"You said you've sent for help?"

"Yes a *Rotoblade's* on its way. It'll take you back to the Institute," said Zeeman looking up into the sky. "Its late!"

Izward had never flown in a Rotoblade and he looked forward to the experience.

"What a field trip this has been," said Izward excitedly.

"You can say that again," answered Zeeman scanning the skies.

Izward grinned and opened his mouth to repeat himself.

"No you don't," smiled Zeeman and they both started to laugh.

Izward realised his left hand hurt and looked at his palm. A strange red symbol had been burnt into it.

"What's this?"

"What's what?" asked Zeeman coming over to investigate.

Izward held out his hand. Zeeman saw an 👁 shape had been etched into the palm.

"Don't know," said Zeeman, "how odd."

A distant roar told Zeeman the Rotoblade was coming and he went to the edge of the river to try to attract the pilot's attention.

Curious as to what had caused the strange mark on his hand Izward started digging. The roar of an approaching aeroplane became louder and Zeeman started waving his hands and jumping up and down in the air.

"Found it!" shouted Izward and pulled a large metal medallion out of the sand. It was attached to a long leather cord.

"Cool!" said Izward examining the symbol on the disc. It was the same as on his palm.

Izward stood up and put the medalian around his neck. Suddenly images flashed into his head. He stood frozen in time while his mind travelled the universe. In an instant he was the *Wizard Master* battling dragons and fighting ogres. Then they were gone and he was left holding the medallion tightly in his hand.

"Cool!"

The noise from the Rotoblade was deafening and above the noise Izward could hear his tutor yelling.

"Over here," shouted Zeeman as the pilot began her descent.

Izward looked up, the thoughts from his vison still racing through his head. The Rotoblade was hovering just above the Lighthouse preparing itself for a landing.

He stared blankly at the Lighthouse then at the cliff edge he'd stepped off. He'd fallen quite a way and realised how lucky he'd been not to have broken his back.

"Quite a drop, isn't it," said Zeeman coming alongside him.

Izward nodded.

Carefully manoeuvring the aircraft around the lighthouse the pilot brought the Rotoblade down. As it neared the ground it kicked up sand and Izward and Zeeman were forced to turn their backs to it.

On landing, the Rotoblade pilot eased down the throttle leaving the aircraft's blades to spin quietly around in stand-by mode.

"Off you go," said Zeeman, "I'll fetch the Jetster."

Izward ran towards the aircraft and Zeeman notice the medallion around his neck.

"What's that?" shouted Zeeman above the noise of the engine.

"An idea!" said Izward.

"For what!"

"A Game."

Izward climbed into the aircraft and sat beside the pilot. She turned to look at him and Izward recognised her immediately. This was the girl of his dreams.

"The name's Elizabeth Jean," said the girl taking the Rotoblade into the air and spinning it around one hundred and eighty degrees. "The youngest pilot in the fleet."

She hovered over the lighthouse for a second then sped off down the coast.

Below Izward could see the peninsula and the abandoned wind turbines that had provided his ancestors with alternative power.

"They call me Izward, the youngest computer wizard at the Institute."

"I know," said the girl smiling.

He'd seen that smile before.

She pressed a button on her control panel and Beethoven's Ninth suddenly blasted through the cockpit.

"Your favourite," she announced.

"How did you know?"

"I know a lot about you," she blushed.

They reached the bridge over the river and the girl manoeuvred the Rotorblade under it.

"Very impressive," admired Izward, "but what are you like with computers?"

"Not bad," replied the girl. "Why do you ask?"

"Well I have this great idea for an adventure game and something tells me you're the girl to help me develop it."

"In that case," said the girl, "you can call me Beth."

THE END

Location   *The Planet Earth*

Time Zone   *The Past*

Extracts From:

The Mysteries Of The Universe Part II

By Wizard Zardo

Chapter 45
The History Of The Dark Zone
(Last Entry)

The Eye of Genesis opened and the oceans of the planet poured in. The water rose and The Dark Zone was engulfed in steam. For forty days and forty nights the oceans of the world covered the Zone cleansing it of all corruption.

On the fortieth day the waters subsided and the Zone was ready for a new beginning.

Location   *The Planet Earth*

Time Zone   *Ancient Times*

Extracts From:

The Mysteries Of The Universe Part II

By Wizard Zardo

Chapter 46
A New Beginning
Eye Witness Accounts

"We all gathered on the northern shores of the island to witness a miracle and celebrate a new beginning."
Hoot: Commander In Chief of the Tellurian Army

"The sea boiled and great clouds of steam swirled over the water then suddenly out of the ocean came an island."
Talon: Commander In Chief of the Terrodac Airforce

"It was a wonderful sight I had never seen the birth of an island before."
Mrs Clutter: Wizard Zardo's Housekeeper

"The new island swarmed with life and I saw strange creatures flying above it."
Utan: A Tellurian Soldier

"At first we were afraid, thinking they were creatures from the Dark Zone. But Zardo had said it no longer existed and we were to greet these new creatures as friends, he was right."
Illa: A Tellurian Soldier and Friend Of Utan

"The new island is called Zarkdon and its creatures Zarkdonians. It is a new beginning for both our species and united we enter a new age of evolution."
Bonn: A Tellurian Philosopher and Friend to the Universe

Personal-Izward

"We no longer have nightmares and I can sleep at night knowing Tellurian has a future.

As I look up at the stars I often wonder what became of you.

I know the truth is out there.

So if you should ever read this chronicle Tellurian thanks you."
Wizard Zardo: Time Warrior Of Tellurian.

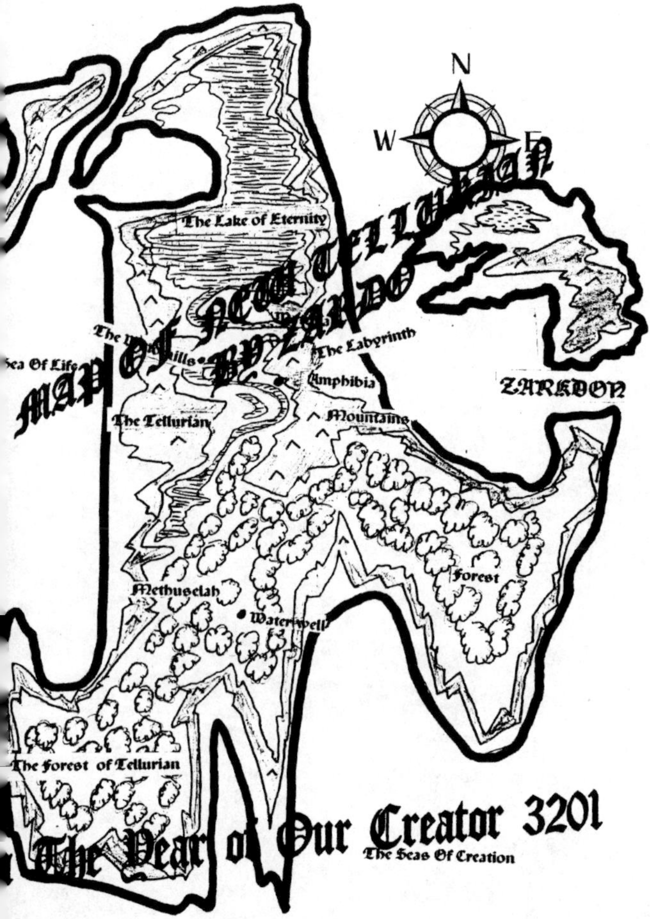

SE ISLANDS OF TELLURIAN AND
RKDON

ALIEN HALL

Author's Note

*Imagination is a Time Machine
It can take you anywhere*

Thank you for coming along.

ALN 1

November 1 2003

ISBN 1-4120-2389-0